OTHER BOOKS BY BETTER HERO ARMY

Plagued: The Midamerica Zombie Half-Breed Experiment
Plagued: The Rock Island Zombie Counteractant Experiment
Plagued: The Ironville Zombie Quarantine Retraction Experiment
Nine Hours 'Till Sunrise

COMING SOON

Girlgoyle Fan-Art & Fan-Fiction Handbook
Girlgoyles (Hollow Mountain Butterfly, Book Two)

GIRLGOYLE

GIRLGOYLE

Hollow Mountain Butterfly, Book One

Better Hero Army

STORYTELLER

STORYTELLER PRESS, LLC

Storyteller Press, LLC and Better Hero Army would like to acknowledge and give special thanks to *Miimork* for her beautiful and inspiring artwork.

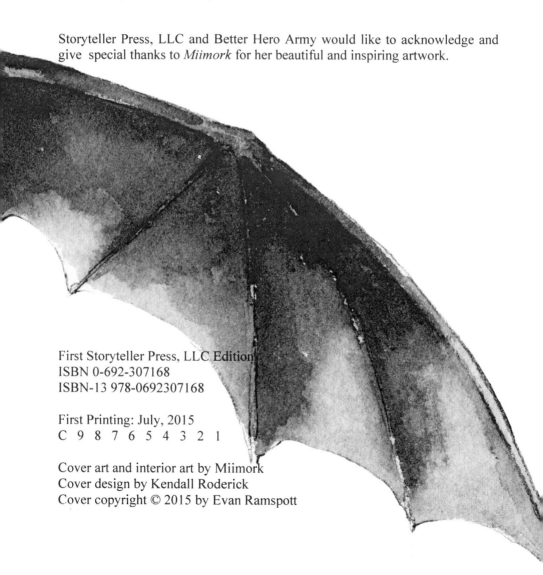

First Storyteller Press, LLC Edition
ISBN 0-692-307168
ISBN-13 978-0692307168

First Printing: July, 2015
C 9 8 7 6 5 4 3 2 1

Cover art and interior art by Miimork
Cover design by Kendall Roderick
Cover copyright © 2015 by Evan Ramspott

For me...for once

ONE

NOT EVERYONE BELIEVES IN GHOSTS. Tiffany Noboru didn't. She may have had a few frightening nights when she was younger, caused by her own dreams—manifestations that felt real for the briefest time after waking up screaming in terror in the dark, yanking a blanket to her chin instead of lunging for the light switch. It accounted for probably ten or fifteen seconds of honest fear, with her heart thumping against the wall of her chest, beating so hard she heard it like an echo all around her that wouldn't fade.

There may have been other sounds, like the raking of fingers against the window pane even though there was no wind and the tree branch had been pruned last week, the hissing of the radiator even though it was a summer night, or the heebie-jeebies—as her mother called them—from feeling some quick spider race over her forehead. Things that went bump in the night, but didn't really exist, banished the moment Mom or Dad turned on the light, fragmented remnants of her nightmarish dreams that dashed to the shadows. Mom's hugs made things right. Dad's vigil at the window and closet did the trick.

Tiffany didn't believe in ghosts because, over time, the nightmares went away and she grew bigger and stronger, and the things Dad gave her for her room seemed to push them all back beyond the reach they once had. No rattling in her closet after he put the vacuum cleaner there, an end to the clicking and hissing from the radiator thanks to a pair of reading glasses missing one lens tucked under the base, no rumbling of the bed or tickety-tack of little clawed feet under the bed thanks to a Hula Hoop, and an end to any scratching against the window thanks to the statue of a gargoyle.

But they were always watching her, and she didn't know it until the summer she died.

TWO

TIFFANY NOBORU'S LIFE ENDED IN ONE MOMENT and began the next. But before her death, she was a sociable fourteen-year-old girl looking forward to her first year of high school. As her name implied, she was of Japanese descent, but tradition and custom hardly mattered in her household. Both of her parents worked, which meant she had the house all to herself most afternoons until they got home. Since she didn't like being alone, she always had friends over, which was what necessitated her drive to be sociable in the first place.

Like any Japanese girl, she had black hair, pale-brown skin, dark brown eyes, and a very small body for what she thought was an unusually large head. Her head was normal, of course, but in the mirror, Tiffany often wondered when the rest of her tiny body would grow to fit it. She lamented being small as much as having a big head, attributing her lack of athleticism to the fact that—as she believed—her body hardly weighed as much as her head. Being competitive in nature didn't help during PE class. Coming in last at everything bothered her to no end. *You've got a competitive streak a mile wide*, her mother always said when Tiffany got frustrated over losing at anything, even *Monopoly*.

At fourteen she was graceful, but as a baby her father nicknamed her Teeter because of how many times she teeter-tottered and fell down when she was learning to walk. Watching home movies around Christmas time, and being thoroughly embarrassed by it, she knew it was because of her big head and small body.

That same small, weak body she'd spent her whole life growing into, but never catching up with, failed to save her in her last gasping moments of life. She should have felt guilty for thinking so, but it was literally the last thing that she thought before her death—she hated being weak.

The thoughts preceding were a little more frantic, a jumble of uneasy feelings and rationalizations to counter the growing fear in the pit of her stomach. Was someone in her room? *Just a shadow.* The slider door was locked. *I checked.* No one could get in. What was that scratching? *A cat?* Was someone in the closet? No, just her clothes hanging awkwardly. *A trick of the light.* Just close the curtains and it will all go away. *Why is the air so cold?*

Her hand trembled as she reached out to slide the curtain shut all the way. Something behind the curtain lunged at her. She tried to yank her hand away, but it grabbed her and pulled her in. Her shriek was muffled by a hand that stuffed a ball of fabric into her mouth—part of the curtain itself. *Mom! Dad!* They couldn't hear her. She couldn't breathe, either. Not through her mouth. Only her nose, and not enough.

A flashlight shone on her face from above. She shook her head to avoid being blinded by it, but it followed her like eyes. She thrashed with her whole body, but it didn't yield. If anything, its grip solidified, constricting to fill in any space she managed to make for herself. It wasn't two arms holding her like a man, but the entire curtain shrinking to fill in every gap.

Mom, please!

Her arms were trapped. She kicked with bound legs. Both feet

4

left the ground and she hovered, kicking and thrashing like a bird in a sack. The curtains constricted more, pulling her knees to her chest, crushing her. She couldn't breathe at all. Her chest burned. The light shining down on her grew more intense as the pain raged. She jerked involuntarily.

Dad!

Tiffany didn't even have the strength left to breathe, much less think herself foolish for hating her body, the same body that convulsed in agony as that bright light faded, first from the edges of her vision, then shrinking quickly into complete blackness.

That life ended, and a moment later, Tiffany lurched up, gasping for air. The curtains were gone. She was free. Her arms flung out in front of her, but nothing was there. She sucked in a deep breath, stretching her lungs to their fullest. Her heart pounded hard, throbbing in her chest. Her head swam from dizziness, but she was alive.

The breathless dream. She hated dreams like that, where she wasn't able to breathe in real life, so to make her wake up, her dreams tried to drown her or…but she wasn't in bed. She sat on a thin leathery substance that covered some kind of hard stone.

And she couldn't see. Her eyes were open, but she saw nothing.

"Dad?" Tiffany called, wincing at a stinging ring in her ears from the sudden noise of her own voice. The room echoed hollowly. Tiffany waved her hands in front of her and felt nothing. She rolled onto her side and tried to stand. The leathery substance hissed as it dragged along the ground with her. *I'm wrapped in it*, she thought, feeling it on her elbow as she rolled. Her legs felt constricted too, but whatever fabric wrapped around them gave easily and she stood. Her vision warmed to the task as well, giving her a bleary glimpse of the room as she straightened and planted her feet. She felt top heavy. Attributing it to her big head, as usual, she leaned forward a little to keep from toppling backwards.

I'm just a little dizzy, is all.

"Mom?" Tiffany whispered.

The room looked like a prison cell, except there were no bars or windows, or even a cot. As she turned around, she found that it was completely void of anything. Just a solid cube of sleek stone.

"I'm sorry, but you've died," Tiffany thought she heard her mother say. She covered her ears quickly, the noise and the ringing coming like a thunderclap. Tiffany forcibly yawned several times, hoping that popping her ears would help. The ringing faded quickly.

"Died?" Tiffany asked, perplexed. Her voice echoed in the dull gray room. She let her hands down now that sound didn't hurt. *Where am I?* This wasn't her room, and as she replayed the words in her head, she realized it wasn't her mother's voice, either. *What just happened?* She spun slowly, looking for a door. "How can I be dead?" Tiffany reasoned out loud. "I'm right here."

No answer came.

She took a step toward the nearest wall. It looked like the other three, with no window or door of any kind. Nothing but solid stone. "Where am I?"

"You're here, with us," the voice said softly. It was a woman's voice, unrecognizable, but attempting to sound reassuring in a way that didn't sit well with Tiffany. She sounded like a nurse, like she didn't really care, even though it was her job.

"Look, my dad is a police officer," Tiffany lied.

"We know everything about you," the woman replied.

Maybe they knew her name and home address, but *everything?* "Really? What's my favorite color?"

The room shifted to a light green hue, the exact color she

envisioned when she asked the question. It wasn't a trick of light from what she could tell. The walls themselves appeared to have actually changed color, as though the light in the room was coming *from* the stone.

"OK, that's weird," Tiffany said softly, stepping away from the nearest wall. "How'd you do that?"

"We did nothing," the woman replied.

"Then why is it green in here?"

"Isn't that your favorite color?"

"Alright, you're…not…any…help." Tiffany sighed and turned to face a different wall. She wanted out, to go home, to find her mother. She obviously hadn't really died. They must have saved her, revived her with CPR or something, but what was this room?

"I want to see my mom and dad, right now," Tiffany demanded.

"I'm afraid that's not possible."

"Why not?"

There was no reply.

"Why can't I see them?"

"It's best that you remain calm," the woman said.

"Why? What's happened to my mom and dad?"

"Nothing. They're home and well."

"Then why can't I see them?"

There was no reply.

It didn't matter. She'd find her own way out, and then a phone. One of these walls had to be different. She approached the next wall and touched it, pushing it gently at first, then harder. It was cold and solid with no seams of any kind, like a single slab. She tried sliding it side to side, then up and down, but it wouldn't budge. Its surface was too smooth to climb, but that didn't matter. She knew she couldn't climb it even if there were foot holds. Not with her little, tiny body. She didn't have the arm strength to climb.

There had to be a way out. How else did she get in here?

Tiffany slid to the next wall, her hands roaming the surface for any unevenness. She pressed her weight against the wall then struck it with the butt of her fist. It thumped solidly. *What is this place?*

"I'm going to find a way out," Tiffany called. "And when I do—"

"We'll be most pleased," the woman interrupted, to Tiffany's surprise. Her voice didn't have that echoing, all-encompassing quality to it anymore. Tiffany turned, able to finally hone in on where it came from.

A tall woman stood near the opposite wall facing Tiffany, her hands clasped behind her back.

"Holy—" Tiffany blurted, startled. Her natural instinct of holding back curse words around adults was the only thing that kept it in.

How did she get in here?

The woman didn't move. In the green glow of the room, her skin, what little of it that peeked out from a long, sleek, tight-fitting red gown, appeared mottled with freckles. Her skin color was odd, too. A gray tint of some kind. With the green light she looked sickly. *Yeesh! You need to get some sun, lady.* Her skin almost resembled granite. She had tightly woven black hair pressed back in a braided bun. She wore some kind of strange cloak that arched and fanned out behind her shoulders, draping a black fabric that nearly touched the ground.

"Where did you come from?"

The woman craned her neck to look around the room, an expression of confusion on her otherwise stony appearance.

"What do you mean?" she asked at last, returning her fixed gaze on Tiffany. "Just now, or when I was alive? We are still talking about your death, are we not?"

"No," Tiffany replied, trying to piece together the logic of her questions. "I meant, how did you get in *here*?" She pointed at the floor.

The woman pointed at the ceiling and smiled, showing a mouthful of thick, fat teeth framed by two long, pronounced canines. Tiffany backed away, repulsed by the ferocity it implied.

She's insane and crazy!

The ceiling was at least twelve feet high, and even though the woman was almost seven feet tall herself, there was no way she could reach it. Even if Tiffany climbed up on her back—*fat chance!*

"How?" Tiffany asked as she looked at the walls in the room. There had to be a door.

The woman raised an eyebrow, then snapped open thick black wings from behind her back. Tiffany cried out, the swiftness of their appearance startling her. It wasn't a cloak!

"Wings!" Tiffany pointed at the woman.

Enormous wings. Twice the woman's size, their weight pitching her forward at the shoulder. The tips of her wings grazed the ceiling then slowly pushed through like a knife cutting butter. A gaping hole grew in the ceiling between her wings, making the rest of the ceiling look more like light through fog, and her wings blocked it completely. Tiffany could see through the shadowy hole between her wings, so it wasn't fog. The woman must have disrupted some kind of hologram.

"It's a trick of light," the woman said.

"Your wings?" Tiffany asked excitedly, astonished by the sight.

The woman said nothing.

"Look, this is all really freaky weird, and all, but I want to go home now."

"That's not possible," the woman said evenly.

"Now, like…now." Tiffany's hands trembled.

"I'm sorry—"

"Please!" Tiffany made fists to control her shaking.

"Calm down," the woman said sternly. "You can go there," she added, pointing at the hole in the ceiling.

Anywhere was better than here, Tiffany reasoned. She took a cautious step closer to gaze through the hole between the woman's wings. A sheer wall of stone several miles away rose to blot out everything. There was no horizon, or trees, or anything between the hole and the looming wall, no clouds or sky. Just solid stone, like the room.

Tiffany sneered. *Why bother?* Except there were lights. Hundreds of them studding the surface. She didn't notice them at first, thinking they were just discolorations in the jagged wall, but they were too regularly spaced. It was some kind of pattern, like rows stitched into the stone.

Tiffany squinted to get a better look. Her vision zoomed in on one hole in particular where a man stepped off the edge and opened his wings to soar into the endless chasm. Her eyes widened, and her vision zoomed out to normal. She stepped back in disbelief, reeling from a dizzying sensation—like standing too fast. *What's happening to me?* She could see miles! *What's happening around here?* That man had wings, too.

"Where am I?" Tiffany asked in shock.

"Spread your wings and I'll show you," the woman said.

"Wings? What are you talking about?" Tiffany looked over her shoulder. "Holy—" she gasped, about to swear again. Furled wings sprouted from her shoulder blades like a cloak affixed to her back. "What the—?"

Words escaped her. Black wings hovered above her head, folded over an elbowed bend at the edge of her arm's reach. The furled wings hung behind her, draping a flowing, loose leathery membrane nearly to the floor. She touched the membrane first. It felt cool. Warmer than the air, but not by much. So this was the fabric that was underneath her when she woke. She reached a hand up to the bend in her wing and felt the soft bone. Her whole body convulsed. She felt it! She felt her fingers touching the wing, but not just through her fingers. She felt it on her elbow—of the wing!

She didn't dare touch it again. It was too creepy to even think about it. She wiped her hands on her chest, against a smooth, satin fabric of some kind that wasn't her nightgown.

"What am I wearing?"

The tight satin gown covered her from neck to ankle, extending down her arms to her wrists, leaving only her bare feet and hands visible.

"It's a flight gown," the woman said.

"Why is it white?" Tiffany hated wearing white.

"So others can tell that you're new here, especially when you're flying. They'll know to fly around you."

"Why is yours red?"

"So others know to stay out of my way. Now, spread your wings. We have work to do."

THREE

AT FIRST, TIFFANY TRIED TO REASON her way out of having wings. They weren't real. This was a crazy dream that she'd wake from at any moment. She pinched herself and held her breath, but nothing changed the fact that the woman in red, whose skin was unmistakably the color of granite, didn't go away, nor did her wings, nor did the dream.

I want to go home!

But she was still stuck in this room. With the woman. And her wings.

I have wings. I have.... She felt dizzy again.

Tiffany reached a cautious hand up to touch her new bicep. It looked a lot like thick bone covered by a thin leathery membrane. The membrane was soft, like her own skin, but more rubbery and tightly bound to the curvature of the bone and thin filaments of muscle. She pushed against the bone and it bent easily, dipping. The wing extended partly, throwing her slightly off balance. She stopped pushing and it righted itself of its own accord. She didn't even feel the things when they were all the way up like this.

Tiffany swallowed at a lump in her throat that wouldn't go away.

There's a logical explanation for this, she assured herself. She clenched her hands tight and took a deep breath before reaching out to touch her wing again. Dangling from the elbow was what she figured to be a forearm. She pushed it and felt it for the first time. The idea of having two arms on both sides made her queasy. She pushed the other side's wing and shivered at the strange sensation.

Tiffany closed her eyes and tried to ignore it, but as the forearms curled behind her again she felt it through her whole body. A chill ran down her spine and gripped her in the stomach. *So gross!* She took a deep, settling breath and opened her eyes. The woman hadn't moved. She still stood with her wings spread high over her head like a statue.

"So let me get this straight," Tiffany said, trying to ignore the sensation of her new set of dangling arms as they swept against her back. "I can fly with these wings, right?"

"That's yet to be determined," the woman replied. "We should begin by *trying* to fly."

"Why? Where are we going?"

"Well, to your home, of course."

Home! Mom and Dad could figure this out. Dad knew what to do when she fell down the stairs and broke her arm. Mom knew what to do when Tommy Briggs broke her heart...but those were normal problems. This was different—she had wings! Maybe there was a doctor. Other kids had plastic surgery! Mom and Dad could afford to have her wings—what? Cut off? She just needed to find them and everything would be alright. She needed to get out of this place.

She sighed heavily. She needed to fly.

"Home?" she asked the woman suspiciously.

"Yes, up there." The woman pointed through the hole in the ceiling. "Although, you can stay here until morning, if you prefer."

"No!" Tiffany held her hands up. "No, I want to go home."

"Very well," the woman said, straightening. "Let's work on snapping open those wings."

Fine. She could do that much. *How hard can it be?*

She looked at her wings and concentrated on opening them, but nothing happened. She opened her normal arms and flapped them and still nothing happened. She threw her head back and closed her eyes, sighing in disgust. It wasn't going to be easy at all.

Figuring out how to just unfurl her wings without falling over took considerable effort. When they were flat against her back, the things were manageable, barely noticeable even, but the moment she finally got them to extend, they didn't hesitate to open—Snap!—and she fell over. First once, then twice, then what felt like a dozen times.

Stubbornly, she hauled herself back to her feet each time, glaring at her wings angrily, blaming them for misbehaving on purpose. Why should they be any different than the rest of her little body?

She snapped them open once more, and fell.

Damn! Tiffany slapped her legs out of frustration. "Why do I have wings again?" she blurted angrily.

"That's how you arrived," the woman answered patiently. "Some have wings, some have tails, some have both, some have neither. It all depends." She gave a tempered shrug. Her enormous wings shrugged with her.

Arrived. Tiffany didn't like the sound of that word. Too much like birth or being sent away to a boarding school. And for as much as Tiffany didn't want to believe any of this was happening, the woman's uncompromising presence—and choice of words—was beginning to erode her confidence that this was only a dream.

And if this wasn't a dream, then it only meant one thing…she *was* dead. This didn't seem like any heaven she'd ever heard of, either. And yet, what else could it be, except…?

Tiffany stood and retracted her wings. Without looking up, she mustered the courage to ask, "So what am I?"

"You're one of us," the woman replied.

Tiffany fought to keep her composure, annoyed by the woman's cryptic answers as much as she was of trying to fly. "Then who are you?"

The woman let her wings down. The hole in the ceiling vanished and the room became quieter. She stared at Tiffany with a blank expression. She obviously didn't want to answer the question. That worried Tiffany even more.

"What's your name, at least?" *And why are you so cold?*

"D.K."

Better than Beelzebub, Tiffany thought. "D.K.? What does that stand for?"

"It is my name."

"Yeah, but you can't be called D.K. What does the D stand for? Danielle? Drusilla? Dagmar? That one's really popular. There are like three Dagmars in my school."

"It's…D...K.," she said with a hint of irritation. "Back to what we were doing, now." She extended her wings slowly, carving them through the holographic ceiling, making a large hole through which Tiffany saw the gray chasm above.

Tiffany took in a deep breath and let it out. So much for getting answers from her. D.K. was as hard as stone, and about as welcoming. A little like her school secretary, who was a mean and grumpy woman that liked frightening the students. She dressed as a witch for Halloween, even.

Tiffany glanced up at the endless catacomb above. She caught movement in the air, a person gliding near the stone façade. Tiffany didn't squint. She knew that made her vision zoom in, and the feeling of it made her want to retch. The idea of flying caused another lump in her throat that she swallowed down. If going up there was what it would take to get to the bottom of things, she'd just have to get it over with.

"Fine," she mumbled and curled her shoulders forward. Her wings snapped out, nearly knocking her backwards again, but she anticipated it this time and put a foot forward to compensate for the added weight. "Hey," she said with a grin. "I got it!"

"Wonderful," D.K. replied blandly. "Now flap."

Tiffany looked at her unmoving, extended wings. "How do I do that again?" Tiffany was sure she heard a frustrated growl out of D.K.

D.K. explained the basics of using her shoulders without shrugging. It felt weird. The wings rose above her head and gently swept down. Her whole spine tingled the first few times her wing's fingers brushed the ground, and worse was that she could move the fingers—straighten them or curl them to stretch or cup the leathery membrane. She couldn't feel the membrane itself, but its tug on her fingers gave her the impression of her skin stretching each time she flapped.

When D.K. told her to sweep harder, she did, and her wings lifted her off her feet and threw her forward, face-first onto the ground. She slapped the cold stone to break her fall. It stung painfully. She glowered at her partly furled wings, but defiantly pushed herself to her feet.

Tiffany bumped into walls and fell head-first to the floor several more times as D.K. instructed her on the basic mechanics of flapping properly. To her credit, D.K. never admonished her nor tired of her failures, but she was equally absent of encouragement, to the point of being testy at times. After every fall, D.K. just clapped her hands once, saying, "Up. Again."

It was getting on Tiffany's nerves. She didn't need a drill sergeant. What she needed was a pair of pants. The dress only inhibited her legs.

"Why do I have to wear this *stupid* dress?" Tiffany snapped.

"Because you're tailless," D.K. replied evenly. "If you had a tail, you wouldn't need a sail between your legs to help steer. When you're wings get bigger, you won't need the gown. Be thankful you're not wingless, too. Now, try again."

I'd rather be wingless. But even that thought depressed her. How hard would it be getting up that mountain wall without wings? She wondered how the wingless got around in a place like this, but didn't bother asking. She already knew D.K. wouldn't answer that kind of question, or she'd say something like, "Back to what we were doing, now!" There were slight variations to D.K.'s stoicism that Tiffany was beginning to recognize, this being an instance of mild irritation. Tiffany had yet to discover D.K.'s look of happiness, mild or otherwise.

Letting her frustration get the best of her, she opened her wings and beat down in a single, quick motion. She careened sideways and tumbled onto her knee. *Ow! Son of a—!*

"Stop," D.K. ordered.

I'm stopped already, Tiffany thought, rubbing her knee.

"Stand."

Tiffany groaned and did as she was told.

"Close your eyes."

"How is closing my eyes going to help?"

"Close them," D.K. said soothingly.

It was the first hint of kindness Tiffany heard from the woman. It made it easier for Tiffany to accept her instruction. She straightened and closed her eyes.

"I want you to put your left hand straight out in front of you. Good. Now bend your elbow and touch your opposite shoulder. Your shoulder, not your—better. Now extend your wings."

Tiffany's wings snapped open and she leaned forward to compensate for the weight. It felt different this time. Her right arm rose to keep balance as she dipped her left side lower, making her wings rise higher.

"Perfect. Now crouch down, flap toward the ground...*hard*, and jump!"

"Alright," Tiffany said uneasily.

"But open your eyes," D.K. said just as Tiffany took in a deep breath to steady herself to the task.

Tiffany opened her eyes right before her wings swatted downward. She leapt into the air, spinning slightly from the force. It rocketed her straight up. Wind rushed through her hair. Her wings swept under her feet and slapped together beneath her, touching nothing but each other. Her wings opened again, revealing the ground—and D.K.—far below.

I did it!

Her heart raced. She stared down through the hole in the ceiling. The hole that had been ten feet above her head a second ago. And then she stopped. *Oh, no.* Dread knotted her stomach.

"Stroke!" D.K.'s commanding voice broke through her fear, but Tiffany didn't know what to do.

She raised her hands for balance as the feeling of weightlessness crept over her body. She had stalled mid-air. She hoped D.K. would catch her or something. Her shoulders flinched at the idea of careening into a wall or the floor and it made her wings haul themselves skyward. Like the instinct to grab something when falling, her mind and body reacted. She swung her wings above her head, turned them, and stroked hard one more time. It catapulted her skyward.

"I did it!"

Tiffany didn't look down. She concentrated on raising her wings again to beat once more. She flapped again and again, rising higher with each hard stroke.

"What do I do now?" she called out, the dread in her heart revealing itself in her voice. D.K. hadn't told her what to do once she was airborne.

"Don't panic," D.K. said, her voice calm and unsettlingly close.

The tall woman dressed in red sailed smoothly just beyond Tiffany's wingspan. Tiffany shuddered, startled to see her so close, their wings nearly on top of one another. Tiffany yanked in her wing, afraid they would hit. She pitched sideways, which caused her to topple onto her back. She fell backwards through the air with her outstretched wings pinned toward the sky.

"Open your legs," D.K. yelled urgently.

Tiffany spread her legs a little. She felt the air pushing the back of her flight gown and with nerve-wracking abruptness she spun full circle, head-over-heels. Her wings and arms snapped wide open to catch the air again. She threw out her legs even more to make a larger fin. Her heart pounded. Her eyes went wide with fear.

"That's good," D.K. said measuredly. "Flap!"

Tiffany nodded and did as D.K. told her, flapping her wings to rise a little.

"Good. Keep flapping. Not everyone survives their first backward aerial summersault. You're doing fine. Do you think you're getting the hang of things enough to follow me?"

Tiffany's heart still pounded with dread, but she nodded. She didn't dare look over at the red-gowned matron.

"Slow and easy," D.K. told her. "Just flap slow and easy."

D.K. dipped below Tiffany to gain speed, then began to stroke the air with the cadence and precision of a row team; reaching forward, dipping her wings into the air, flapping with graceful power, and arcing ever higher as they circled the interior of an enormous cavern that was as big as a mountain. Dotting the cavern walls were perches and landings that jutted out from the base of cave openings. Most of the caves were lit a dull grey that seeped from their depths, only enough light emanating to make them noticeable against the twilight blue of the rest of the mountain.

As the fear of falling slowly faded, Tiffany began to embrace the excitement of flying—*flying!* Not as well as D.K., whose gait was smoother and stronger. The red gowned matron flew with the ease of a nightingale compared to Tiffany's rough and uneven meandering. D.K. could have easily outdistanced and out-maneuvered her a hundred times over, but she flew slowly and constantly looked back to make sure Tiffany was still there.

Oh, these wings are cooler than I thought. I'm actually flying! Caitlyn would freak if—but this wasn't right. Tiffany's elation drained as she began to think about home, her friends, and her parents. She chastised herself, angry that she felt any kind of joy when Mom and Dad were somewhere worried sick. *Just get home.*

She set her sights above, and put her mind and focus on getting there. The higher they flew into the cavern, though, the narrower it became, and she didn't think home was anywhere up here. Maybe if they flew out of the top, but it didn't look like it opened up. She couldn't tell, though. The top was too far away, and as unsteady as she was at flying, she didn't dare risk zooming her vision in on anything. She might run straight into the cavern

walls that completely engulfed them, or faint and fall out of the sky. Making matters worse, they weren't alone in the air.

Others flew by, moving majestically to avoid D.K. and Tiffany, giving them both wide range. They raced by at breakneck speed, making it impossible for Tiffany to make out anything about them. Were they men or women, and what did they wear? Even the nearest wall seemed a blur to her. She knew there were caverns dotting the interior of the…what was this place? *A hollow mountain?* That was the only way Tiffany could describe it if she had to. The inside of a cone, and not a narrow cone like for ice cream, but a fat, wide mountain that spanned ten to twenty miles at its base. And everywhere she looked, caverns dotted the interior walls, most all of them lit by a dull gray inside. From big caverns as wide as a semi-truck all the way to small holes no bigger than herself, some with lip-like ledges, and some without. There was hardly anything to tell them apart, except—

"We'll be landing there on the next pass." D.K. pointed out one of the cavern holes. It was much larger than most and painted yellow, or maybe the rock itself was yellow. As quickly as they passed by, Tiffany couldn't be sure.

"Landing?!" The idea sounded both good and bad. Her wings were tiring. She *wanted* to land, but she had no idea how, and worst of all, she worried she might kill herself trying.

"It's easy. Throw your feet forward and cup your wings to slow yourself, then flap just before you touch down."

"That doesn't sound easy," Tiffany called ahead.

D.K. took the lead and guided Tiffany half way around the circumference of the hollow mountain, then banked and crossed through the center. Tiffany flapped furiously to climb to D.K.'s level. D.K. glided now, and Tiffany tried to do the same, but she dropped out of the sky much faster, so she began flapping to stay even with D.K., gaining on her. Suddenly D.K.'s wings flared out and she swooped upward. Tiffany did the same, mostly out of fright, and it felt like a parachute had grabbed her. D.K. swept aside and Tiffany found herself falling into the mouth of the yellow cavern. Her heart stopped as it swallowed her whole. She flapped furiously to stop herself from falling, but the air in her wings gave out and she fell backwards.

She closed her eyes out of fear. Her whole body jerked as she struck the ground, expecting a great, walloping pain, but instead she bounced gently. She opened her eyes, hoping the dream was over. *The falling dream! Please just be the falling dream.* As much as she hated the sensation of falling and jerking suddenly awake in her bed, she begged for it to happen now.

What the—?

She lay breathless and half-submerged in a pit of sponges, thinking she probably died again. D.K. stepped into view above her. The tall red-gowned woman still showed no sign of emotion.

"Are you hurt?"

"What happened?"

"You overshot the safe landing zone and hit the crash pit. Are you hurt?"

Tiffany thought a moment then rolled to try to climb out, adjusting and furling her wings to make sure they were still functioning. She didn't feel any pain. "I don't think so."

"Good, come meet your roommates."

Roommates!? Tiffany didn't like the sound of that. She struggled with the sponges. Each time she pulled her legs free of one spot, she'd slide forward a little and sink into another. It took all her strength to reach the edge, her heavy breathing making it too hard to protest the idea of roommates yet.

There were several rope ladders dangling into the pit along the edges. She grabbed one and stuffed her foot into a rung. She caught her breath a little and climbed out.

As soon as Tiffany reached the top, though, D.K. turned and walked deeper into the cavern.

Tiffany groaned in frustration and staggered to her feet, the weight of her wings more trouble now that she was tired. She looked back out the mouth of the cavern. The hard yellow stone was only some kind of perch for landing and takeoff, with the wide and long pit filling most of the cave.

Five doors lined the back wall, spread far apart, each with a large number on it. D.K. walked for the door in the middle.

"I thought you said I was going home," Tiffany finally protested, still a little winded.

"This *is* your home," D.K. replied evenly.

What!? Tiffany stared incredulously at D.K.'s back. *You've got to be kidding me!*

"You've been assigned to Barracks 3." D.K. pushed open the door and started down a tall hallway, ignoring Tiffany's silent protest. Her wings nearly touched the ceiling until she shook them, curling them tightly to her back.

Tiffany knew she wouldn't have the same trouble in the confined space, but that wasn't what irritated her. Tiffany wanted to tell D.K. she didn't want to be part of some barracks, or have roommates, or anything—she wanted to go home!—but D.K. was walking away so quickly. Tiffany rushed to catch up, arriving on D.K.s' heels as the hallway opened into a polished stone room filled with beds lined like store aisles. Along the far wall were lockers and book shelves. A fireplace with a small red glow of embers warmed a corner of the long chamber. A few dozen girls of various sizes were spread throughout the room.

"Dorm Three, *attention,*" a girl's voice called out and every girl lurched up from what they were doing to stand erect, arms at their sides, wings at the ready, heads held high.

"Good evening, Commander," a girl wearing a yellow gown called out. She was tall with black hair and peach-toned skin. Most of the other girls appeared to have mottled stone for skin, and not one in the room had a tail. One other girl wore yellow—a pretty girl with blue skin—but the rest wore silver gowns with black or red stripes ringing the sleeves. Tiffany recognized it at once as rank, similar to belts in karate or stripes on military uniforms. She was the only girl in white.

Great, Tiffany thought dejectedly.

"Good evening, Corinne. Good evening girls," D.K. said as she came to a halt and let Tiffany step up beside her. Tiffany wanted to complain, but D.K. spoke as if she wasn't in the room. "We have a new recruit. Her name is Tiffany. I expect you all to show her around, make her feel at home, help her with protocol, and be responsible for her well-being. Her mentor will collect her in the morning."

"An honor, as always," Corinne replied. Tiffany resisted the urge to roll her eyes, already thinking the girl a real suck-up.

D.K. nodded and turned around, almost bumping into Tiffany as she took a step toward the door.

"You're leaving me here?" Tiffany asked D.K. "I thought you said we had work to do?"

"By we, I meant me," D.K. told Tiffany evenly. Past D.K., Tiffany saw the tall girl in the yellow gown named Corinne smile out of the corner of her mouth. "You have work to do here as well, just not as urgent as mine. Your mentor will come fetch you in the morning. He'll explain everything then." D.K. glowered over her shoulder at the other girls in the barracks before adding, "Don't...wander."

FOUR

TIFFANY NEVER LIKED BEING THE CENTER OF
attention, a role suddenly thrust upon her by D.K.'s departure. A
dozen girls pressed forward, Corinne in the lead. Corinne wasn't
the tallest of the girls, but she definitely towered a head-and-a-half
over Tiffany. Another girl, made all the more terrifyingly brutish
due to the chiseled appearance of her speckled, dark gray and
white skin, stood to Corinne's left. On Corinne's other side was a
girl a hand taller than Tiffany—short by their standards—with
bright, silvery eyes that stood out against her brown-and-gray
spotted skin. Both wore silver gowns like all the others
surrounding Tiffany.

"My name's Corinne." She pointed a thumb at herself. "I'm
the Bay Chief. Whatever you need, you come to me, OK?"

Tiffany nodded.

"Where'd you come from?"

"Phoenix," Tiffany said.

"You're not Japanese?" Corinne asked, a hint of
disappointment in her tone. A hint of a European accent came out
with it. Not as strong, but noticeable.

"I *am* Japanese."

"Oh, well, welcome to Bay 3. This is Karla." She tilted her
head toward the big one. "And Priya." She tilted her head the

other way, at the girl with silver eyes.

Tiffany nodded to both and Corinne continued naming off several other girls in quick succession, pointing them out as she did, each nodding and saying hello, but their names and faces blurred into a single, giant, impossible catalog in no time.

"That's a lot of names to remember, I know," Corinne said with a friendly smile. "For now, just remember me and the girls you sleep next to."

"OK. Where will I be sleeping?" Tiffany asked meekly. She was afraid to know the answer. Her stomach turned like it wanted to squeeze her heart. If Corinne made Tiffany bunk close to her, she'd have no reason to decline. She didn't even know if she was allowed to. D.K. left before mentioning *anything* about what was going on, what to do, or even what had happened to her. No, that wasn't true. D.K. said she died. *But I can't be dead. I'm right here.*

Corinne looked around the bay, waving indiscriminately. "Just pick an empty bunk. We've got plenty."

Tiffany held back a relieved smile.

"You're the first white-robe we've had in a long time. How'd it happen?"

"What do you mean?" Tiffany asked.

"How'd you die?" Karla interrupted. Corinne slapped Karla on the arm with the back of her hand. "What?"

"You didn't have to say it like that," Corinne replied.

"It's OK," Tiffany said, trying to sound as accommodating as possible. "I don't know, really. I mean, I vaguely remember," she lied. These girls seemed too eager to hear about it, which frightened her a little.

"She's already forgetting," Priya said, throwing her hands in the air and pushing her way out of the ring of girls. Several others frowned in disappointment and began disbanding with her.

"Forgetting?" Tiffany asked.

"Most girls forget what happened by the time they're brought up. I mean, who wants to remember their own death, right?"

Tiffany nodded, but she wasn't forgetting. Tiffany would never forget the icy touch of that thing. *What was it?* She'd call it a ghost if she believed in such things. In the darkness of her bedroom, though, she hadn't been able to tell. Some man behind the curtain, with a flashlight to blind her—no, to watch her die. She knew it was a man because she heard him when she woke up. He called her name, a distant voice for as close as it felt. "Tiffany. Tiffany," he'd said in her ear and she jolted upright in bed, but there was no one in her room. The red glow of the alarm clock said it was three in the morning. "Dad?" she'd asked. "Over here," the voice had called from the window.

"Don't let them bother you," Corinne said, breaking Tiffany's recollection.

Tiffany took a deep, shaky breath to settle her nerves.

"Do you remember anything?" Corinne asked invitingly.

"You don't have to tell them," a girl said from one of the nearby bunks. Some of the girls turned to look at her, sneering. The girl who spoke up was the only other one wearing a yellow gown, with two black stripes on her sleeves. Two stripes fewer than Corinne. She sat still, staring at an open book propped up by her raised legs, her neck and head leaning against her black wings, which leaned against the stone wall. She was a small thing by height, probably about as tall as Tiffany, but solid, almost dangerous looking, with bluish-tinted, mottled skin resembling granite.

Corinne didn't turn to look at the other girl. "She can do what she wants, Hedika," Corinne said irritably.

30

"That's my point, Corinne," Hedika answered, mocking her tone.

Corinne let out a trying sigh as she recovered her smile.

"If you want to talk about it, we're here to listen," Corinne said softly. "We all went through it."

Even though Corinne donned a warm smile, Tiffany didn't believe it. That other girl, Hedika, was warning her about something without saying so, and it already gave Tiffany a chill to think about how her anguish could be used against her in the future, to mock her or taunt her.

"Thanks," Tiffany replied. "Is there a bathroom?"

"Yeah," Corinne said, pointing toward another hall. "Don't make a mess."

"What?"

"Keep the bathrooms clean. We get inspected regularly. Don't be sloppy washing your hands, clean the water off the sinks and floors with the hand towels before you come out."

"Oh, OK."

Tiffany went into the bathroom and fought with her wings to get through a stall door before sitting down, alone. She only came in here to get away from the others long enough to try to figure things out. Funny how she came in here to be alone. Even with all these girls, she felt so alone in the first place. D.K. abandoned her as though she thought being in a room full of others might comfort her, but all it did was remind her of the time her father moved them to a new school and she had to walk into a fifth-grade class full of boys and girls who stared at her, judging her before she even reached her new and unfamiliar desk. Those unsettling nerves fluttered in her chest again.

The dorm itself reminded her of sixth-grade camp. That was the last time she bunked with a bunch of girls she didn't know, and that was just eight girls and lasted only a week. Everything about this dorm, from its size, to its occupants—every girl at least a year older than Tiffany—gave her the distinct impression her stay was going to be far longer, and there wouldn't be any juvenile antics or all-night giggling. Their demeanor veiled a hierarchy that wasn't apparent in the color of their gowns or the stripes on their sleeves, either.

It would have been nice if D.K. could have mentioned *something*.

"Tiffany," Corinne said as she knocked on the outside bathroom door.

Tiffany caught her breath and jerked in her seat. How long had she been sitting in the stall?

"Some of the girls and I are going to stretch our wings, maybe go look out over the Endless See. I thought maybe we could show you around."

"Sure," Tiffany said, swallowing hard. If that wasn't an initiation test, Tiffany didn't know what was. The last thing she wanted right now was to be excluded from the group, or pitied, or stand out for anything like failing her initiation. "Hold on, I'll be right out."

Tiffany remembered to flush and wash her hands so the others wouldn't think she had gone to hide, or at any rate, they wouldn't know with certainty. As she came out into the hallway, she found Corinne leaning against the opposite wall, a smirk propping up one side of her lips.

"Sorry, I'm not used to these wings in there with me," Tiffany said with an awkward smile.

Corinne snorted a laugh. "You ready?"

"Born that way." Tiffany wasn't sure what possessed her to choose those words, but they seemed appropriate. It put a smile on

Corinne's face.

The bay had emptied of the pack of girls who circled Tiffany earlier, and Corinne led her toward the long hall. Tiffany looked back at Hedika, who didn't budge or peel her eyes from her book. The other remaining girls didn't seem the least bit interested in her either. Tiffany thought if this was a bad idea, they might at least watch her the way a herd of sheep does a straggler walking toward a pack of wolves. None of them did, which made her worry all the more.

The girls she was going out with were lined up at the edge of the yellow perch. Several looked back at Tiffany and Corinne as they came through the door marked with the big number 3. Tiffany glowered at the pit full of sponges between them, remembering her earlier crash, and thought maybe this wasn't such a good idea.

"Are we going or what?" Priya called back irritably.

"We're coming, we're coming," Corinne replied.

"Where are we going?" Tiffany asked, trying to fight off the worry in her tone. Backing out now was probably what they all expected of her, but they didn't know her yet.

"Wherever," Corinne shrugged. "Maybe get a snack. Maybe just fly."

Tiffany's stomach complained. She wondered what constituted food around this place. She still craved all kinds of things like hamburgers, a chicken salad, a burrito, and even fish tacos, so she hoped they didn't eat raw caribou or sea lions.

"Let's go," Priya said as Corinne and Tiffany joined them. She dove off the ledge with her wings still furled and opened them as she fell, swooping away from the wall and turning with ease. Other girls began jumping after, their wings outstretched first in a less dangerous manner.

"Ready?" Corinne asked.

Tiffany nodded. She leaned forward and snapped open her wings. She struggled to keep her footing even as she felt herself tipping sideways. Instead of falling onto the ledge, however, she decided to lean forward more and fall out into the dark sky. Her heart beat with such fervor she thought it might push through her chest. Her wings didn't catch the air. She fell straight down, feet first, her wings straight up behind her. Her mind raced, thinking of what D.K. told her to do. She opened her legs and bent her knees, causing her head to dip forward. Her wings suddenly caught the air. She swooped out of her freefall in a startlingly fast arc that shot her out toward the center of the cavern.

"This way," Corinne said from above.

How embarrassing. She craned her neck to see the rest of the girls banking to follow the curve of the conical cavern. Tiffany began to flap to gain altitude and join them as they passed in front of her. She turned and fell in behind them. The girls hardly flapped their wings, gliding slowly in an uneven formation, sweeping side to side, amusing themselves by swatting each other's wings, trying to disrupt each other's flight or push each other around. The girls sometimes played at dodging one another, or a variant of tag, darting this way and that through their ranks, circling each other, giggling as they chased another with aloof pursuit tactics such as acting bored, or ignoring the others altogether, until making a sudden lunge.

Tiffany hoped none of them would include her in any of it. She was having a hard enough time just flying straight and keeping up with them. Her gait was wobbly, causing her to tilt left or right with every beat of her wings. When she tried to glide, she felt herself falling out of the sky, drifting downward so quickly she wondered if her wings had holes.

Priya held the lead of the formation most of the time. She darted forward, dropped down abruptly, or threw out her wings to stop in mid-flight whenever another girl tried to get near her. She was acrobatic and quick, and all the other girls obviously knew she was the best flier. Eventually, however, Karla swooped up from beneath her. They came together and Priya grappled Karla around the neck. Both began to tumble out of the sky. It looked like a big bird being harried by a smaller, faster bird, but the big bird finally got hold of it and was making it pay. As they fell, Priya let go. Karla didn't. Then Priya's voice crying 'Uncle' echoed up and the two separated, swooping from each other in different directions.

Corinne laughed at the sight of the two girls' short tussle, as did the other girls.

Tiffany fought off yet another updraft, struggling to keep balance as her wings wobbled and shook her entire body. She widened her legs and that seemed to calm things down, but it slowed her even more.

"Don't worry. You'll get the hang of it," Corinne said as she circled around behind Tiffany and passed her slowly. "Do you want to see something cool?"

Tiffany nodded as she caught herself from an uneven flap of her wings that threatened to make her spiral out of control. It unnerved her, but she managed to keep the fear from rising to her face. "Sure," she said with as much confidence as she trusted to come from her voice without it breaking.

"Priya," Corinne called ahead. "Go to the See."

Tiffany thought Corinne had said "sea" and wondered where an ocean might be hidden inside the enormous cavern. The ground below showed no sign of water anywhere. If anything, it just looked like uneven rock lit up like a big town.

Priya nodded her head and banked, leading the way for the other girls, who soared down ahead of Tiffany much faster than she thought safe. They cruised down, always down, as though they intended to fly to the ground. The lights and uneven ground quickly revealed itself to be a city with buildings and lanes ringing a dark center. Nothing seemed familiar, and with all her concentration on flying, she had no time to sort it out.

Half-way down, Priya turned and they raced toward a nearby ledge at break-neck speed. Corinne winked at Tiffany and dropped suddenly from her side, gaining speed to join them. As each approached the wide ledge, they arched their wings to swoop upward at the last possible moment, throwing their legs out as they flapped in quick succession. Priya landed first, her feet touching down gracefully. She stepped forward out of the way of others, snapping her wings shut behind her.

So that's how it's done.

Tiffany tried the same maneuver, although much slower than the others, coming in beneath the landing perch and arcing over it at the last moment, curling her wings to make them into a parachute, snapping her legs out. She landed on unsteady feet, nearly falling backwards, but managed to swirl her arms several times to regain balance. She felt relief. Crashing in front of the other girls would be embarrassing, and probably what they were all expecting.

Priya turned her back on Tiffany, disappointment apparent as she sauntered away from the group toward the opposite end of the long cave. The other girls followed her coolly.

"Where are we?" Tiffany asked. Her voice echoed down the long, dark passageway. It was perfectly rectangular, as though chiseled out of stone, and about twenty feet wide and ten feet high. By the way Corinne held up a finger to her lips, Tiffany realized they probably weren't supposed to be here.

"One of the passages out," Corinne whispered. "They leave this one open at night."

"Outside?" Tiffany asked, fighting to contain her voice. A sudden vision of her bedroom and her parents caused her heart to throb, and her throat constricted as she fought off a growing desire to cry. The idea of seeing the world again hurried her pace. She caught up with the other girls, but stopped short of the group. She didn't want to appear too eager, especially if this was some kind of prank.

As she followed the girls, they began to spread out and crouch low behind thick bases of stone supporting a huge barred gate. Two enormous, unguarded floor-to-ceiling hinged doors were wide open, revealing a gray haze in the far distance that appeared like a wall of fog bearing down on them.

Tiffany stopped, gawking at the sight.

A hillside descended into the fog. Row upon row of enormous medieval walls curved with the landscape, spaced out evenly with vast ranges of emptiness between them. Where the land and fog met, an enormous invisible barrier held the billowing haze in check. Tiffany blinked her eyes in disbelief. The walls may have only been thirty or forty feet high, but compared to the endless shroud of fog rising to the height of Tiffany's sight—up over the mountain itself by the looks of it, like a dome surrounding them— the walls appeared as toys.

Towers and strongholds dotted the landscape, giving form to the walls and reminding Tiffany of the Great Wall of China, replete with glowing, hooded lanterns and torches. In the grayness of what appeared to be night, orbs of blue-white light shone like streetlights seen from an airplane, illuminating the entirety of the maze.

"Take a good look at the world we live in," Corinne whispered into Tiffany's ear.

"What is this?" she wondered aloud. She squinted and her vision zoomed in on one of the walkways atop the nearest wall. She still couldn't get used to the feeling of her vision doing that. A wave of dizziness made her knees feel weak. Thoughts of fainting flew out of her mind, though. A large statue facing the billowing fog captured her attention. It held a tall pole in its hand, the end of it glowing in a strange blue-white light that pulsated and swam like churning lightning. The statue moved, turning its head to the side, then the other way, before looking ahead toward the great fog looming in the distance. Her eyes widened, zooming her vision back. She stumbled backwards a step, recovering her balance while shaking her head in disbelief. The statue was a stone-skinned man without wings or a tail. She zoomed in her sight on another man and he appeared the same, like a living statue. It looked like medieval castle walls being guarded; *but against what?*

"This is the Endless See," Corinne said softly.

"I thought you meant an ocean," Tiffany whispered honestly. Corinne snorted softly and stepped past Tiffany to join the other girls, breaking Tiffany's sightline. Corinne sneaked ahead to crouch against the stone base of the gates. All the girls held the bars and leaned over one another like children trying not to get caught watching a ball game from outside the park.

Tiffany gazed in wonder at the wall of fog, stepping toward the center of the passageway to get an unobscured view of it through the open gate. The fog swelled behind what seemed to be a wall of glass, like an enormous aquarium that arced up and over the mountain. *Some kind of dome*, she thought as she stepped closer to the gate.

The entirety of the fog billowed, undulating with movement within. It reminded her of fish swimming through muddy water. Their passing churned up roiling filth in the form of smoke and ash.

Enthralled by the bizarreness of it she hardly noticed her vision zooming in, drawing her sight closer as she took small, cautious steps forward. The forms in the fog seemed to be wraiths, mere shadows of flying beings, and she wondered if there were others like her out there.

A face suddenly appeared, pressing against the glass barrier holding back the fog. It stretched the surface of the glass like it was made of latex, pushing its enraged face toward Tiffany as groping hands flailed in a wild attempt to dig through the pliable clear surface. Blue-white lightning danced all over it. Its rage turned to a look of agony and it retreated as quickly as it appeared.

Tiffany gasped and her eyes widened, zooming her vision back out.

"Shh," Corinne hissed.

Tiffany swooned from dizziness. Everything around her appeared vague and dark, as though her eyes were crossed.

"Too late," Priya groused. "A Sentinel spotted us."

"What?" Tiffany asked, wondering what a Sentinel was.

"Come on," Corinne said, leaping into the air. The other girls followed quickly, abandoning their hideouts as they turned and threw themselves into the air. Priya blasted by, streaking only inches above Tiffany's wings. The wind of her passing knocked Tiffany to her hands and knees.

"Fly," Corinne called urgently.

In here!? There was no room, and yet the other girls were doing it.

Tiffany watched the girls lift off around her with ease. She stretched her wings out and lunged forward, flapping wildly, only to fall flat on the ground.

"Come on," Corinne shouted. The other girls retreated with her, all of them calling back, urging her to flight.

Tiffany's heart raced. Whatever had them all running had to be bad. *One of those things trapped in the clouds?* She got up and started running, her hands stinging from her fall. All she needed was a little speed.

The ground in front of her bubbled over and a thick man rose like a wall. She screamed and tried to stop, but he appeared so suddenly she slammed face first into his hard body. He caught her in one arm to keep her from falling backwards. When she looked up at his dark gray, brutish face, he scowled down at her. He held one of those tall poles with its fiery blue-white globe of light casting an eerie shadow over his glowering expression.

Well, now I know how wingless get around.

FIVE

TIFFANY SAT ON THE BED IN THE HOLDING CELL for hours, too afraid to close her eyes. She expected D.K. to come get her, wearing a heavy scowl of utter disappointment, but no one came—not even to check on her through the bars of the gate—and she found herself alone with only her thoughts for company. Thoughts of home, her death, and the loss of her family mostly. Other little things like never seeing her friends again, wanting to go to the mall, and dying for a Chipotle bowl gnawed at her too, in more ways than one. She was starving. Mom and Dad would have come to get her out of jail. How would she ever see them again? How was she going to get out of this place and get back to them, to tell them she was still alive?

I am *still alive. I can't be dead. I'm right here.*

Tiffany closed her eyes and imagined her mother's hand stroking her hair, the warmth of her mother's palm resting on the back of her head as she worked on homework at the kitchen counter. Mom always hovered, watching her write her words and numbers, correcting her gently. And when Tiffany did well, she leaned forward and kissed her forehead, telling her, "That's my girl."

Her father liked to sneak up on her and grab her around the waist, then he would swing her around like he did when she was a little girl, her feet straight out, and even though she complained, she still giggled.

The sting of her first tear worked its way through her tightly shut eyelids. She blinked at it and more began to fall. *Where are they now?* Not here. They wouldn't come to rescue her this time. They couldn't protect her from this place.

What a rotten place, too. A small, solid stone room with a single iron gate locking her inside. Outside her cell, an eerily quiet hallway. If there was anyone else in the jail, she couldn't tell. Her jailors abandoned her too, but then again, she refused to call out for any of them. Big stone-skinned brutes in blue uniforms with no tails or wings, all scowling at her since the moment she arrived. Even the women were huge, and grim.

Tiffany leaned her head against her wings. They were warm; the folds of leathery membrane soft like a pillow. She curled them around her shoulders, hugging herself as she sobbed into her hands, lamenting everything in life and death until she had no more strength. She gave in to her anguish knowing that, at least here, alone, in as wretched a condition as she was, at least it wasn't in front of the girls in Bay 3.

When the tears ran out, so did her strength, and she slipped into a deep slumber, wishing that when she woke she would be home again and the nightmare would be over. She even clicked her heels like Dorothy in the *Wizard of Oz*, just in case it would help.

She slept so hard she didn't hear the gate screech open in the morning.

"Get up," a man's voice said, startling her from an empty dream. His tone sounded like he was tired of repeating himself. "Come on, get up."

She lurched upright, her heart racing. The cell radiated a

warm, white glow instead of the ominous gray-black it had been last night.

The man stood above her with his hands on his hips, holding open his black leather overcoat, which draped to the floor. She noticed immediately his round belly stretching out the fabric of a white shirt, the same belly that hung over his blue jeans where they were lashed to his waist by a black belt. His tanned skin appeared as leathery as the overcoat, weather-worn from years of exposure to the elements—the kind of skin her father always pointed out to Tiffany, saying it meant the man was homeless or a transient or someone who worked in the sun. In any case, he was likely crazy and someone to avoid. She wasn't sure if those same rules applied here.

"You want to get out of here?" he asked. His huge wings stood neatly folded behind his back. At least he wasn't a Sentinel. Tiffany knew what that meant now. Cops. Still, this one might have been a cop too, just with wings.

Tiffany squinted and nodded. Of course she wanted to leave. Being in prison was the worst experience of her life—her new life, at any rate. She didn't even care who he was so long as he got her out of this crummy place.

"I'm Franklin, by the way," he said while holding out a hand. "Your mentor."

D.K. said something about a mentor last night. She pictured a tutor or someone her own age. Franklin seemed more like someone's father. Tiffany stood and took his hand to shake it. Thick callouses covered his fingers and palms. His hand engulfed hers as he gently shook it.

"I'm Tiffany—"

"Noboru," Franklin finished for her, pronouncing it perfectly. "I know all about you. Sorry I wasn't here to pick you up myself when you arrived. I was…hunting."

Tiffany didn't say anything, but wondered what he meant.

He was the first winged man she'd met, and so far she didn't feel impressed. It may have been how his jeans flared like bell-bottoms, although not as pronounced—what kind of fashion statement was he trying to make? But as he turned she realized he was tailless, like her.

"The night watch girl in your bay said you'd been picked up by Sentinels. Not the best first day, huh?"

Tiffany shook her head when Franklin stopped outside of the open cell door.

"Did D.K. treat you well, at least?"

Tiffany shrugged.

Franklin chuckled knowingly, waving for her to follow him. They walked through a hallway lined with other empty cells, and into a larger room where several wingless men and women were working at desks. Some looked up, nodding at Franklin. A few glowered toward Tiffany. Maybe Franklin was one of them after all.

"Don't let them get to you," Franklin said under his breath as he led her across the room. They passed through another iron gate and Tiffany found herself under the now brightly lit cavernous interior of the hollow mountain. It looked different under the spell of daylight. The holes that were lit up at night were now dark so that they appeared equally conspicuous against the soft white of the stone. *What a strange place.*

She squinted to look for the yellow strip somewhere above, zooming in her vision over large areas until she found it. She expected to see Corinne and the others perched up there, laughing and pointing at the sight of her, but the landing platform was thankfully empty. She retracted her vision and felt dizzy.

Franklin squinted to look up as well. "What're you looking at?"

"Nothing," Tiffany said, shaking her head.

"Well, let's get some chow, then, and get you up to speed on things. Can you fly?"

"A little."

"Fine. Follow me and try not to crash when we land. They know me where we're going, so don't embarrass me."

Tiffany sighed. So far, her mentor was turning out to be a big disappointment.

SIX

THE MOMENT SHE LANDED BEHIND FRANKLIN she nearly tumbled over. Thankfully he caught her. "Don't go dying on me twice," he said. He held her arm until she steadied her feet beneath her and retracted her wings. "There's no coming back from the afterlife. If you die now, you're gone."

"So I'm really dead?" It still made no sense. How could she be dead if she was still alive?

"Bah," Franklin said with a dismissive wave. He led her toward a long counter fronting the broad landing ledge. Men and women of all sizes and colors, with and without wings, sat on stools at the counter. Behind the counter a long grill sizzled with cooking food as smoke rose up into a stone chimney built into the wall. A sign above the chimney read FLY & DIVER GRILL. A tall, alabaster colored woman took people's orders while two stony fry cooks worked the grills. Franklin picked two seats side-by-side along the counter and motioned for Tiffany to sit with him.

Tiffany sat down, but Franklin stood, leaning with both hands on the edge of the counter, hovering.

"Look, the other world, you know, where we came from, it's, well, it's not…there's things you don't know, and…shoot, the thing of it is—" Franklin stopped and took a deep breath. "I know

what you're going through. I was eight myself when I died. It's…it's been a long time."

Tiffany stared at him blankly.

Franklin sat down with a huge sigh. He slid a menu in front of her. "Don't get the sausage, by the way. I'm not sure what they make it out of here, but they are *not* pork links."

"Morning, Franklin," the tall alabaster waitress eventually chirped as she slid in front of them, putting out silverware and two glasses of water. "Who's your friend?"

"Tawny, meet Tiffany. Tiffany, Tawny."

"Wait. Franklin, are you mentoring? He's not your mentor, is he?" Tawny asked, giggling and grinning ear to ear.

"As a matter of fact," Franklin replied, obviously offended.

"Shoot, Franklin, when was the last time you trained anyone? Or did field work?"

"I was in the field yesterday," Franklin grumbled, his eyes glowering at Tawny.

"Oh," Tawny said with concern. She leaned forward over the counter, looking side to side at the other patrons. Tiffany looked as well. None of the other customers seemed interested in their conversation. "What's going on? I thought you were just a protector now. Don't you have too many chimera in your collection?"

"I did," Franklin said. He eyed Tiffany then looked back at Tawny. "Can we just have some flapjacks and eggs?"

"And bacon, please," Tiffany added softly. "And orange juice. Is there orange juice here?" she asked Franklin. She hadn't even looked at the menu.

"Sure thing," Tawny replied with a smile turned toward Tiffany. She wrote up their order and shot them both a worried look again before leaving to help other customers.

"You're probably wondering about that," Franklin said.

Tiffany shrugged, even though it piqued her curiosity. After dealing with Corinne and D.K., she didn't feel like getting duped. *Just play it cool.*

"I'm not an old wash-out, if that's what you're thinking," Franklin grumbled. "When you've been doing this as long as I have—hunting ghosts—you get a collection of people and places you need to protect, keep an eye on, watch over. You get too many, like me, and you can't keep an eye on everyone all the time *and* keep hunting. Sometimes it's hard enough just keeping an eye on them. They make you a protector, and newbies—someone like you—come in and take over with the hunting and start your own collections.

"Only we don't have hardly the number of newbies we used to. Some say it's because we're over-protecting the living. I didn't used to believe it, but—"

Franklin sat up straight and stared at Tiffany. "Do you even know what I'm talking about?"

"Not really," Tiffany replied honestly. "I'm still just trying to figure out why I have wings."

Franklin took in a deep, serious breath. "Right, baby steps. I suppose starting from the beginning is the best thing for you. Stop me if you already know this, but the long and the short of it is that for as long as people have been praying, they've been seeing angels and devils. That's us. Angels. Devils. One in the same. About the only difference is that the stone-skins—like those two cooking our breakfast—look a lot more devilish than you and me. You, they'd call an angel. Me, when I was younger, they called me an angel...sometimes."

Franklin grinned and raised his eyebrows. Tiffany smiled even though she tried to keep a straight face. His grin slowly faded.

"We're neither, of course," Franklin said sharply, turning in his seat to scrutinize her. "Gargoyles. That's the best word to describe what we are."

Tiffany snorted, stifling an involuntarily laugh.

"What?" Franklin glowered.

"Gargoyles? Seriously?" Tiffany shook her head at the insanity of such a statement. "I liked the angels and demons thing. That…that one sounded convincing, but gargoyles? Gargoyles are statues they put on the sides of buildings—"

"To protect them," Franklin pointed out. "There's a bond between those *'statues'* and our kind. Anything made of stone will work, really, but somewhere along the line people got the idea to make the things look like us. And it stuck, and we've been calling ourselves gargoyles to new-comers like you for as long as I can remember.

"Now, if you had a tail, well, those high-and-mighty Seraph would be filling your head with a bunch of malarkey right now about truly being angels, but you're tailless. We're hunters. In the good old days, they called us Valkyrie. And what we do is claim the dead, the dangerous ones, at least, and send them packing."

Tiffany stared at him with a raised eyebrow, completely unconvinced.

"You don't believe me."

Tiffany didn't answer.

"I'll take that as a no. Look, Tiffany, you're a new cadet, whether you like it or not. Just like you were born into the old world without a choice of what you were—the color of your hair or eyes, or your skin—you've been born here a flier. You're tailless, so you're never going to be part of the Seraphim, but you've got wings, and that means that right now we need you in the other world. Badly."

"Flapjacks," Tawny said as she slid two plates in front of Franklin and Tiffany.

Tiffany looked down at her plate, avoiding Franklin's stare.

"Tawny," Franklin called as the waitress retreated. "Can you tell my young friend here what we are?"

"What do you mean?" Tawny asked.

"What are we called? By the other world."

"What, gargoyles?"

"Yeah, thanks," Franklin told Tawny. He leaned closer to Tiffany. "You can ask anyone. They'll all say the same thing."

Tiffany frowned, her mood soured by the waitress's confirmation. She didn't want to be a gargoyle. "I want to go home," Tiffany told him.

Franklin sighed and put a hand on her shoulder. Tiffany shrugged it away angrily.

"Hey, I'm on your side," Franklin snapped. She felt his hard glare soften, but he turned his body to face the counter. He picked up his fork and reached for the syrup. "Eat your breakfast before it gets cold. We have a lot of work to do."

SEVEN

TIFFANY ATE BEGRUDGINGLY even though she was starving and the food tasted delicious. Franklin didn't say a word as he cut up his pancakes and shoveled the slices into his mouth. He leaned sideways with his hand on his thigh, his elbow pointing up and out so that the wingless beside him didn't get too close. There was something predatory about the way everyone protected their food, which made Tiffany think in other circumstances they might actually curl their wings around their plates to keep it hidden.

Franklin stopped eating suddenly, becoming still as a statue, staring at the wall with his fork midway to his mouth. Tiffany finished her bite and drank her juice, wondering if he was having a seizure. She looked up and down the counter at the other patrons, but none of them paid Franklin any attention.

He dropped his fork suddenly, growling, "We've got to scoot!" He stood from the stool and pushed himself back urgently. "Come on."

"What's going on?" Tiffany asked, putting her fork down and sliding from the stool to follow him.

"We need to get topside right now." Franklin reached the edge of the landing platform and looked down, waving for Tiffany to catch up. She hurried to his side and looked where he did.

In the center of the cavern floor was an enormous dome, ringed by the thousands of buildings and streets of the city. Unlike the rest of the interior of the immense hollow mountain, which glowed a warm off-white, the dome was pitch black on the outside, reflecting the other light off its arcs as though made of polished glass. Tiffany imagined it forming out of a great bubble of obsidian rising out of the earth, hardening as it expanded. She remembered seeing the thing last night only as a dark patch, but when Franklin retrieved her from jail this morning she hadn't looked for it or noticed much of anything around her. Now she wondered how she could have missed it.

"Have you done a free fall yet?" Franklin asked. Tiffany looked hesitant. "That's a no. I'll do the flying. Keep your wings in tight."

"Wha—" Tiffany began, but with two quick moves Franklin stepped behind her and grabbed her around the middle. "Hey!" She put her hands on his arms to try to pry herself free, but he stepped off the ledge before she could resist. Tiffany screamed. They fell away from the ledge and began diving face first. The wind rushed by, flattening her hair. Instinctively she tried flashing out her wings, but Franklin's hold around her waist pinned them to her back. She stopped struggling at the sight of the ground closing in on them. Her scream died out. The dark cave entrances along the mountain's interior walls rushed by in a blur, like lights in a train tunnel. Her eyes widened out of fear, forcing her to watch the ground rising at them. Franklin's wings remained tight to his back, open only enough to keep them facing straight down. With every second they gained more speed.

"If I drop you," Franklin yelled loud enough for Tiffany to hear over the wind buffeting against her ears. "Just open your wings half way at first to slow down. Got it?"

Tiffany hardly registered his words. *Drop me!?* The ground came up at them too fast. She'd never be able to stop, even with wings. She squirmed, tying to free herself from his grip.

"Quit that," Franklin shouted. "And hang on!"

The elbow of his wings above their heads spread slightly. Their bodies lurched as his wings filled with a loud pop. His grip around her waist held firm, like a seatbelt, but her feet and arms snapped forward, leaving her hands and feet dangling as they continued to fall toward the ground. After catching her breath, Tiffany screamed again. Franklin straightened his wings and shifted trajectory. Instead of a straight drop, they began to arc and race toward the dome. The change in angle forced her legs back again, and she felt an exhilarating tingle in her belly. Tiffany's scream rose in pitch. She yelled with excitement.

"That's the fun part!" Franklin shouted over her calls. The raw force ebbed as he banked them to begin a circle of the dome. Tiffany went silent, grinning ear to ear. Tears caused by the wind and her hair lashing at her eyes trickled along her temples. He slowed as he came around, giving Tiffany a chance to take in a deep breath to help calm her pounding heart. Her face felt flush, her fingers and toes tingled.

She saw where Franklin intended to land, a large flat courtyard alongside the dome. He swooped in and flapped his wings repeatedly to bring them down gently. Once grounded, he let her go and checked his wings before curling them against his body.

"That was—" Tiffany began, breathless, still smiling widely.

"Can you walk and talk at the same time?" he asked, taking her by the hand and dragging her toward the dome.

That's rude, she thought until a seam split apart in front of them and black doors began to open of their own accord, but so slowly Franklin slipped in sideways to get through, pulling her in after. He rushed down a long hallway, letting her hand go as he pushed open one of the side doors. The room they entered looked like an enormous library, its racks filled with small statues about a foot tall. Thousands of square, hollowed shelves supported the figurines, each in individual slots. Most slots were occupied, but she saw an entire section of empty cubbies.

"Wait here," Franklin said and leapt into the air. He flew across the room and landed on a ladder next to a wall of statues. He climbed up a little and looked over the little figurines quickly, his eyes hunting for one in particular. Tiffany zoomed her vision in on the figurines in front of Franklin. She saw a name placard beneath the statue that Franklin grabbed, which read:

CRAFT, FRANKLIN
BAKER, JOSHUA K., 1938—

Franklin leapt off the ladder and swooped back toward Tiffany as she retracted her vision. Her head swooned with dizziness, but she tried to hide it as he landed in front of her, his huge black wings blocking out the sight of the room.

"Come on," he said as he brushed past her, pushing his wings against her as he furled them, which made her spin.

"What was that place?" Tiffany asked as she caught up with him out in the hallway, shaking her head to clear her vision. Franklin continued his fast pace toward the end of the hallway, the center of the domed complex.

"Our collections." Franklin held the statue in front of him so she could see it better. The miniature gargoyle had a wide face with an enormous mouth showing four thick teeth meant to represent fangs. Tiffany remembered how D.K.'s teeth looked large too. She felt her own canine teeth, wondering if they had grown any bigger since her death. They felt normal, though.

Along with its big head, the figurine had a round belly like a Buddha statue that made it look no more menacing than a fat cat. A lot like the figurine she used to have by her window.

They passed through a set of tall double-doors at the end of the hallway and Tiffany came to a halt. Ahead of them stood an enormous, circular pillar reaching from the floor to the top of the domed ceiling. The room was likewise circular, with several platforms protruding from the walls where empty clear-glass offices overlooked the floor space. The floor was strewn with clusters of desks and half-walls that gave the whole place the look of a garden maze.

"Dispatch," Franklin called as he crossed the room, holding his statue above his head. A tall, ash-white wingless woman stood from a desk and turned to regard him. Tiffany snapped out of her doe-eyed shock and jogged to keep up with Franklin.

"Franklin?" The woman seemed surprised at seeing him. "What's wrong?"

"I need an emergency gate. Right now."

"I need authorization," the woman said. "Where?"

Franklin shook his statue.

"No, no, no," she replied, throwing out her hands. Her fingers were long and thin, much like her body. She stood two feet faller than Tiffany, almost as tall as D.K. Even her head was longer than normal, but in a beautiful manner that spoke of wisdom and refinement.

"Kendall—"

"I'm not going to do it," the tall woman interrupted.

"Open the gate right now or I'll cut off your tail, Kendall."

Tiffany looked Kendall up and down and noticed a tail as long as her legs twitching behind her. She wasn't sure if that meant

Kendall was angry at him, or afraid he might do it.

"No one goes alone. You *know* that's the new rule."

"I'm not going alone."

"She doesn't count!"

"She just did a free-fall getting here. She's rock solid."

Tiffany nodded enthusiastically. "You should have seen it," Tiffany said, grinning ear to ear.

"I can't authorize it."

"Please," Franklin said softly, his shoulders slumped forward as he held out the figurine with both hands. "I know I screwed up the last one, but that's because I've been out so long. I won't let it happen again."

Kendall didn't say anything. She crossed her arms and eyed him.

"We can't let him take them." Franklin held the figurine higher so it stared Kendall in the face.

She sighed, holding her hands out, motioning for the figurine.

"Thank you," Franklin breathed, putting the statue in her hands. He stretched to kiss her cheek. "You are now, literally, a life saver."

"Go before I change my mind," Kendall said, not looking at him. "And I'm calling D.K."

Franklin grabbed Tiffany by the hand and led her toward the pillar in the center of the dome. "Call the National Guard while you're at it."

"Where are we going?" Tiffany asked as she jogged to keep his pace.

"1944," Franklin said. "Or thereabouts."

"What?"

"You'll see."

The base of the pillar had an opening that Tiffany hadn't

noticed. A trick of the eye, maybe, like the changing color of all the stone. Franklin led her straight inside and let her hand go as he walked to the center of the hollow pillar. Tiffany stared up at the endless tube. The tube appeared longer inside than the dome itself. *Another trick of the light?* She wanted to walk back out and double-check. There was no tube in the middle of the hollow mountain that she'd seen.

"You may want to stand over here in the center," Franklin said. Tiffany looked at him and he motioned for her to come closer. Tiffany backed to Franklin, looking up again, squinting to zoom in on the endless point of light above, but she couldn't focus on it.

"Where does it go?"

"Top side."

"How?"

"Ever been shot out of a cannon?"

Tiffany shot Franklin a look of concern. Breaking her concentration on the tube above made her dizzy. He grinned a second, then looked straight up, taking in a deep breath. Tiffany did likewise, figuring whatever he did probably made more sense than anything else.

The light above raced toward them as though someone flicked on a switch in a dark room. Her hair stood on end. She heard a cackling *zot* and all her skin felt stretched, as though it were being pulled toward the top of the endless pillar by long elastic tendrils. It yanked her so hard she thought her body stretched a hundred miles before her feet snapped free of the ground to catapult her even faster into the coming light. As she collided with the light there was a metallic *bang, clang*, and she felt something hit her in the head. She fell back to the ground, her feet bound in something that interfered with her balance, and she careened sideways. Still blind, with her arms flailing, she struck cold, moist ground.

"That's not right," Franklin complained from somewhere nearby.

Tiffany rubbed the knot on the top of her head as the darkness of her vision faded. They were under a canopy of ominous gray clouds hanging low overhead. A chill crept up her spine as though something vile watched her. A disturbing presence. Maybe from the window—*where did this house come from?* She looked up at the window, but saw nothing looking out.

How did we get here?

She tried to roll onto her back, but her wings were in the way, and her legs hardly moved. She looked down to find her legs buried up to her thighs in an old-time aluminum trash bin.

"Yuck," she said. An empty box of Boraxo Soap rolled to the ground as she began pulling her legs free. Banana peels and a lump covered in gray-green mold tumbled over her hip. "Gross!" She pulled her legs out and sat upright, swatting at bits of refuse clinging to her gown. Franklin tumbled off the top of a wood pile stacked against the house opposite her, several split logs falling with him. He landed squarely on his feet and stood straight, arching his back with his hands on his hips. She heard a cracking sound from his back.

"Criminy," he said, stepping next to Tiffany. He held out a hand for her and helped her to her feet. As she stood, he let her hand go and reached down behind her. He picked up the statue that they gave to Kendall.

"What's this doing in the trash?"

"Why were *we* in the trash?" Tiffany asked.

"Because we're rooted to this," Franklin replied, rolling the figurine in his hands, turning it to inspect it. "Huh," he said with a puzzled look. He handed the figurine to Tiffany and crouched down, swatting at the trash littering the ground. Tiffany turned the figurine over to look at it too. It wasn't the same one from the library. This one was smaller and didn't have a belly. This one looked a lot more like the one she used to have.

"What the—?" Franklin stood up straight, holding a pair of old glasses for her to see.

Tiffany recognized the glasses. Not that exact pair, but something like it from her own home. Her father always left a pair just like it under the radiator. Both this pair and her father's were missing a lens. "So they can't see," Tiffany whispered, echoing her father's words from long ago. She sucked in her breath to fight off her guilt. She'd thrown out the pair under her radiator a few days before her death. She swallowed a lump in her throat and it became a knot in the pit of her belly.

Franklin looked at her sharply. He shoved the glasses into her hand. "This way," he said, grabbing her by the arm and leading her to the back of the house. That strange, cold presence seemed to follow them. *Not following us*, she thought. *It's in the house.*

The back yard sloped down toward a large lake. The property had its own small dock with a rowboat tied to it. Across the lake, Tiffany saw four or five other homes spread widely along the shore. She looked to her left and right, wondering how close the other homes were. She couldn't see any through the trees.

Franklin turned her toward the house and let her go as he looked it up and down. *Does he feel it too?* Tiffany shivered involuntarily. Maybe it was just from being barefoot in the cold, wet grass.

The house hunched under low, gray clouds. It was an old style two-story with a porch that wrapped around one side, supporting a balcony and two sets of double-doors that probably led to bedrooms. A haze-like fog roamed the tips of the nearby trees, depositing a fine mist that brushed against her wings.

A muffled scream rose from somewhere inside the house.

"Wait here," Franklin said tersely as he rushed toward the back door.

"But—"

"Wait!" Franklin snarled and drew what looked like a pistol from his coat pocket. He bounded up the eight porch stairs in two strides with his wings slightly cupped. He stopped outside only long enough to retract his wings tightly and yank open the door. He shook the pistol in his hand, which flared with blue-white light and filled out into a larger shape—that of a crossbow.

"What the—?"

Franklin could produce the same blue-white lightning that the Sentinels used on their poles, but his light didn't look like it was for seeing in the dark. His was a weapon.

Tiffany sidestepped in the hopes of seeing through the big window under the balcony. She wanted to know where Franklin went, but something in the grass caught her eye. She squinted and her vision zoomed in on a pile of something next to the house. It made her head swim a little. *Would she ever get over that feeling*, she wondered? She felt sick to her stomach, and not just because of her eyes.

Five long rib bones were stabbed into the ground as though someone had been playing with them. What a gruesome thought that was. She grimaced, repulsed by the sight. She looked away, widening her field of vision as she shuddered involuntarily, shaking off the mild dizziness that followed.

Up on the balcony an insistent banging on the door drew her attention. Through the glass, Tiffany witnessed a terrified boy beat on the door frame with one hand as he shook the lock with the other.

"Franklin," Tiffany called out worriedly.

The boy stopped pounding and turned his back to the door. Tiffany squinted and her vision zoomed in, seeing right through the glass panes as though looking through the boy's eyes.

Her head swam as a shadow moved across the wall, rippling under the paint like an enormous, flat bubble. It had a smoldering eye that left a trail of smoke rising from the burn marks it scarred into the wall at its passing. It dove suddenly toward the floor and a second later the boy disappeared, as though he fell into a hole that opened up beneath him.

"Holy—" Tiffany gasped. A wave of past terrors crashed into her, staggering her backwards as her vision recoiled. She shook her head briskly, pushing aside memories of her own death and the hauntings that led up to it. She didn't know what that thing was in the boy's room, but she recognized it as what killed her. The cause of all this. The thing that took her from her parents, and meant to do the same to that poor boy.

Rage and fury welled in her chest, but she couldn't move. Her puny body hadn't changed. That thing killed her once already.

That was before I had wings.

She gnashed her teeth. She had to do something. Bending low, she sprang into the air, her wings stretching forward as though she could grasp the balcony rails to catapult her into the room. One enormous flap surged her forward with such speed that the glass door rushed at her like a speeding car. She covered her head with her arms, pulling in her wings just before crashing into the door. It burst open and she threw her arms out to break her fall, dropping the figurine and glasses Franklin made her carry. She landed squarely on top of the boy. Her wings swatted the floor at the last moment to help brace her and keep her from crushing him. She let out her breath in relief and rose to her stinging hands and knees, her elbows aching from where they hit the door frame.

Tiffany had to take a second to orient herself to the room. She felt a little unstable after crashing into the door, either that or the room was moving. The boy slid on his back beneath her toward the closet. He stared at her in utter horror then desperately grabbed her by the arm. She felt a cold chill dig into her skin and rush through her body, then it vanished and the boy stopped moving. Several thumps and crashes circled the room. Tiffany felt keenly aware of a presence that moved like the wind, effortlessly drifting around her, almost pacing. She straightened, still kneeling, as she dragged the boy closer. Her wings retracted against her back, curling in tightly. The boy began whimpering.

"Shhh." He stared at her finger as she reached out to touch him on the lips with it. "It's OK," she whispered, turning her head side to side, tracking the feeling of dread that moved around the room, evaporating from one place to manifest in another.

The door leading to the balcony slammed shut behind her. The boy cowered, covering his head with his arms, curling into a ball as he cried out.

Tiffany shook the boy's grip off her arm and stood. The presence charged. She turned to face it, expecting to see or feel something substantive, but it wavered and dove beneath the floor just as she put a hand out to try to stop it, as though she might be able to deflect it or grapple it in some way. She wanted to fight it. She wanted to strangle the life from it as it had done to her.

The boy began sliding beneath her, dragged away once more toward the closet. She lunged on top of the boy, grabbing him by the arms as she rolled with him away from the closet, closer to the bed. She felt an ice-cold chill against her wings that stabbed throughout her body, and she felt the presence recoil beneath her.

What was that?

"What's this?" she heard a dark and familiar voice echo from the closet. "You're not Franklin."

EIGHT

TIFFANY SANK LOW, HOVERING OVER THE BOY, suddenly afraid and cold. The boy continued whimpering, covering his eyes with his hands, not daring to look at her. For the first time, she got a good look at him—only six or seven years old, thin, with short brown hair and big ears. Curled up and fetal as he was, he hardly seemed more than a baby.

"Why are you hiding?" the voice asked, this time from somewhere near the balcony doorway. Tiffany quietly turned to face it. The curtains began to slide across the rod even though nobody was there, slowly darkening the unlit room. The curtain fabric stretched and bunched near the middle as though a hand clutched it. No wind or drawstring moved it; no one was standing there, nothing at all except a shadow cast over the fabric. As the room darkened, an orb of light resembling a fist took shape where the curtain fabric bunched, and the shadow darkened into the outline of a looming man.

"Ah, there you are," the voice purred menacingly. The chill of his words dug straight to her bones. The truly unsettling thing of it all was that she recognized his voice.

The other curtain began to move, sliding across the rod, tugged by the same glowing fist attached to the spectral shadow that undulated on the curtain. The wraith had long arms and what looked like flowing, draping cloth covering its enormous form. The nearest wall wept a chill as though made of ice, sending a shiver down Tiffany's spine. The curtains came together, drowning out the gray daylight beyond. Only the light from the glowing fist remained, and then it too snuffed out, allowing the bunched fabric to fall.

Darkness, cold, and silence reigned. The boy shrunk into a ball beneath her.

Tiffany felt the presence hovering next to the curtain, unmoving and silent, glaring at her with a malice that made her fingers tingle. The ball of light lit again, brightly, appearing in the thing's head like a Cyclops' eye. She squinted and held a hand up to block the intensity of the light.

"Who are you?" it asked curiously.

Tiffany didn't dare answer. She held her breath, afraid of the presence just like she had been afraid of things that went bump in the night as a child. Her parents assured her they weren't real, that she was dreaming, but she knew better. She wouldn't fall asleep because she knew things hid in the dark.

The ball of light blinked out again and Tiffany felt the presence moving, dissipating from in front of her only to reappear in front of the other door, the one leading into the hallway. Tiffany spun to face it as the light shone again. The ball of white light glowed where what looked like two hands gripped a big chair. The chair slid across the wooden floor until it reached the door. The hands winked out and the chair fell to lean against the door just under the knob.

"Alone at last," the voice said ominously. Again, she felt the presence move, this time to the bed beside her. She turned with it, facing it, still crouching, her hands on the ground, wings tucked in low. She didn't know what to do. In a way, she felt as helpless as the boy, but in the back of her mind she kept thinking that whatever this thing was, it was afraid of her. She just wished she knew why.

"We don't have a lot of time," the voice purred. "And you shouldn't be here…alone."

Tiffany wanted to reply, to tell him she wasn't alone, that Franklin was coming, but her childhood fears crept up on her, clawing across the floor, digging their cold fingers into her back as they reached her, weighing down her wings so much that her arms and legs felt the strain.

"I know you're afraid," the cold voice whispered in her ear. "Let's have a look in those memories of yours to see why."

The weight of darkness sank through her flesh, suffocating her…until she pushed herself up and threw the covers off her back. Somehow she was on the bed, kneeling. She didn't hear the whimpering boy anymore. *Where am I?* The chill in the air made her think the heat was out again. She heard a scratching at the window and spun to see the branch outside raking its skeletal fingers across the glass. *Home*, she thought. *It* was *a nightmare.* She looked over her shoulders. *No wings!*

"Mom?" Tiffany called out nervously.

The scratching at the window grew louder. *Damned tree.* She kicked her legs out of the blanket and rolled off the bed to slide the curtain shut. The moment she did, she froze. The room became *too* dark, and that presence she'd felt in her dream somehow followed her here. She shivered in the cold even though a hissing noise rose from the radiator. It came with a clicking of small, sharp claws that tacked their way across the dark floor. In the dimness, she barely made out small, animal-like shadows swimming toward her along the ground. She jumped back on top of the bed, afraid they were rats or some other pestilence trying to bite her bare feet.

If only she still had the Hula-Hoop, or the broken glasses, but she'd thrown them away when she cleaned her room just a few days ago. She was fourteen years old now. She didn't need stupid things like that to help her sleep anymore. She'd laughed to herself when she found them both. Dad said the Hula-Hoop kept the creepy crawlies away. Mom put the broken glasses under the radiator years ago so anything that came out would be blind. Tiffany remembered her mother pretending to bump into the wall as she wore the glasses, and Tiffany giggled even though the fright of that night's nightmare still clutched her heart. *Wait. Mom didn't put them there! Dad did.*

"Do you miss them?" the voice asked impishly. "Your parents?"

It's not a dream.

Tiffany swallowed a hard lump in her throat.

The presence rose along the wall behind her and she spun to face it. It appeared as only a darker shadow hanging on the wall, its head exactly where her poster normally hung. She tried to reason that it was just Justin Beiber and not an apparition.

"Their little protections were amusing," the voice said, somehow emanating from the wall. "Of course, your *real* protector was that figurine. Oh, but where is it? I don't see it anywhere."

The presence swam across the wall, turning the corner toward the window. The curtain fluttered as the presence pushed past it, revealing an empty window sill.

"Oh dear," it said as it continued its course around the room. "It seems you threw out your little friend. Tsk-tsk."

Tiffany faced the shadow as it moved, feeling it rather than seeing it in the dark.

"You're a curious one. You see me in the dark."

"You don't scare me," Tiffany replied bravely, even though her voice broke.

"Oh, but I think I do," the voice said. It stopped at the open closet and sank inside. "Do you see your pretty dresses in the closet?"

Not the dresses. She hated the dresses, the way her clothing hung like headless figures milling about in the closet, their shadowy forms nudging against one another for space, as though a hundred wraiths stood inside, each vying for a look at her, pushing and shoving the others for air to breathe.

She gasped. She wanted to leap for the light switch, but the things began to shuffle out of the closet to block her path to the door.

"Mom!" Tiffany called, begging for her mother to come save her, even in this nightmare.

Clothes without bodies moved in the dark, substantive, yet empty. The arms along the front ranks rose toward her, groping across the edge of the bed. Tiffany looked back at the floor between the bed and the window. The things that scurried along the floor retreated now that the creeping clothing was out, leaving her a safe path to the window. A blouse groped her leg. She kicked it away and jumped for the window. She just needed light.

She grabbed the curtain, feeling the presence rise in her hand as the curtain swept around her, spinning her and enveloping her within its folds. It constricted against her body. She tried to push it away, but it wrapped itself around her, closing out the last of the light.

"I remember this," the wicked voice said.

So did Tiffany. This was how she died.

The fabric of the curtains wrapped her in a cocoon. She

reached above her head and tried to climb out, but the curtain sealed tighter around her waist and chest, constricting against her like a giant snake.

Please, no.

The vile presence only tightened its grip. Her breaths came quick and shallow. The darkness swam in a dizzying emptiness and her grip on the fabric closing in above her began to wane. Death was coming again.

No.

The curtain opened suddenly, dropping Tiffany to the floor. She sucked in a deep breath and fell to her hands and knees. Her wings sagged to the floor beside her. A bright light burned in the center of the room and she squinted to see through it. A streak of cackling blue-white light chased the retreating presence, swinging to follow its dark form as it dove for the closet, where it suddenly vanished.

"Where's Franklin," the form holding the blinding light asked. Tiffany recognized the voice, but looked through her fingers to make sure. It was D.K. She stood as tall as the ceiling, her wings outstretched from wall to wall. In her hands she held a long spear made of ash wood or ivory, the end of it a piercing blue-white tip of glowing lightning. The same light as the sentinels, and like Franklin's crossbow.

"Downstairs," Tiffany managed to say between quick breaths.

D.K. kicked the gargoyle figurine at her feet. It slid across the hardwood floor to Tiffany's knees.

"Take it," D.K. said. Tiffany put a weak hand on it to drag it closer, wondering about its significance. *Why is this so important?*

D.K. turned her spear tip toward Tiffany and jabbed the gargoyle. Tiffany recoiled. A surge of fire filled her body. She yanked her hand from the figurine and fell backwards onto cold stone. The bright light faded, and as her vision returned, she stood again, realizing she was back inside the gargoyle tower. She looked up through the endlessly long, hollow pillar, trembling.

NINE

TIFFANY CROUCHED with her back against the cold stone outside of the pillar, hugging herself, waiting just by the entrance where the dispatch woman Kendall had put her, her body numb and shivering. Kendall asked what happened, but Tiffany didn't answer. She couldn't speak. She shivered and hugged her arms to herself, too stunned from the ordeal to think of words, much less retell her story. *That poor boy*, she thought. He'd suffered through it right alongside her, only it didn't try to kill him like it did her.

Kendall offered her a blanket.

"No," Tiffany snapped. She shook her head, her eyes wide with terror. "No blankets."

"Oh, honey, you faced one, didn't you?" Kendall asked softly.

Tiffany stared at her and gulped, then nodded.

"You're safe now, alright? They can't come here. Do you understand? They can't."

From what Tiffany could tell, that 'one' could go where it wanted. It went inside her head after all. It forced her to relive her own memories, putting her back to the night she died, and it almost killed her, *again*.

She wondered what that meant now that she was…what was she? A gargoyle? What did that mean? She looked up at Kendall, specifically at her ash-white skin. The color gave the tall woman a smooth appearance, like a polished fountain statue in a garden. Tiffany looked at her own skin and saw the same naturally tanned color of her Japanese heritage she had always in life, and as she turned her hands, she realized they were trembling. Her heart still pounded. She barely felt her body through the chill lingering beneath her skin.

"Someone's back," Kendall said, looking toward the entrance to the hollow pillar. Tiffany shuddered. What if it was that thing?

"—of the stupidest things you've ever done," D.K. roared! Her voice echoed out of the hollow pillar like a megaphone, charging ahead of her brisk pace as she emerged. She walked with a wooden staff, the same one that earlier glowed with a blue-white lightning spear tip. She slapped it down in cadence with her words. "That was a trap, and you walked right into it. And worst of all, you took *her* in with you!"

D.K. pointed the staff toward Tiffany. Tiffany leaned away from it, expecting an eruption of lightning to stab at her. Franklin opened his mouth to object, but D.K. cut him off.

"You're grounded, Franklin. *Notify* the shift commander when you sense another haunting."

D.K. stared down any response. Franklin took in a deep breath while gnashing his teeth, the muscles on his jaw twitching. D.K. turned her cold glare on Tiffany. Tiffany shrank, hunching her shoulders and drooping her head like a scolded dog.

"Kendall, he's not allowed out again," D.K. growled, pointing at Franklin.

"Yes, Commander," Kendall said softly.

D.K. thrust out her wide wings and leapt into the air, shouting "No more unauthorized travel for anyone!" She rose above the desks and beat her wings several times, banking away, lifting herself higher as she flew up toward one of the top glass offices overlooking the interior of the dome. She landed and pushed open the office door as her wings curled against her back. Once inside, she threw her staff into a corner of her office and shoved the door closed behind her. Because there was only glass between them, Tiffany had no trouble seeing D.K. pacing furiously.

Now I know what she looks like when she's pissed off.

"Thanks, Franklin," Kendall said glibly as she turned her back on him.

"Kendall," Franklin pleaded apologetically.

"Put your own chimera back in the collection," Kendall added, pointing toward a pedestal as she walked past. The figurine sat on top of it, watching them stoically.

Franklin growled to himself, but stood still as she walked away, then he turned to regard Tiffany. She still sat against the pillar. With D.K.'s arrival, though, the numbness she felt earlier had dissipated. Now she felt the weight of his frustration and anger pressing down on her and it made her uncomfortable.

"What the heck were you doing in the boy's room? Didn't I tell you to stay put?"

"No," Tiffany replied innocently, scrunching her eyes as she looked up at him. "You said *wait*."

"It's the same thing!" Franklin threw up his arms and started walking away. He favored one leg, limping. Tiffany wondered what happened to him. He grabbed the figurine off the pedestal and curled it under his arm.

Tiffany climbed to her feet. "Is the boy OK?"

"What?" Franklin looked over his shoulder at Tiffany, but kept limping toward the main door.

"Is the boy alright? Is he—?"

"Frightened half to death? Sure enough, but he'll live. For now." Franklin lifted the figurine in front of himself and stared at it closely, then nodded. "He's fine."

Tiffany followed Franklin as he moved between the scattered empty desks. The desks weren't arranged in any particular order or lined up in rows. Instead, different sizes of desks were interspersed throughout. A small, round, coal-colored man sat on a high stool in front of a nearby desk, his long black tail wrapped around the stool legs. Like Kendall, he didn't have wings. Kendall walked past him and stopped in front of one of the larger desks. Stacks of files and papers littered the top. She glanced at Franklin before turning her back on him and sitting down in front of a tower of paperwork.

Franklin marched toward the door, his eyes straight ahead, and his pace quick for being encumbered by his new limp. Tiffany hurried her step to keep up.

"What was that thing up there in the boy's room?" Tiffany asked, shuddering.

Franklin pushed open the door and held it for Tiffany. "What'd he do to you?"

"Who?"

"The *thing*! Bones."

"Bones?"

"That's his name, or at least that's what he's called. Did he hurt you?" Franklin looked over her shoulders at her wings, then looked her up and down.

"No. He tried to—" She took a deep, steadying breath. "He tried to suffocate me in the curtains. Like he did the first time."

"He got in your head, huh?"

She nodded, fighting back the glistening of tears in her eyes.

Franklin took a quick look back through the room, then put an arm around her shoulder to ease her through the doorway. "Come on, not in here," he whispered. He guided her out into the hallway and let the door close behind them. They were alone. He started to pull her closer, but she pushed back with her elbow and he let her go, holding his arms up as he sighed.

"I'm sorry," Tiffany said, hugging herself, looking down at his feet to avoid his stare. She didn't like feeling vulnerable to begin with, but in front of Franklin—a man she didn't know—it just felt wrong. She breathed deeply several times to calm herself as he shifted his weight off his left leg. A blood red stain darkened his jeans and his brown boot had dark red streaks leaking from somewhere under the cuff. "You're hurt!"

"Bah," Franklin growled with a wave.

"You need to have that looked at," Tiffany said, pointing at the holes in Franklin's pant leg, evenly pierced as though a large dog bit him.

"I intend to. Come on."

He led her back to the library of figurines and, with audible effort, lunged into flight to return the small statue to its slot. Tiffany waited for Franklin to return, hardly thinking to look around this time. Her thoughts kept replaying her encounter with Bones.

He couldn't see her at first. Not until it was dark. She wondered if that was because she was a gargoyle, or if it had something to do with the broken glasses Franklin had given her, the ones she dropped when she crashed into the room. Her Dad used the same thing in her room.

"Are you ready?" Franklin asked and she leapt with a start.

She hadn't realized he'd flown back. She nodded hastily.

"Come on, then."

Franklin led her back out of the dome and sat on a bench, groaning all the way down. The light emanating from the stone of the interior of the hollow mountain felt like noon, both in brightness and heat. She looked up to see hundreds of fliers at different elevations and courses. Amazed by the ease of their flight, she wondered how long it would be until she could fly as well. She tore her vision away from the sky, trying to remind herself that she didn't belong here. She belonged back in her own home. There had to be a way to get there.

Franklin gingerly raised his pant leg to inspect his wound. Several small punctures in his skin ringed his calf like a mouthful of fangs had grabbed him. Each hole was dark red and oozed blood. "Damn," he growled and leaned back, squinting up into the distance. Tiffany followed his sight and easily picked out the yellow perch of her barracks. "Do you think you can make it there on your own? I need to get this looked at."

Tiffany didn't want to go back to the barracks. She retracted her vision, feeling a little disoriented as she looked at Franklin's leg instead.

"That looks awful," Tiffany said to avoid the question. "Where's the hospital? I'll go with you to make sure you make it."

"I'm not going to the hospital," he groused. "These are bite marks. One of the five ghosts Bones brought with him bit me. I know someone who can figure out who it was."

"There were others?"

"Five of them. Downstairs."

Why did the number five seem so familiar, she wondered. "Why do you want to find them? Why not just find Bones. You know who *he* is."

"He didn't bite me. Look, Bones is enlisting others to help him out. That means they know what he's up to, or at the very least what he's planning to do next. I want to get a step ahead of him. I need his scent to find him," Franklin said, pointing at his leg. "I only have this to go on."

"I have his scent," Tiffany said. "All over me."

"What?"

"Bones tried to suffocate me. He wrapped me in a curtain. I would have been dead if D.K. hadn't arrived. He let me go the moment she appeared and he ran for the closet and vanished. Poof."

Franklin stared at her suspiciously, with one eye on her.

"I'm not lying."

"I don't doubt it," Franklin said, shaking his head half way. He slid his pant leg down and gingerly stood up. "Let's go. It's not far."

TEN

TIFFANY FOLLOWED FRANKLIN as he glided over the tops of the city buildings that ringed the dome. During their free-fall earlier, she hardly noticed its design, but now she had time to see ahead of them as she concentrated on Franklin and the rooftops. She saw the contours of the wide city, the way it was mostly made of four- and five-story tall rectangular stone buildings. Large gaps opened in places that seemed at first to be abandoned or empty, but as they swept down into one, she realized they were village squares. At the edge of this one were several small stone kiosks with clothing, grain foods or spices, and wooden trinkets on display.

Franklin hobbled with his landing, turning on one leg to face Tiffany the moment he touched down. She saw him grimace in pain then realized she was coming in too quickly. She flared her wings and flapped hard. As her feet touched down, the weight of her outstretched wings caused her to fall backwards.

"Ouch!" She landed square on her rear.

Franklin gave Tiffany a hand to her feet before looking around to get his bearings.

"This way," he grumbled with a wave. He limped and led them into a narrow alleyway. Tiffany could nearly touch the walls with her outstretched hands, so she knew her wings were useless in here. It seemed like one of those back-alleys of some Middle-Eastern city like in *Raiders of the Lost Ark*, with rough buildings made of sandstone and alabaster rising to blot out the sun. Only there were no shadows. The buildings, like the hollow mountain itself, cast a dull sense of afternoon everywhere.

They reached the end of the alley and stepped into a wider road, still too narrow for flight, but at least Tiffany could walk beside Franklin out here. A few stores lined the street. Grocers stood beside their crates of fruits and vegetables on display. A barber's stripes were painted over a small pillar at the corner. Like the tight-packed cities she'd seen in T.V. and movies, outside stairs led down to basement apartments while inner stairwells gave access to the three and four story apartment buildings above. The smell of hot and spicy food cooking not far off carried in the air.

The few people they passed were wingless, some with tails, some without, and invariably, each one looked at Franklin and her with suspicion or curiosity, and not one said hello.

Tiffany had no idea where the dome was. She looked up to the sky to get her bearings, searching for the yellow ledge of the barracks. She hoped there was only one yellow ledge up there.

The delicious smell of food turned out to be an open-faced diner like the Fly & Diver Grill. This one had a sign over it reading EGG ROLL STATION. Several hulking gray- and brown-stone colored wingless sat at stools along the counter. Some were looking over their shoulder at Tiffany and Franklin, their scowls making the distance between them seem far too little.

"You coming?" Franklin stood at a stairwell opposite the grill with a hand on the rail. He didn't wait for an answer, turning to hobble down the steps.

The first flight of stairs led to a dimly lit walkway beneath the street. Three doors lined the building side of the hall. Franklin turned behind the stairwell, walking into a dark recess, as Tiffany reached the landing. Another stairwell led down into a pitch black, passageway.

"Duke never turns on any lights," Franklin complained as he sank deeper into the blackness, the tips of his wings scuffing the underside of the first set of stairs. Tiffany looked back up toward the street, wondering if she should wait up there, but the thought of those big men at the grill scared her as much as the darkness. Maybe she could wait right here. She looked down the empty, quiet, eerie hallway and shuddered.

A small glow of blue-white light suddenly emerged from the darkness. It came from a small twig Franklin pinched between his fingers, holding it above his head so she could see. A candle, only this was made of the same light he used to make his crossbow.

"Come on," Franklin said, looking up at Tiffany from half-way down the stairs. "It'll be fine."

He hobbled down the stairs and Tiffany rushed to follow, not wanting to stray far from Franklin's circle of light. The hallway on the second floor was likewise unlit, with only a single doorway halfway down. Franklin limped ahead of Tiffany, holding the light over his wings to shine behind him as well as in front. They reached the door, which was wide open, and Franklin turned to wait for Tiffany. He waved for her, nodding that it was alright to come closer.

"Come in, Franklin," a welcoming, albeit aged voice said from within. "And who is with you? A newborn?"

"My pupil," Franklin said as he stepped through the threshold ahead of Tiffany. "Can you turn the lights up?"

"Oh, sorry. I forget sometimes." A light grew within the room. Franklin shook out his little candle-sized torch and stuffed it into his pocket.

"Tell me, Franklin, is that Bones I smell on you?"

Franklin wiped his feet at the doormat before stepping into the room. Tiffany peered around the doorframe, but didn't go inside. It was a large, inviting space with the feel of a well lived-in home. Two couches stood between a large coffee table next to a fireplace and mantle that didn't burn wood, but instead appeared to use large chunks of coal. The un-burnt rocks were kept in a bucket beside the fireplace. A dining table and chairs took up a section of the room across from the fireplace, and a large, wide kitchen filled the entire far end of the room.

A hallway from the kitchen led further back into the home, out of which came an old, squat, wingless and tailless form, swaying as he made his way. With each step he leaned the top of his shoulder against a long walking staff for support. He stopped to take a deep breath through his large nose, which was the most prominent feature of his oval head—wider than tall, having two deep cavities where eyes should be and a low forehead that seemed to have collapsed into the empty eye sockets. Tiffany straightened at the sight of the gray-skinned old man, appalled by his deformity.

Franklin watched her reaction then shook his head with what seemed like disappointment and walked further into the apartment.

"I take it by your silence that you've had a run-in with him again, and lost his trail...again."

"He ran away," Franklin grumbled.

"Of course he did," Duke replied, shuffling ahead toward the nearest couch. "Why else would you be here?"

"As a matter of fact, I'm not interested in Bones this time."

"Aren't you now?"

Tiffany stepped into the apartment a little ways, but stopped and tried to stand perfectly still. She didn't want to be part of the conversation if she could avoid it. She stared at Duke's empty eye sockets, wide open as though he were looking at Franklin, but completely absent of any eyeballs. Black holes in his head that served no purpose except to gross her out.

"Well, of course I'm *interested* in him," Franklin said, crossing the room toward the couches. "But I mean I'm more interested in finding his colleague at the moment."

"I see," Duke said, putting a hand on the couch to steady himself. Tiffany recognized the walking staff Duke leaned on. It was the same kind the Sentinels used to hold up those balls of blue-white light out on the walls facing the Endless See. Or maybe *they* were the Endless See. No one explained it to her yet.

Franklin sat down on the opposite couch and pulled up his pant leg. He thumped his foot onto the coffee table to show the blind old man. Duke turned and side-stepped closer, then leaned forward to take deep breaths through his nose, inhaling the air around Franklin's leg as he waved it up toward his large, round nose.

"Do you smell it?" Franklin asked.

"Quiet," Duke replied. Tiffany noticed a bulge at Duke's lower back just below his belt line where it looked like a pocket had been turned inside out. It wiggled a little as Duke inhaled deeply once more through his nose.

"Well?"

"I've got his scent," Duke said while straightening. The pocket at his lower back straightened too, like the nub of a tail reacting to a shift in balance.

"And?" Franklin grumbled.

"And I'll have to look around."

"And how long will that take?"

Duke shrugged. "Come back tomorrow. I should have found him by then. And bring me some egg rolls this time."

"Tomorrow," Franklin agreed firmly. "Don't lose his scent."

Duke stared with his empty eye sockets directed at Franklin, the insult plainly visible.

"Sorry," Franklin said as he rolled down his pant leg over the bite wounds. "What about Bones?"

"I smelled him before I smelled you, old friend. He's not trying to hide."

ELEVEN

CLIMBING UP THE STAIRWELL from Duke's home was easier because of the light above, even if Franklin's big body blocked most of it. The door didn't close behind them when they left, but the light from within faded away. *What did a blind man need light for anyway?* She also wondered how he had been so hideously deformed in the first place. It looked like a huge stone wall had collapsed on his head, crushing his forehead into his eye sockets, probably squishing them flat. Tiffany shuddered. Given what she had seen and done since coming to this place, she didn't think it an unrealistic likelihood.

Franklin reached the top and groaned in relief, stepping aside for Tiffany.

"Why the stairs?" Tiffany wondered aloud.

"Huh?" Franklin asked as he straightened, his hands on his lower back to rub his muscles after having to crouch forward the whole time down there.

"The Sentinel that caught me came up from the ground. He just—poof!—appeared. Why are there stairs going down everywhere?"

"Not everyone is a Sentinel," Franklin said. "And besides, we didn't fly all the way here, we walked. Just because you can doesn't mean you do all the time, you know?"

Tiffany didn't argue the point. "Was Duke a Sentinel?"

"Ask him," Franklin replied, waving for her to follow him. He hobbled toward an intersection down the street.

"What happened to his tail?"

"Look, your orientation got a little disrupted by recent events," Franklin said, limping and looking to the sky. She looked up as well. The buildings were too narrow for flight. "One of the things you need to learn is to stop asking questions about other people. It's just not done here, you understand?"

Tiffany stared at him in disbelief. He looked over at her and sighed.

"Just believe me on this one. Some basic rules to live by here are don't tell stories about your past just because someone asks. Don't offer anything, even your name, without a reason. And don't tell stories you know about others."

"What? That's absurd. How do you ever make friends? How do you—?"

"It's our way of life," Franklin told her sharply. "It's like an insult not to honor it. As a Japanese, I'm sure you can understand custom."

"I'm American."

"Alright, think of it like this: if you're open about what's inside your head with people down here, then when you meet someone like Bones up there and he starts toying with your thoughts, how are you going to be able to tell when he's in your head or not?"

Tiffany swallowed the lump in her throat.

"They play mind games," Franklin said, pointing toward the sky. "You have to know the difference between what you truly know, and what *seems* real. You have to harden your mind to resist them. *A heart and will of stone.* That's our way."

"I—" Tiffany began, but couldn't think of what to say. She didn't want to admit that she didn't understand completely, even though deep inside she had an inkling of what he meant. Having Bones inside her head, playing on her fears the way he had, she understood that the reality she *believed* had been different than what actually happened. Nothing crawled across the floor the night Bones *actually* killed her. And her father was the one who put the glasses under the radiator.

"He'll play tricks on you now that he knows you. He'll show you me, doing something horrible or put me in terrible danger, something I wouldn't do, saying something I wouldn't say. That's why we all live by the same code, so there's no ambiguity. You have to know me solely by what you know of me, and trust that I will always, only, ever be that way. And I have to trust that you will too, because it's not just *your* mind he'll try to get inside of."

Tiffany nodded.

Franklin came to a stop at an intersection. The road was wide enough to spread his wings and then some.

"I'm going to the hospital. Don't talk about Duke to others, especially D.K. She'd have a fit if she knew we came to him. You fly back to the barracks, OK?"

"Alright. But what do I do?"

"Try to sleep. Don't worry about Bones. He can't get down here."

That was the second time she'd been told that, but for some reason she just didn't believe it.

"Don't dwell on things," Franklin went on. "Just get some rest and I'll pick you up for breakfast. And whatever you do, *don't* go flying around with those other girls again. D.K. doesn't know about last night, either, and she doesn't need to know."

"More of the gargoyle code?"

"No, this is you and me trying to stay off her radar. Look, my leg is killing me. We'll talk in the morning. I need some pain pills or something. Now go on home."

"I wish I could," Tiffany said under her breath.

Franklin jumped into the air, flapping his wings as he banked away, leaving her alone in the middle of the street. She looked down the street at the Egg Roll Station grill, at the row of wingless who stared at her. Their eyes felt predatory, mostly because their faces resembled ferocious beasts more than they did men. She crouched low. *Please don't crash, please don't crash.* She took a deep breath and jumped, her wings lashing out and scooping the air to hoist her up. She sighed with relief, but concentrated to keep her wings flapping and to avoid hitting the side of a building. She flew over the building tops and banked to start her slow, easy ascent toward the yellow deck of her barracks somewhere high above.

TWELVE

TIFFANY CRASH LANDED, tumbling into the pit of sponges nearly the same as she had the first night. *Was it only yesterday?* She curled her wings tightly and fell sideways, throwing out an arm instinctively to protect them, but the sponges gobbled her up. She lay still for a moment, seething over her inability to land well. Even though nobody was around to laugh at her or make a smug remark, she didn't want to stick around for them to show up. She clambered over the sponges to a rope ladder and hauled herself out of the pit.

The things Franklin said about their way of life didn't sit well with her. She didn't like the idea that everyone around her, for the rest of her life, would remain a mystery to her, guarding their life stories so that they couldn't be used to hurt them. And yet, it made sense. If Bones tried to get into her head and pretend Corinne knew something about her, tried to torment her with her own memories, Tiffany would know them to be lies, that Bones was tricking her. It made sense, and she hated it.

She scowled as she approached the five doors, her new home. She wondered who lived in the other four. Were there more girls? Boys, maybe? Or what if they were completely empty? She walked toward the door to Bay 2 and hovered near it, holding her breath and listening, nervously looking around the large landing bay of the barracks in case someone else was there. The empty silence bothered her. She retreated back to her own door, upset with herself for being afraid. She pushed open the door to Bay 3, scowling deeper at not having the courage to push open the other door and go see for herself.

Franklin didn't want her wandering, though. He wanted her here, and this is where she would wait, even though her stomach growled in protest.

Only a few girls were in the barracks. Two of them were fast asleep on their beds. Another was pushing a soft broom across the polished floor. Two sat across from each other at a chess board, concentrating on the pieces. Another girl sat on a ledge on the wall with a stick firmly held in her hand as it fizzled with blue-white sparks. She shook the stick and the sparks popped out of it, but it wasn't a solid blade of light like she had seen from D.K.'s spear or the Sentinel's staffs.

Hedika sat on her bed, her back to the wall, knees propped up with a book resting in her lap, her head craned forward to read. The whole bay was quiet. Maybe that's why she hadn't heard any noise through the other door.

Tiffany took a deep breath, determined to defy convention…just a little. She walked down the row of bunks until she reached Hedika. She turned and stepped between Hedika's bed and what looked like an empty bed beside it.

"Is this one taken?" Tiffany asked.

Standing close to Hedika for the first time, she was able to see the girl's full features. Hedika was a little taller than Tiffany by height, and fuller of body with strong, taught shoulder and arm muscles, the kind that came from physical training. Even her thighs under her yellow dress appeared cut with muscle. She had blue tinted skin, mottled with gray and black like granite. A thick vein of black coloration scarred her from temple to chin, giving her what looked like a permanent shadow over her right eye. Tiffany was staring at it as Hedika looked up from her book.

"Sorry," Tiffany said, looking Hedika in the opposite eye, realizing she was being rude. "I'm new. I've just...I never—"

Hedika sighed. "You don't want to sleep by me," she said irritably and returned her attention to her book.

"Why not?" Tiffany asked, trying to keep her tone cordial. "Do you snore?"

Hedika didn't reply.

"Thanks, by the way," Tiffany went on. She wouldn't be deterred by a sour expression and grumpy disposition. Hedika had to be nice under all that or she wouldn't have been nice the night before. Tiffany sat on the empty bed and leaned forward, whispering, "For warning me last night. I should have listened to you."

Hedika eyed her a moment, then went back to reading.

"Wow, these beds are a lot more comfortable than they look." Tiffany lay down on her side, facing Hedika, looking at the black mar on her cheek and wondering if it was natural or a scar. She looked at Hedika's neck, bare hands, and feet where only mottled blue-gray skin showed, made more prominent by her yellow dress. It made her appear statuesque, and Tiffany had the impression Hedika would make a great gargoyle outside of a library.

"Can I ask you a question?"

"You just did," Hedika replied blandly. The girl hardly moved an inch, her breathing the only thing that gave any indication that she was alive.

"Do you listen to music here?"

"What?" Hedika asked, turning her eyes to look at Tiffany, but otherwise unmoving.

"Is there music? You know, like a radio."

"We don't get any stations. Batteries and electronics don't survive travel." She turned her head slowly to look squarely at Tiffany. For a moment, Tiffany thought Hedika would dash her hopes, but Hedika held her breath before saying anything. They stared at one another and Tiffany noted Hedika had hazel-colored eyes, even though she expected them to be blue. Hedika's eyes softened. "There are several old Victrola hand-crank record players they use at the dances or at parties," she said softly. "Sometimes they bring back instruments; guitars, things like that. There's this one hunter that built several pianos by hand, bringing back one piece at a time over the years. They keep books on the subject in the library. If you're interested."

"Yeah," Tiffany said, smiling. "I'd love to see the library."

Hedika considered Tiffany, staring at her but saying nothing, holding an expectant expression on her face, as though she didn't believe Tiffany to be sincere. Perhaps that was just because of living in this place, always on the defensive around the other girls, never letting her guard down lest she be hurt. Following the gargoyle code.

Tiffany rolled onto her back and let her wings fan out and drape to the floor. "Oh, that feels good."

Hedika returned to her book, acting uninterested in Tiffany again.

"I think it's cool, by the way."

"What?" Hedika asked.

"That we have a library. How long does it take to learn to read gargoyle?"

Hedika chuckled to herself. Tiffany turned her head with a puzzled expression.

"You have a lot to learn about being gargoyle," Hedika said.

Tiffany frowned, ashamed of her inexperience. "If it's written, you can read it. Your only limitation is that you need to know what the words mean in the first place."

"Really," Tiffany said with a little skepticism. She'd have to try it for herself before she believed that. Still, Hedika didn't seem like the kind of girl to lead her astray. "So you read a lot," Tiffany went on.

Hedika, her nose still in her book, turned an annoyed eye at Tiffany, then went back to her book.

"Right," Tiffany said with a smile. "Have you read much about all those figurines they have in the dome?"

"You mean the chimera?" Hedika asked blandly.

Tiffany shrugged.

"I know enough," Hedika said.

"So how do they work? I mean, they do something, right?"

Hedika took a deep, frustrated breath and turned to stare at Tiffany. "Are you going to talk all day?" Hedika asked. "Because I've been reading the same sentence since you sat down and it's not *that* interesting."

"Sorry," Tiffany replied timidly.

Hedika didn't look away or bury herself in her book again, though. She stared at Tiffany suspiciously. Tiffany looked away, avoiding Hedika's eyes at first, until she summoned the courage to look back at the stone-skinned girl.

"How do you know about the room in the dome?"

Tiffany squirmed under Hedika's scrutiny. "I saw it today," she whispered.

"Your mentor took you to the dome?" she asked with even more skepticism. "On your first day? Who's your mentor?"

Tiffany didn't get a chance to answer. A loud procession of laughter came down the hall and Hedika rolled her eyes and leaned back against her wings so she could return to reading her book. Several girls emerged from the hall, led by Corinne. Corinne glanced over the room and her eyes landed squarely on Tiffany. Tiffany felt a lump in her throat. The dread of facing Corinne and the other girls poured over her from her head to her toes, draining her of courage.

"Oh good," Corinne announced loudly. "You made it back."

THIRTEEN

THE OTHER GIRLS STOPPED TALKING amongst themselves and fanned out to get a good look at Tiffany. They hovered by her bed as though expecting her to be wearing some kind of prison clothing or shackles, or have scars from a whipping. They seemed only mildly disappointed by her appearance. Tiffany forced her wings off the ground and sat up.

"Your flight gown looks horrible," Corinne announced. "What happened?"

Tiffany looked at herself. The bottom half of her dress was stained from rolling in the trashcan, and one of her sleeves had a rip along her forearm, probably from when she crashed into the balcony door. She had a long abrasion beneath the tear sporting a swollen bruise as well.

"I've been practicing flying," Tiffany lied.

"You need another gown. That one's ruined. I'll show you the spare wardrobe. I'm sure we have something that'll fit you. One of Hedika's old things should be small enough."

Hedika ignored the comment.

Tiffany got up and followed Corinne to the back of the barracks. The wall was filled with different lockers and several large free-standing wardrobes. Corinne explained that each bed had a number and the number matched the locker. Tiffany found the one for the bed next to Hedika and she opened it to look into the empty shelves and hanging rod.

"You aren't planning on sleeping next to her, are you?"

"Well," Tiffany shrugged. "I didn't know which beds were empty, so I—"

"She was disowned by her mentor," Corinne said softly. "It happens," she added with a sympathetic shaking of her head. "You're paired with whomever they have available when you arrive. They don't try to find the best mentor to suit your abilities. Some girls get lucky, others, well, they get ditched."

"What happens to them after that?"

"They wait," Corinne said bleakly. "They wait until another mentor is willing to take them under their wing, so to speak. But once you've been disowned, nobody wants you. I hope you got a good mentor."

"So do I," Tiffany said, purposefully avoiding telling Corinne who her mentor was. She nodded gravely for Corinne's sake, though, then quickly changed the subject. "How do I get this gown mended?"

They had several sewing kits she could use to do basic mending, Corinne explained. She explained a lot more, too, mostly about the rules. Don't make a mess, keep clean gowns hung when not in use, dirty clothes went in a bag at the bottom of the locker, and so on. Then Corinne helped Tiffany dig through the common clothes in the wardrobe until she had two other flight gowns, and undergarments to last a week.

"You might as well throw this one out," Corinne said while lifting Tiffany's arm to look at the rip.

"I think I'm going to keep it for a little while, as a memento," Tiffany replied.

"Suit yourself, but leave it in your dirty bag until it's clean and mended."

Tiffany nodded and went into the bathroom to wash and change. Having wings made it difficult to just take off the gown. She looked in the mirror to see her back. Two straps with Velcro crossed her shoulders just above her wing notches to hold the gown up. Once she ripped them off, the gown fell to the floor. She didn't like seeing herself naked in the mirror, with or without wings. She quickly put on her underwear and the other gown.

When she came out, the other girls were sitting around Corinne's bed, giggling as Priya joked about a flying maneuver she conducted over a group of wingless stone masons today. Tiffany retreated from the ring of girls, listening to them talk back and forth with wild statements, besting each other with one joke after another. She didn't understand their banter yet, which made her less inclined to join them, and after what happened today, she didn't feel in the mood for laughter.

She hung up her old dress in her locker next to the other white flight gown. The collar of the spare gown and the one she now wore had the letters H.G. stenciled in them. Corinne said the gowns were Hedika's first gowns, making Tiffany wonder what Hedika's last name might be.

She dragged the ends of her wings back to the bed next to Hedika and sat down. She didn't look toward the other girls, but she felt the chill of Corinne's stare. She didn't want to deal with those girls, or let them try to get her into trouble again, or put her in the middle of whatever competition or jealous in-fighting that was going on in the bay. She didn't even want to get up to go eat even though her stomach protested. She was too tired.

"Thanks for the dresses," Tiffany said quietly as she draped her wings over the bed to lay down on her back. Her wings unfurled to the floor.

"That's not good for your wings," Hedika said.

"It feels good," Tiffany replied weakly, her eyes already closed. "You don't mind if I sleep here, do you?"

"Only if you snore," Hedika said under her breath.

Tiffany grinned. She liked Hedika.

FOURTEEN

"WAKE UP," Hedika told Tiffany softly, nudging her. It was nearly pitch black in the barracks except for a small nightlight near the main door that shimmered with the blue-white glow of lightning. "Your mentor's here."

"Franklin?"

"I don't know. He asked for you."

"What time is it?" Tiffany groaned softly, trying to lift herself up with her elbows, but only pinning her wings to the bed, making it impossible to get up.

"Before dawn."

"Why are you up?" Tiffany asked, rolling on her side to retract one wing, then doing it with the other as she turned to sit up.

"I'm the night watch," Hedika told her at a whisper. "Did Corinne give you any duties?"

"What? No. What do you mean?"

"Duties to perform in the bay, like cleaning the bathrooms?"

"Not yet."

"Then you should go—quietly—before she wakes up and gives you one. Come on."

Hedika held up a small piece of wood the size of her pinky and shook it. A thin, blue-white spark ignited at the tip like a candle, illuminating Hedika's blue skin and yellow gown eerily against the otherwise pitch black bay. Hedika cupped the light with her hand as though it might blow out, but Tiffany realized she was only trying to keep the light low so it wouldn't wake up any of the others. Tiffany stood and followed Hedika down the hall to the main door.

Hedika slid a peephole open and held her light to it.

"Is he your mentor?" Hedika asked quietly.

Tiffany stood on her toes to look through into the dark landing area where a shadow lurked. The shadow turned and stepped closer, his large face coming into the light.

"Are you ready?" Franklin asked quietly.

"Yeah," Tiffany told them both, nodding toward Hedika.

Hedika put her hand on the wall beside the door and a clack echoed softly through the bay.

"Go on," Hedika whispered urgently, pulling the door open wide enough for Tiffany to squeeze through. As she pushed Tiffany out, she explained, "Everyone wakes to the noise of the door. They think it's a snap inspection.

"False alarm," Hedika called down the hallway toward the bay as she closed the door behind Tiffany.

Tiffany stood in the dark. Franklin's form was a black shadow breaking up the meager light pouring in through the mouth of the landing cavern. With his wings looming over his shoulder, his silhouette felt even more ominous.

"How's your leg?" Tiffany asked softly.

"It hurts like—" he started moodily, then sighed, softening his tone and asking, "Are you hungry?" His voice had a familiar and comforting ring to it, an assurance that broke apart the spectral shadow that he appeared to be.

"Starving," Tiffany replied.

Franklin led her to the yellow perch and stood at the edge,

looking out into the gray morning glow of the hollow mountains' interior. At this hour even the landing perches were dim, having abandoned their light hours ago. It reminded Tiffany of a campout with her father a few years ago, rising before dawn and walking on the shore of a big lake near their home. It had been peacefully quiet there, broken only by the warbling and chirping of birds waking. For a moment, Tiffany wondered whether Franklin would start chirping like a bird, but just as her father had on that morning of the campout, Franklin simply stood quietly still.

Tiffany stood beside him, worrying about the dizzying heights, wondering what the day ahead held.

"We're going to break a lot of rules today," Franklin said, as if knowing her thoughts. She turned to regard him, looking up and wondering how it would be any different than yesterday, or what the repercussions might be. "It's not a good idea for you to come with me. You can get into a lot of trouble, and I don't want that for you. You'd probably even be better off with a different mentor, one that won't—"

"I don't want the others thinking you disowned me," Tiffany said sharply.

"Disowned? How do you know—? Oh, that's right. You're in the same bay as Machiavelli's—" Franklin held his tongue, staring hard at Tiffany. "She wasn't disowned, and if you leave me, no one will think less of you, especially after what happened yesterday. We can fly down to D.K. right now and get you reassigned."

Tiffany didn't like the idea of changing mentors. She *knew* Franklin, or at least she knew enough about him to know he wasn't all that bad. Her encounter with Bones hadn't been his fault. She was the one that flew into the boy's bedroom even though Franklin told her to stay put, outside where it was probably safe. And she hadn't met any other mentors yet to know if they would be better or worse. She suspected the latter.

What she really wanted was not to feel defenseless the next time she ran into trouble.

"I want to know how to make light," Tiffany said.

"We don't have that kind of time. Manifesting your inner light is a skill that takes—"

"Then I'll tell D.K. about Duke."

"What?" he asked incredulously. "Are you trying to blackmail me?"

Tiffany folded her arms in front of her, trying to keep a straight face. Franklin's glare didn't waver. She knew it wouldn't. She sighed, her shoulders drooping in resignation. "Come on, aren't you supposed to teach me that kind of stuff?"

"Eventually."

"Why not today?"

"Maybe disowning you might be a good idea after all," Franklin grumbled half-heartedly.

Tiffany glowered at him.

"I'm kidding," Franklin said with a grin. Tiffany's eyes narrowed. "Really, I'm kidding. We can afford a few hours in the pits to get you started, but let's get some breakfast first. And don't expect much."

FIFTEEN

FRANKLIN SAVED TIFFANY FROM CRASH LANDING
at the Fly & Diver Grill, which was nearly empty so early in the
morning. He mumbled something about 'no one seeing her'
before they took seats and ordered. She wasn't sure if he meant it
for her sake, or his own. Tiffany let it slide, too famished to be
angry. She wolfed down everything on her plate, even the
sausage, which tasted like pork to her. After breakfast, Franklin
pointed toward an enormous square on the ground near the
mountain wall. It had several buildings along one side, and when
she zoomed her vision in on it, she saw what looked like normal
homes, the kind she expected to find in the outside world.

"What is it?" Tiffany asked as they stood on the ledge next to
the grill.

"Training grounds."

"Why are there normal looking houses like with wood and
paint?"

Franklin sighed. "For training. Just follow me in, and keep a
respectable distance whenever you fly over the place. You never
know what they're practicing in the red and yellow sections. Stick
to the blue and green paths once we're in, alright?"

"Green and blue, gotcha," Tiffany said, an anxious weight
pressing against her lungs.

Franklin glided down the distance, slowly circling the entire interior of the mountain, taking wider turns as the mountain expanded, until he banked in the opposite direction high over the pits and began circling tighter, descending over a large complex of buildings. Tiffany followed, her heart racing at both the difficulty she still had with flying as well as the uncertainty about the place they were heading. She had to flap to stay aloft, falling like a brick each time she tried to glide the way Franklin did. Her flight was unsteady too, each stroke of her wings making her bank to one side or another. She felt like a wobbly toddler trying to stand.

A squad of wingless and tailless marched along a blue path, their boots striking the stone in unison with an echoing clap, their gray uniforms menacing. Two winged men with tails wearing blue flight suits stood near the building Franklin was landing in front of. Being so close to Franklin as she had been flying, she didn't have room to react when he decided to land. Tiffany fully extended her wings and let her feet shoot out in front of her, free falling several stories of the building before flapping her wings vigorously. *Please don't crash, please don't crash.* Franklin, already on the ground, tucked in his wings and turned around to catch her just before she crashed into him. He staggered backwards under her weight.

"Sorry," she said.

"Don't follow so closely next time," Franklin grumbled, setting her down on her feet.

"I didn't want to lose you."

"I'm not going to ditch you," Franklin said into her ear. "Let's go inside."

Franklin walked around the two men without looking at them. Tiffany followed with her head down, hoping to avoid seeing their mocking grins. He pushed open a door and held it for her. Once inside, she looked up to take in her surroundings. A large room shaped in an "L" held a long counter running its length down the left side. Behind the counter were several different knife handles, sticks of various width and length, staffs, and longer rods. A jet-black wingless woman with a tail came out from behind the counter as Franklin approached her.

"I need to start her training," Franklin said with a thumb pointed in Tiffany's direction. "Do you still have used practice batons?"

"Sure, over here," she said and led them to a huge stone bin filled with sticks of various sizes, all heavily scarred with dents and burn marks. "Take your pick, they're all the same price."

Franklin thanked her and waited until she walked away, then leaned in to Tiffany saying, "Some of these were here when *I* was in training, so let me pick one out for you."

Franklin bent over the lip of the bin and started moving sticks around. He held one up and looked at it, then tossed it toward a corner with a scowl. He dug deeper, shoving sticks aside in bunches. Tiffany was certain he wasn't looking at them all. She picked one up, just to feel if it was really made of wood. She half expected them to be petrified.

"That one's garbage," Franklin grumbled, waving a finger at Tiffany's selection.

It looked like it. Big burn scars and dents ran its length. She tossed it back into the bin and Franklin covered it with a bundle of other sticks he cast aside. Tiffany noticed one on top that looked interesting. She grabbed it just before Franklin buried it too. It fit her hand perfectly, thin enough that she could wrap her fist around it, but thick enough that it didn't feel flimsy. It was longer than the other sticks—the length of her forearm—and hardly wore any scarring or dents. She turned it over looking for cracks, but didn't see any.

"That's two-sided," Franklin told her. "You should—"

"Cool," Tiffany said excitedly.

"Not cool. Two sides is twice as hard to control, and you can cut off your own wings if you're not careful. Give me that. Let me show you."

Tiffany handed Franklin the stick and he shook it. Three feet of blue-white light emerged from both ends. Franklin turned the stick in his hand and swung it slowly as though he were chopping with it. The bottom blade of light swept just above the ground, then almost touched his wing when he stopped mid-stroke to show her.

"See? If you follow-through, you'll cut—"

"Cool!"

"What?"

"That's so cool. It's just like in *Star Wars*, do you remember Darth Maul?"

"What are you talking about?" Franklin asked, staring at her like she was crazy.

"*Star Wars?*"

"What's *Star Wars?*"

"Seriously?" Tiffany asked in astonishment. Franklin stared at her blankly. "How long have you been dead?"

Franklin tossed the stick onto the pile as its light went out. "Not that one," Franklin said insistently.

Tiffany reached for it.

"Leave it," Franklin said.

"Let me at least *try* it," Tiffany said, fishing it out and holding it reverently. She expected it to do something magical, but it just felt like warm wood.

"Fine," Franklin agreed, folding his arms in front of him. "Go ahead."

"Go ahead what?"

"Go ahead and try it. Go on."

Tiffany looked at the stick in her hand, then at Franklin. "What do I do? To make light?"

"Concentrate on something that gives you joy. Happiness is a powerful emotion that manifests physically throughout your body. Channel that feeling into your hand and wrap the wood with it. A properly crafted weapon will complete the circuit and your light will flow into its veins."

"So the Sentinels on the Endless See are *happy*?"

"In a way," Franklin replied. "They channel their inner light. Once you've learned to trigger it, you'll understand what I mean. It's something that just flows from within. I don't even have to think about it and, poof, it's there. Just like breathing."

"So think of something that makes me happy," Tiffany said, thinking that nothing that happened recently would bring her joy at all. Thoughts of her mother and father only agonized her. Knowing that they were out there mourning her death and she couldn't do anything to reach them, to let them know she was still alive, infuriated her.

"It's tough for new-comers," Franklin said. "You come here with nothing but grief."

Tiffany couldn't argue the point. She'd arrived afraid and full of sorrow, but D.K.'s stern and steady ways managed to redirect her attention to other things, like learning how to fly.

"I think I have something," Tiffany said, remembering that first moment she flew, and then again when Franklin jumped with her to free-fall to the dome. She closed her eyes and relived the thrill of each moment, feeling her face go flush and her arms and legs tingle. She felt her chest warm and she pushed it toward her

hand as her heart pounded heavier. She concentrated on the grains of the wood under her thumb, pretending to switch it on like a light saber.

"Jumping Jiminy," Franklin exclaimed.

Tiffany opened her eyes and nearly dropped the stick. A blade of blue-white light three feet long radiated out both ends. She lost her concentration the moment she realized what she was doing and the two sabers of light fizzled out.

"I did it," Tiffany said. "I actually did it!"

"It looks like we've finally found something you're good at," Franklin announced, impressed. "Do it again."

Tiffany closed her eyes and concentrated on that feeling again, focusing it on the stick once more, flicking her thumb to send the power she felt in the palm of her hand through to the wood. She didn't have to open her eyes to know she'd done it again. She could feel it coursing through her fingers, warming her hand.

"That's...really good," Franklin said with genuine surprise. "Better than your flying," he added quickly.

Tiffany opened her eyes and glared at him. The light winked out as her concentration broke.

"Your lesson's over for the day," Franklin said. "But you should get a different—"

"I like this one," Tiffany said, gripping the stick in both hands.

"Fine," Franklin said. "But don't say I didn't warn you."

SIXTEEN

FRANKLIN AND TIFFANY STARED DOWN the dark staircase leading to Duke's home. The only difference between the men and women sitting at the Egg Roll Station since yesterday was color and size. Their menacing stares were the same, so Tiffany didn't need encouragement to go down into the dark this time.

As they descended, Franklin held a candlestick over his shoulder, waving it for her to take it. "Practice," he said. "Work on keeping it going. I don't want to fall down these steps."

Tiffany glowered at his back, but took the candlestick and thought of flying, closing her eyes only long enough to direct the warm feeling from her center to her skin, down her arm, and to her fingers. The candle lit with a small shaft of blue-white light, the same way Hedika and Franklin made it work. She marveled at it, concentrating on keeping the feeling alive. Her joy shifted from the thought of flight to the amazement of making light from nothing.

With her focus so heavily on the light, she didn't notice Franklin leading her all the way down to Duke's home under the street. Franklin called out and ducked through the doorway. Tiffany's light faltered briefly, but she regained control and held the candle in front of her to light the room as she followed him inside.

"Are you back so soon?" Duke's weak voice called from deep within the home.

"You said you'd give me his location today," Franklin replied.

"And you said you'd bring eggrolls," Duke pointed out as he shuffled from the hallway into the meager glow of Tiffany's light.

"Damn," Franklin said. "I'll get them later."

"No better time than the present. I haven't had breakfast yet, and my old legs—"

"Fine, fine," Franklin agreed begrudgingly. "Wait here," he told Tiffany softly. Franklin brushed past her and out the door, climbing the stairs quickly for having an injured leg. Tiffany wondered if their pain medication was better down here or if gargoyles healed faster. She wanted to look at her own arm, but knew it would disrupt her concentration on the light. It already flickered with her wandering thoughts.

"You met Bones face-to-face," Duke said. Tiffany shivered at hearing the name. Her light went out. "I still smell him on you. Has Franklin told you about him yet?"

"Who? Bones, or himself?" Tiffany closed her eyes and tried to restore the lost light, but couldn't shake the thought of Bones invading her mind.

"Oh, I doubt he'd tell you anything about himself. What's your name, by the way?"

She immediately remembered what Franklin said about sharing information, but disregarded it. "Tiffany," she answered. A lot of other people already knew her name. She couldn't see the harm in letting Duke know hers, especially because she knew his.

She heard Duke shuffling through the pitch black room, coming closer. She shook the candlestick, hoping to bring light, but her mind still conjured the horrible thoughts Bones unearthed—scurrying things under the bed, fingers clawing at the window, the bodiless clothes coming out of her closet, and the suffocating drapes.

"I'm Duke." By the sound of his voice she knew he stood so close she could touch him. "It's a pleasure to meet you."

Tiffany took a deep, steadying breath and wished she could bring light with the ease Hedika did. She wished she had Hedika's confidence at the very least, or her physical strength, or even a portion of her knowledge. Just having Hedika by her side would be enough right now.

The candle began to glow, startling her a little. What startled her more was the visage of Duke only an arm's length away, his hand extended, his empty eye sockets black under his flattened head. She sucked in a breath and her light winked out again.

"Are you alright?" Duke asked.

"No, I mean, yes, it's just that I'm having trouble with my candlestick," Tiffany said, steadying her voice as much as she could muster. "Can you—?"

The room began to glow. With light emanating from every direction, Duke's malformed face didn't appear nearly as gruesome, nor as frightening. He smiled, showing his fat teeth, one in front broken in half.

"How do you do that?"

"You *are* new, aren't you?"

Duke still held a hand out and she took it, shaking it slowly. His skin was soft and aged, loosely fitting over his thick frame. His thumb was huge—three of her own fingers thick, wrapping over her hand to give her a firm shake. He didn't let her hand go, but stared straight through her with his empty eyes, and she wondered if he could see her the same way bats did.

"It's unfortunate one as new as you had to face Bones. Did he touch your mind?"

Tiffany nodded. "Yes."

"I'm sorry," Duke told her. "But you're not alone in that regard. Bones has been menacing our kind for as long as I've been around, and he was old when I first came along. A great deal of rumor surrounds him, because no one knows for sure when he died or who he was before. I do know he's not like other ghosts. He doesn't have remains in the other world that anchor him to any one place or time, or at least no one has been able to sniff them out yet. Not even me," Duke said, pointing to his large, round nose. He grinned and let Tiffany's hand go as he turned to shuffle toward the pair of couches.

Tiffany swallowed hard, afraid to follow him, much less take a step from where her feet felt riveted to the ground. Duke wore the same pants as the day before, with the same outward facing pocket below his belt line.

"Do you mind if I ask you something personal?" Tiffany asked.

"About my face?"

"No, actually. About your tail."

Duke turned slowly and glared at her with his empty eye sockets. The way he glared directly at her even though he had no eyes was spooky.

"I saw the nub yesterday," Tiffany pressed, her voice wavering. "When you leaned over Franklin to smell his leg. My friend has this pit bull with a cropped tail..." Tiffany held her tongue. Only after the words left her mouth did she realize she was comparing Duke to a dog. *Dummy!*

Duke nodded and turned away, continuing his slow shuffle toward the two couches. He sat with his back to her and put his big, rounded feet on the table.

"It's cropped," Duke admitted, popping his toes as he curled them slowly. "I wanted to be a Sentinel from the day I arrived, but I had a tail. I asked to be transferred and even though I passed all the requirements, they denied me twice, so I hacked it off."

He sighed and leaned his head back.

"Did you get to be a Sentinel?"

Duke didn't answer at first. He leaned his long staff on the couch beside him and touched it reverently. She knew it was a Sentinel's staff, the kind they used on the walls facing the Endless See to make the light.

"I got what I wanted," Duke grumbled, then sniffed the air. "Franklin's back."

SEVENTEEN

FRANKLIN CARRIED A PLATE full of eggrolls into Duke's home. He limped now from all the climbing. He looked Tiffany up and down as if making sure she was alright then slipped past her.

"Three dozen," Franklin said as he put the plate on the table. He sat down opposite Duke and leaned forward to rub his leg, wincing. "Two bowls of sauce, too."

"Ah, thank you, Franklin," Duke said, dropping his feet from the table. He leaned forward and grabbed two eggrolls then stuffed them whole into his huge mouth and crunched on them loudly. Franklin was silent as Duke shoveled more eggrolls into his mouth, chewing loudly, smacking his lips, licking his fingers. Tiffany smiled at the sounds, fairly certain Duke was doing it on purpose to prolong Franklin's visit.

"Did you hear the Seraph are opening positions for a few qualified *commontry* to train under their mentors?"

"Fat chance of that happening," Franklin replied. "No one ever qualifies. They keep saying that to keep us in line."

"I think they're finally afraid of our dwindling numbers."

"I think you read too much into things."

"What does 'commontry' mean?" Tiffany asked.

"Huh?" Franklin asked, lifting his head to regard her. She still stood near the door. "Partials. That's us. Anyone without both wings and a tail. The Seraph have both so they think they're special."

"They *are* special," Duke said.

"Especially irritating," Franklin replied. "There are no Seraph among the commontry, and you know it. It's a myth. They talk about it to keep us in line. It's just politics as usual."

"Still, wouldn't it be nice?" Duke asked whimsically, smacking his lips as he crunched another egg roll.

"I suppose," Franklin said quietly. Tiffany could tell he was letting Duke dream a little. "Maybe we'll get a rock-head up there with half a brain out of it all, huh?"

"Or a hunter with some vision," Duke replied.

"Speaking of hunting, I don't mean to cut the visit short or anything, but I'm kind of in a hurry to figure out what Bones is up to before he goes after another chimera, so did you find that fellow who bit me?"

"I did. He's on the mantle, there." Duke pointed toward the fireplace. On the mantle was a small figurine that looked hideous. Tiffany zoomed in on the thing, although she wished she hadn't. It was a small figurine, grotesquely shaped with a deformed, melted wing on one side and what looked like a tattered sail or drape on the other, its head covered in burlap with a rope around its neck which looped around its chest and waist. The face pushed against the sack, a long snout and a dog-like mouth with teeth ripping through the burlap. Franklin crossed the room to pick up the figurine.

"Who's this pretty fellow?" Franklin asked, turning the figurine in his hand.

"Say hello to one Matthias B. Thorp, deceased. This will take you to the church outside the cemetery. You'll have to find his plot yourself. Best to wait for nightfall, though. It's in the middle of town."

"Wonderful," Franklin said dryly. He weighed the figurine in his hand, frowning at it. "It looks like we've got some time for a visit after all. Hand me one of them egg rolls."

EIGHTEEN

TIFFANY CRASH LANDED into the barracks perch again. Her approach was fine, swooping in beneath the ledge, rising and slowing with her wings out wide, and flaring her legs at the last moment, but when her feet touched down, the weight of her wings staggered her forward until she stood on tip-toes, pitched over the crash pit, swinging her arms to try to regain her balance. Then she whacked her wing with her training baton and it recoiled instinctively from the pain, causing her to fall forward. She landed face first on the sponges. She swore and crawled through the uneven pile of sponges for the nearest ladder to haul herself out. It irritated her how close she was to doing it right, for once. Halfway up the ladder she swung her baton over the lip so she could pull herself out. The baton began rolling away and she scrambled to get out to stop it.

"Nice landing," Priya said with a smirk. She put a foot on Tiffany's baton to stop its rolling.

"Thanks," Tiffany said breathlessly, wondering where the girl came from. Tiffany managed to lift her weight above the pit and throw her leg over to climb out completely. She stood and swept her hair back. "Flying isn't my stronger suit."

"You already got a training baton, huh?" Priya asked, picking it up and handing it to Tiffany.

"Yeah, my mentor said—"

"This one's two-sided. Only wingless use this kind."

"I don't know, I thought it was—"

"You're going to cut your wings off with it, but I doubt that'll make a difference."

"Right," Tiffany said with an accommodating smile, not sure if Priya was being mean or joking. "I'll keep that in mind."

"Well, I've got things to do," Priya said and snapped open her wings. She leapt to Tiffany's side, flapping once to clear the crash pit, then banked sideways out the mouth of the landing cave, dropping out of sight. Tiffany shook her head, wondering about Priya's gruff nature. Was she just mean because Tiffany was new? Tiffany didn't think so. The way she flew spoke of her arrogance.

Tiffany found Hedika sleeping in her bunk. Several other girls were also sleeping, two girls were reading books at a table, and one girl was mending her silver gown. Tiffany went to her locker and put her baton away, then went to her bed as quietly as she could. She eased the sheets out of the way and lay down, unfolding her wings to let them drape onto the floor. She sighed softly and closed her eyes.

"I made your bed," Hedika said quietly.

"What?" Tiffany asked, startled wide-eyed.

"I made your bed this morning. You're supposed to keep your bunk and locker in order."

"Thanks," Tiffany said. "I'm sorry. I didn't mean to wake you just now."

"You didn't. Priya did."

"Oh, I ran into her out in the crash pits."

"She crashed?" Hedika asked with surprise, opening one eye.

"No, I did. She laughed at me...I think. She wasn't laughing, though."

"Was she being mean?"

"A little."

"She was laughing at you," Hedika said. She sat up and pushed her bed sheets aside. She wasn't wearing her yellow flight gown. Instead, she wore a sports bra and shorts. Tiffany's eyes widened. Hedika had sharp, strong muscles like a gymnast, and with her blue-granite skin beneath her white underclothes, Tiffany couldn't help but stare. There was something curiously beautiful about it that drew her eye.

Hedika glared back at her. Tiffany felt self-conscious and lowered her gaze, sitting up in bed with effort, dragging in her draped wings, but she still stared at Hedika's calves.

"I'm sorry," Tiffany said. "You just look so…"

"Blue?"

"Yeah, but in a cool way. I mean, look at your skin."

Hedika held her arm out. She appraised it only for a moment and scowled.

"It's like smooth granite, but it looks—" Tiffany realized she was reaching a hand toward Hedika's arm. She withdrew her hand quickly, ashamed and a little confused about why she'd done it.

"I'm going to get something to eat," Hedika said.

"Oh, where do we eat? My mentor keeps taking me to the Fly & Diver Grill, but I don't have any money and I'm starving."

Hedika sighed with mild annoyance. "I'll show you, but make your bed while I take a shower."

"Right," Tiffany said.

NINETEEN

TIFFANY MADE HEDIKA'S BED as well as her own. She had nothing to do while she waited for Hedika, so she stood near the door and drew back her sleeve to look at her forearm. The abrasions had become long, flat scabs with blue and black bruising around the edges. She touched the wound tenderly, but it didn't hurt as bad as it looked.

"How did you do that?" Hedika asked, appearing out of nowhere beside her.

"I...crashed," Tiffany said, tugging the sleeve of her gown back over the wound. "I'm not really that good at flying yet."

"Well, the mess hall is just a glide across the way."

"I'm not good at gliding either."

Hedika shrugged and quietly led Tiffany to the barracks landing perch. She stood at the edge and rolled her shoulders, waiting for Tiffany to step up beside her.

"It's right there," Hedika said, pointing. Tiffany followed her finger with her eyes, zooming in on a perch that had several silver-gowned girls standing next to two silver uniformed boys, all winged like herself. Another boy wore a yellow uniform. He was tall and charcoal-skinned with long streaks of powder white carving veins down his neck into his shirt.

"It looks crowded," Tiffany said, gulping.

"It *is* lunch time," Hedika said. She let her wings open slowly as though she were stretching off her slumber. The leather of her wings wasn't black like Tiffany's, but the same dark blue as Hedika's skin, only without the silvery speckles that made her appear granite-like. Hedika dove off the perch and caught the wind with a single beat of her wings, then she began gliding across the hollow mountain.

Tiffany took a deep breath and jumped off the perch as well, flapping her wings furiously to keep from free-falling. Her clumsy strokes sent her side to side as she rose again to be slightly higher than the opposite perch. Hedika swept in and landed on one foot, hauling in her wings slowly and gracefully as she stepped away from the ledge. Tiffany marveled at it a bit too long and was forced to throw her legs forward abruptly to avoid crashing headlong into Hedika. She flapped her wings and nearly fell backwards off the perch, but Hedika reached a hand out and grabbed Tiffany by the arm to haul her in. Tiffany was surprised by Hedika's strength, feeling like a feather in her grip.

"Watch it," Hedika hissed, pushing one of Tiffany's wings off her head.

"Sorry." Tiffany's face flushed with embarrassment. "Sorry."

The boys and girls that had been standing near the perch laughed at her and she felt even more embarrassed. She drew in her wings and lowered her head, looking away from everyone.

"Sorry," she whispered to Hedika.

Hedika shook her head, clearly frustrated, but led Tiffany by the arm past the others and into the large cavern. It had several entryways all linking to a huge room, and the noise of hundreds of conversations poured past them. Inside were long stretches of benches and seats. Clutches of winged boys and girls wearing a wide assortment of silver, yellow, and blue filled the rows of benches. Tiffany noticed only five others wearing white, two of them boys.

"Well I stick out like a sore thumb," Tiffany said under her breath. Hedika let her arm go and got into the short line for food. Hedika picked three plates and a stack of muffins on her tray, so Tiffany didn't feel bad about taking two plates for herself. Hedika found a secluded spot and sat down across from Tiffany. Hedika ate her first plate without a word. Tiffany didn't eat as quickly, but she was equally ravenous.

"I noticed you have a training baton," Hedika said as she shuffled her plates. "Normally girls don't get one this soon."

Tiffany thought of what Franklin said about offering too much information, but dismissed it, angry at him for making her think that she shouldn't make friends. She would rather have Hedika as a friend than anyone else in Bay 3; that much was certain.

"My mentor says I'm pretty good at making light."

"Really?" Hedika said while chewing. She wiped her hands with a napkin. "Show me."

Tiffany took out the candlestick Franklin gave her and closed her eyes, thinking of…but Hedika touched her. Tiffany sucked in a deep, nervous breath and opened her eyes wide, startled to find Hedika's hands cupping hers.

"Don't close your eyes," Hedika said. "Never close your eyes in the face of danger."

"But you're not a danger," Tiffany said, her voice shaky. Hedika's deep blue skin felt warm and soft, nothing like the cold stone it appeared to be.

"Just don't," Hedika said with a firm squeeze of her hand before letting go. "Now show me."

Tiffany took a deep breath and stared at her hand where Hedika had touched her. She still felt Hedika's soft stone-colored skin radiating its warmth, and the sureness of Hedika's fingertips against the back of Tiffany's hand. She grabbed hold of the thought and guided the feeling into the candlestick, which began to glow a blue-white light.

Hedika smiled and leaned back in her chair, a look of awe creeping into her stony façade. "Wow," she said. "It's solid. And unwavering. Do you know how hard that is for a newbie?" She leaned forward, allowing her eyes to inspect Tiffany's light more closely. "Look at that." She took out her own candlestick and shook it alive. Her own blue-white light began to glow next to Tiffany's, not nearly as bright, nor as tall. "Look at that. How did you do that?"

Tiffany smiled and her light flickered out.

"I just think of the things that amaze me," she said. "Like that," she added, pointing at Hedika's own light. "And flying. Do you realize how awesome it is to fly?"

"Yeah, but I wouldn't call what you do flying," Hedika said, letting her own candle die out. Tiffany frowned. Hedika smiled, and Tiffany realized it was a joke. She smiled too and they giggled. It felt good to laugh, even at herself, but most of all, it felt good to finally have someone she knew she could trust.

TWENTY

"I'M FULL," Tiffany said, turning sideways on the bench to lean against the wall with her wings. "Now I don't want to go to bed."

"Where's your mentor?"

"He's...busy. He sent me back to get some sleep for tomorrow. Actually, tonight. He's going to come get me tonight."

"You two are keeping some odd hours," Hedika said.

"I don't think he sleeps," Tiffany said honestly.

"Well, since you don't have to be anywhere, you can come to the library with me. I need to get a new book for tonight."

"Really?" Tiffany asked excitedly, sitting up in her chair.

"It's kind of a long way," Hedika said sarcastically. "Can you make it to the ground without slamming into it, or should I get a rope?"

"Ha, ha," Tiffany replied sourly. She frowned, wondering aloud, "Am I really that bad?"

Hedika shrugged. "I've seen worse."

Tiffany sighed.

"Don't worry. You'll get the hang of it. Nothing beats practice."

Tiffany followed Hedika to the ledge and watched her dive off casually, sweeping out away from the wall to circle closer to the center of the hollow mountain. Tiffany took a deep breath and snapped open her wings, leaned forward, and jumped. She didn't catch the air as well as she hoped and began freefalling. Her heart pounded as she batted at the air with her wings to right herself, opening her legs to help catch the air currents rushing up at her. She began to straighten as Hedika swooped beneath her, diving fast as though she meant to catch her.

"Are you alright?" Hedika asked after arcing back up and circling to join Tiffany. By then, Tiffany's heart had calmed enough that she could breathe again.

"Fine, just—"

"You scared me to death," Hedika called out irritably.

"I'm sorry."

"We'll take it nice and easy, OK? Circle and descend as fast as you feel comfortable. No more freefalls. You're going to hit someone."

Tiffany nodded. She didn't want to mention her freefall with Franklin the other day. If Hedika believed her in the first place, she might think her mentor was crazy.

Hedika stayed beside her the whole way down, easing them with the currents and helping her by pointing out what was causing her to flail and thrash against the wind instead of using it to glide. By the time they came in for a landing, Tiffany thought she might have learned something. The thought dashed away the moment she crashed. At first, she landed on her feet, jogging awkwardly to try to stay upright, but then she tipped to the side and fell over. Her wing swatted the ground to slow her fall and she felt a spike of pain. She sat up and curled the wing close to inspect it, touching it and bending it to see if she'd broken the rigid knuckle, but it looked and felt fine.

"Got a stinger, huh?" Hedika asked, holding a hand out to help

Tiffany to her feet.

"Yeah."

"It looks fine. Does it hurt?"

"No, not now."

"Welcome to the library, then," Hedika said, sweeping her hand toward the four story high building. It looked like a Roman cathedral with its tall spires and huge archways carved in the stone face of the building. Three enormous sets of stairs led up to the entryway, which had a massive gargoyle face carved above the door. Its tall ears, long snout, and great teeth were softened by a mane of hair and a pair of glasses over its eyes. It didn't appear fearsome, but instead had a scholarly, welcoming look.

Hedika led Tiffany up the stairs and through the main doors. The floor was a mixture of clear and opaque crystal that looked to be five feet deep, with no sign of a seam or change in pattern anywhere. Beneath was a radiant blue, giving the illusion of a glass-bottom building floating in the clouds. The walls were polished limestone. Twenty pillars supported the roof, each made of basalt with ridges plated in electrum. The interior glowed a pale, soft white that showered onto enormously tall book shelves with ladders and walkways in front of each. Winged and wingless alike sat with books or moved quietly through the collections.

"We should probably start you with the Book of Order," Hedika suggested, pointing the way. Tiffany followed her like a wide-eyed child in a toy store. She wanted to stop and look at everything, but Hedika trekked them into a far corner of the building and climbed a ladder to retrieve a book. Tiffany stood below and watched, zooming in her vision to read some of the bindings. There were several copies of the Book of Order, as well as a Basic Flight Tactics, Basic Training, Mathematics, Stone Working, and Light Manipulation.

"What's the Book of Order?" she asked, shaking off a bout of dizziness after retracting her vision, leaning against the book shelves for support.

"It explains everything you need to know about being a gargoyle, at least the things they think are important."

"It's big," Tiffany said, weighing the book as Hedika dropped it in her arms.

"Put it down there," Hedika said. "Give it a look. I'm going to go find something. I'll be right back."

Tiffany sat down and turned the huge leather-bound cover to open the book. The runes on it were unfamiliar, nothing like English or even Japanese. It looked like ancient biblical lettering she once saw in a museum. She sighed and stared at the first lines, wondering how she was supposed to read it. One of the runes looked familiar to her, though, then another, and she found that she could piece together one word, then one more. She leaned back in her chair with her eyes wide in amazement.

"Getting the hang of it, I see," Hedika said with a grin as she sat down opposite Tiffany. She slid four books onto the table. "Kind of weird, huh?"

"That's an understatement," Tiffany whispered. She looked at one of Hedika's books. It was an old hard cover of *Othello* that looked fifty years old. "Where do all these books come from?"

"What they don't write they bring in from up top. Like this," Hedika said, holding up the hard cover. "This would be a pretty boring place if we didn't steal from the real world."

"Huh," Tiffany said. "But they write books too, right?"

"Sure. The training manuals mostly, and all our histories. Stuff they wouldn't know about up top. There's a whole section cataloging the adventures of all the old hunters."

"Do they mention ghosts?"

"Sure. All the time."

"How do you find them? I mean, is there a Dewey Decimal System or something?"

"Kind of," Hedika giggled. "What are you interested in? Your mentor?"

"No," Tiffany said, her mind wandering with an idea. "But I need to find a book about someone. Can you help me?"

"Sure," Hedika shrugged. "I know this place inside and out."

"But you've got to swear not to talk about it to anyone, even D.K."

"Why?"

"Swear."

"No. You tell me why and maybe I'll consider it."

"At least don't tell Corinne."

"Please," Hedika scoffed. "Why would I tell her anything?"

"I'm looking for the history of a ghost named Bones," Tiffany whispered.

"Bones!?"

"Shhh," Tiffany said, waving her hands at Hedika. "Keep it down."

"Why do you want to know about Bones? And who told you about him, anyway?"

"How do *you* know about him?" Tiffany asked.

"I do *read*," Hedika said, waving a hand at the shelves. "How do you know about him?"

Wincing through every word, Tiffany said, "I kind of went up top with my mentor and ran into him, and D.K. had to come save us."

"You've seen Bones?" Hedika asked flatly.

"Kind of," Tiffany said.

"Bones?" Hedika asked again, this time incredulously.

"I said that, yeah."

"Do you even know who he is?"

"An ancient ghost that no one knows much about, but he's super powerful—oh, and he can move things with a white-light like hands." Tiffany clenched her hands into fists in front of her. "And he likes closets," she added excitedly, but then became detached from herself as she thought aloud, "And he can invade your mind and kill you with your own dreams."

"Bones," Hedika said, still completely stunned.

Tiffany shuddered. "And he bubbles paint like he's crawling under it. It's really freaky scary."

"You've *actually* seen Bones, haven't you?"

"More than seen him," Tiffany said. "I think he killed me."

TWENTY-ONE

HEDIKA DROPPED another large wood-bound book onto the table in front of Tiffany. It had strange, cryptic runes drawn all over it, only half of which she could make out.

"What's this one?"

"Demon Chronicles of Vlad Dracul."

"That says 'dragon'," Tiffany said, pointing at one of the words on the cover that she could recognize.

"Dracul, yeah. It means dragon. Vlad was given the name because he was part of the Order of the Dragon. He was also the father of Vlad the Impaler."

"I know that name. Who is that?"

"Dracula."

"Are you kidding me?"

"No, I'm not. This book was drafted by Vlad during his years as a demon hunter. Back then, they called them demons instead of ghosts. You'll see that a lot. This book has a section about Bones, though. It's considered one of the first sightings of him, depending on who you ask."

"How do you know all this?"

"Basic history and lore is required reading."

"Yeah, but how do you know about *this*," Tiffany asked, tapping the book.

"Vlad is an icon. They spend a lot of time talking about him because he was one of the first to chronicle everything he did. They have a lot of icons, though," Hedika added, shrugging. "But I've always been a bit of a book worm, and I thought I'd learn something about Dracula by reading all this garbage. Vlad never even mentions his son."

"Just like a gargoyle," Tiffany muttered.

"Ain't that the truth," Hedika replied softly.

They smiled at one another and Tiffany felt a little closer to Hedika. They weren't that much different, at least she hoped not. Aside from the two or three year difference in age, they were both lonely. That much was apparent. Tiffany hoped Hedika was as desperate for friendship—an honest friend she could trust. Someone to just *be there*. She didn't need anything else. Everything else would come, in time.

"Here, let me find that section," Hedika said abruptly, grabbing the book and lifting open the cover. She scanned the pages, avoiding looking at Tiffany's eyes as she rummaged through the book.

"Bones doesn't have a real name, at least none that anyone knows," Hedika explained as she flipped pages slowly, glossing over whole sections. "Vlad just named the demon 'Bones' because of how he found him. He was hunting in this river valley, searching for a specific heathen burial site with underground caves that—oh, here it is. Here it is. Listen to this:

On my right the river coursed an even flow, tumbling loudly over stones the size of anvils at my feet. To my left rose a blackened wall, a sheer height of thirty spans of my wings that was the gorge through which the river dashed. Ahead, the scratching I witnessed ceased abruptly and the dim white light vanished as though the lamp had been blown out. This was certainly not a peasant worker as I had considered earlier. At once I smelled a foul stench of rot and decay, and somewhere ahead of me I heard wolves begin to cry out. False manifestations, each and all. A rock tumbled down the sheer wall beside me, clacking loudly in the dark shadows.

I approached the site nonetheless, unafraid by such simple effects. Between the stones at the edge of the water I found the worn-down length of a forearm's bone, having its wrist joint partly scoured away. The bone was wet and gritty with its own scrapings, but otherwise sturdy and of little age.

A cold wind lashed across my back accompanied by moaning from upriver. I indulged this noise and continued in its direction, carrying with me the bone I had found. I ignored the cries of wolves and the raven's scream from the shadows above. I ignored the clacking of small stones tumbling over me, and the stench of death that came with it all. Even the growl of a bear did not deter me in my quest for the heathen burial site I knew should be near.

Eventually, I tired of the petty hauntings and discarded the bone, leaving it behind as I advanced further into the dark recesses of the gorge. As the sounds and smells disappeared around me, I looked back to see a weak light dragging the bone away over the rocks, struggling with its weight. Such a meager demon, I had no heart or stomach for killing it. I still had my sights on the forgotten son of Mehmed. The heathen crypts were surely hidden close by.

I scanned the dark shadows of the gorge up and down each side to no avail, then looked again to the progress made by that pitiable demon *Bones*. His path did not lead him back to the river, but instead toward the sheer rock wall, and thanks to

his dim light, behind an enormous boulder that seemed part of the wall itself, I found the narrow path into the mountainside. *Bones*, in his demonic cowardice, had shown me the way to my prize.

Hedika looked up with a grin. "Spooky, huh?"

"A little," Tiffany agreed, shuddering. "I used to like ghost stories."

"Me too," Hedika said. "I still do."

"Have you seen one? A ghost?"

"No," Hedika said hesitantly, shaking her head and looking away. "It's my next stripe, but—" She took a deep breath. "I don't have a mentor anymore."

"What happened? Why don't you—"

"I was disowned," Hedika snapped.

Tiffany froze, frightened that she may have just ruined everything between them by prying too deeply.

Hedika turned away, eyes closed. All her muscles tightened as though she meant to leap into the air and fly away. Her jaw clenched. She took a deep breath and Tiffany expected her to jump out of her seat, but instead her body sagged.

"They don't think I can kill," Hedika admitted softly. "I failed the assessment."

"What assessment?"

"Before you're allowed to go up top, they test you. I'm borderline, as D.K. put it. A split decision by the review panel. So I was disowned to receive a new mentor, and restart training."

"Restart? From the beginning?"

"No," Hedika said with a weak smile. "Just this stripe," she said, pointing at her sleeve.

"Well, if you don't want to be a hunter, why not switch? I

heard they have positions in the Seraph."

"Nobody goes up," Hedika said while shaking her head in disgust.

"I've heard that too."

"How do you know so much and still know so little?" Hedika asked, her eyes narrowing as she pondered Tiffany from across the table. "Where do you hear all this stuff?"

Tiffany shrugged. "You wouldn't believe me."

"Try me."

"A blind Sentinel."

"A blind Sentinel?"

"See? I told you you wouldn't believe me."

Hedika shook her head in disbelief, but smiled. Thank goodness they were getting along.

TWENTY-TWO

EVEN WITH HEDIKA'S INSTRUCTION and encouragement, Tiffany still toppled into the crash pit full of sponges at the landing ledge. She swatted a big sponge from in front of her, punching another out of frustration. Hedika didn't laugh, but she looked down at her with an amused smile. Tiffany sighed and rolled several times to the wall. She had crashed enough to know the easiest way out of the pit was to get on top of it. Her abdominal muscles were sore, nonetheless.

"It's too narrow," Tiffany complained about the yellow landing ledge, grunting to pull herself over the edge of the pit.

"When you're better at flying, you can just fly past it and land deeper in the cave."

"That's impossible," Tiffany thought out loud. Someone tall like D.K. barely had enough room to walk through the cave without the tips of her wings scraping the ceiling. "There's no room."

"Are you kidding? There's tons of room. Priya flies tight circles in here sometimes to let off steam."

"Can you do it?"

"Not as many," Hedika shrugged. "Not as long. You'll get the hang of it." Hedika held out the book she carried up from the library for Tiffany.

"Thanks," Tiffany said, slipping it under her arm.

They walked to the barracks together and went inside. Only a few girls were there, one fast asleep on her bed, one coming out of the bathroom with a towel around her torso, hair still wet.

"What a long day," Tiffany said under her breath as she dropped her book on her bed.

Hedika dropped the three books she brought from the library onto her own bed and stretched. "I'm going to take a nap. Everyone will be coming back soon. You should get a shower before the hot water is all used up."

"Good idea."

Tiffany took a change of underwear and towel from her locker and went into the bathroom. It was a big, open room with several toilet stalls, a line of sinks, and a wide shower room with four nozzles coming out of the ceiling. At first she felt embarrassed undressing in the big, open room, but no one else was in with her, so she folded her things and stepped in front of a mirror to look at her back. Her wings sprouted from her spine, articulating over— and independent of—her shoulder blades, but sharing the same thick, stretched skin. The pale tan of her normal skin darkened in streaks as though a hundred fingers fastened the wings up and down her spine, each pumping some kind of black pigment into the very core of her being. Or was it leaching the darkness from her?

One thick bone the width of her leg rose and tapered the frame of each wing, jointing in two places above her head to allow her to stretch the leather of her wings. She opened her wings and raised her hand as high over her head as she could, only just touching the first joint. Sliding her hand down the length of the bone tickled, sending a shiver through her spine and to her neck. The bone wasn't hard beneath her fingers, but instead it had a certain combination of resilience and softness that felt hollow and pliable. It explained how she hadn't broken them crashing into the pits as often as she had.

Her fascination didn't last. The things were still too foreign. She retreated to the showers to hide from the mirrors.

The water came out of a wide shower head when she turned on the faucet. Warm, fat droplets fell gently over her wings, pattering onto them like rain over huge leaves. The sensation of water flowing over her wings felt a lot like wind as she flew, but heavier and more relaxing. She swept her wings slowly through the showering droplets as though flying in slow motion, catching waves of warm water that she lifted and poured like buckets. It washed away everything that had happened to her these last few days.

The moment didn't last. So much water triggered thoughts of drowning, a reminder of her death at the hands of Bones. She hugged herself and stepped out of the stream of water, shivering a little.

The door to the bathroom snapped open. Two girls burst in, laughing and leaning close to one another. Their laughter halted the moment they saw Tiffany. Tiffany felt awkward, standing naked and on display with nothing to hide her tiny body and big head. One of the two girls started laughing again, dragging the second toward the bathroom stalls.

Tiffany curled a wing around herself. Death didn't seem to dilute the insecurities and self-conscious feelings any. She still hated the twigs she had for legs and arms. She shut off the faucet and went for her towel.

She covered herself as best she could and stretched out her wings behind her. They were soaked. Pools of water began to grow where her wings dragged over the cold stone floor, spreading the water like a squeegee. She walked back into the shower area and tried to shake her wings by swinging her body side to side.

"Snap 'em," one of the girls said as she came out of the bathroom stall. She was one of the girls from Corinne's circle, but Tiffany couldn't remember her name. She had warm gray skin the color of an andesite paver, awash with veins both light and dark.

"Huh?"

"Your wings. Snap 'em open a few times to dry them."

The other girl came out, giggling again as soon as she looked at her friend, and the two left, giggling together as the door closed behind them.

Tiffany collected her wings and snapped them out. Water shot everywhere, like a wet dog shaking clean. Tiffany nearly fell over from the shift in weight. She furled her wings and steadied her stance, then snapped them again. Less water flew off, but her wings still felt heavy, so she snapped them again and again and again until she had to sit down from dizziness.

Dry and dressed, she went back out to thank the girl who helped her, but there were others around her now. Five in all, and another just arriving in the bay whom they all waved to. She felt embarrassed again, thinking of herself from the girl's perspective; a scrawny little thing who didn't even know how to dry her own wings. Tiffany walked past the group of girls instead and put her dirty underwear and towel into the laundry bag in her locker.

The girl who had been practicing making light the other day sat up on a perch above the lockers as she had before, shaking a candlestick that fizzled each time. She had skin the color of brick, and short black hair.

"Where's Hedika?" Tiffany asked quietly, looking around for her friend's blue skin and yellow gown.

"Probably went to a study room," the girl above her said, pointing to the four doors on the other side of the bathroom hall. Tiffany had wondered what those doors were for, but had been reluctant to ask, or even look. "To sleep," the girl added.

"Oh," Tiffany said. She couldn't think of anything else to talk about. She didn't want to try to help her with her light, thinking it would only make the girl resent her for being better at it even though she was brand new, so Tiffany went and sat down on her bed.

She didn't like being alone, but she didn't like the way the other girls were treating her so far, either. Even if it was just the attitude Franklin had been trying to foster in her, to be cautious of everyone and everything, it didn't mean these girls didn't make friends. There were small groups, sides, and subtle fences erected all over the bay. Tiffany needed a little time to sort out which girls to watch out for, like Priya. That girl was clearly in a camp of her own; both rude and arrogant. Another rude one was Karla, the big one. She had the disposition of a pit bull. Both were friends of Corinne, so that lumped them all together, and every girl she'd met who sided with them was probably trouble.

Thank goodness she had Hedika.

Tiffany opened her book and sat cross-legged in front of it. She didn't read. Instead, she watched the other girls from the corner of her eyes and listened as best she could. The one who helped her with drying her wings in particular. She had been nice, at least, even if she was part of Corinne's circle. *Go say thanks,* Tiffany scolded herself. She took a deep, steadying breath, closed her eyes, and put her feet down from her bed to stand up. Hedika had been like a wall too. These girls were no different. *Just go talk to them.*

"Listen up," Corinne called out to everyone, clapping her

hands together. Tiffany's eyes popped open, her heart thumping hard from the surprise. Corinne and Karla sauntered into the bay, stopping at the head of the beds. "Karla caught wind of an inspection tomorrow, so you know what that means. After dinner, I want everyone on their assigned duties and making this place spotless."

Several girls sighed or groaned, but no one voiced their displeasure. Corinne patted Karla on the shoulder and the big girl nodded appreciably, then stalked toward the ring of girls Tiffany had been about to go join.

"And that reminds me," Corinne went on. "We're making some duty changes. Monica—"

"Yes," one girl said excitedly, pumping her fist.

"—you're switching up to laundry. That means the laundry team now has three girls, so I want laundry done three times a week instead of two."

Tiffany sighed, knowing what was coming next. Corinne looked Tiffany's way as she said the rest of her announcement. "And that means our newest recruit, Tiffany, is responsible for bathrooms."

Of course I am.

"Monica, show her what to do tonight."

Monica stopped pumping her fist to nod, a beaming smile carving deep dimples into her jade-hued cheeks. Monica was one of the girls in Corinne's circle. The other girls sitting around her smiled and patted her on the shoulder or knee, slapping her hands in congratulations. It made Tiffany apprehensive about getting stuck on bathroom duty all the more.

This is really going to suck.

"Hey," Corinne said, startling Tiffany slightly. She'd been concentrating so much on the other girls she hadn't noticed

Corinne walk up to her bed. "Sorry to drop it on you like that. You weren't here this morning to get your task assignment."

"It's alright," Tiffany said, trying to act unaffected. *Be strong. Hide your true feelings.* At least in front of Corinne and the girls she didn't trust.

"Come on and sit with us. You haven't been in here much these past few days."

Tiffany closed her book and followed Corinne to a line of beds occupied two and three apiece by the girls in Corinne's circle. Monica was the center of attention now. The other girls giggled as Monica said, "I thought I'd *never* get off bathrooms."

"Pipe down," Corinne said to the girls as she sat down amongst them. "Don't make it sound so bad around the newbie."

Tiffany didn't like being called that, but didn't say anything. She sat down on the end of one of the beds and put her hands on her knees.

"It's easy once you get the hang of it," one of the other girls said.

"Are you kidding?" Monica asked incredulously "What? Did you have bathrooms for all of a month?"

The other girls laughed.

"Hey, it's not my fault I came in ahead of a big surge of girls," the first girl replied.

"So Tiffany, do you have any questions you want to ask us?" Corinne asked at a lull in the conversation.

She had a thousand. She had a million, but she didn't want to sound stupid or frightened or...or anything. She shrugged.

"Oh, come on," one of the other girls said. "Something's got to be on your mind."

Tiffany shrugged again, but opened her mouth, asking, "Do mentors teach us everything, or are there classes to attend?"

The girls giggled again almost all in unison. She felt embarrassed immediately for asking.

"Who's your mentor?" Corinne asked, laughing lightly.

Tiffany's heart stopped. She knew nothing of the other girls and already they were prying information from her, using her as a source of entertainment.

"It's OK," Corinne said. "Look, my mentor is Amanda Paulson. Karla's is Tom Latimore. It's no big deal."

"Well," Tiffany said, her voice breaking. She coughed to clear her throat. "My mentor is Franklin. Franklin Craft."

"Craft?" Corinne asked, her eyes widening.

"He's still alive?" one of the other girls asked.

"I heard he killed someone," said another. "He's been to prison six times," said a third. "You two are cut from the same mold, I guess," Priya said under her breath. The group giggled. Tiffany frowned. "I heard he fell in love with a human and she turned into a ghost he refused to kill," one of the two that barged into the bathroom on her earlier said—the one Tiffany didn't think nice. "I heard he broke all Eight Edicts," Karla put in. "I heard he was caught in possession of forbidden artifacts."

"Would you all shut up?" Corinne stood and glowered at everyone, turning in a circle, stopping when she reached Tiffany. Her eyes softened. "I'm sorry, but there is some truth to all that."

"What?" Tiffany asked hesitantly, staring up at Corinne, fighting her fear both at the thought they were making fun of her, and that they might be telling the truth.

"Franklin Craft got a cadet he was mentoring killed."

"I knew it," one of the girls whispered, sounding vindicated. Corinne glared at her, as did some of the others. The girl shrank.

"What are you talking about?" Tiffany managed to ask without her voice breaking.

"As far as hunters go, he's legendary," Corinne said. "But they don't let him mentor anymore. Ever since that cadet was killed because he took him up top before he was ready. I'm really surprised they let him mentor you. Tomorrow I'm going to ask my mentor about it, alright?"

Tiffany stared up at her like a doe gazing into the headlights of an oncoming truck.

"OK?"

Tiffany nodded.

"At least you're not going up top with him any time soon," one of the other girls said, shivering.

"Yeah," Tiffany said with a weak smile.

"Don't worry," Corinne said, putting a hand on Tiffany's shoulder. "I'll get it straightened out in the morning."

Tiffany nodded again, knowing the morning wouldn't be soon enough.

Tiffany hardly listened to the girls as they spoke in spates around the circle, laughing and giggling at times, whispering at others. Once dinner time rolled around, Tiffany retreated to her bed and lay down rather than go eat with the girls. She worried that the girls were playing a trick on her, but harbored a deeper fear that they may be right. No wonder Franklin told her not to talk about anything with anyone. Now she doubted both sources, and she had no idea how to find out the truth.

When the girls returned, Monica told Tiffany to wait until everyone was settled for the night before starting any work, so Tiffany sat with her book open, staring at the unread page, waiting and hoping someone would tell her it was all a joke. Girls came and went from the bathroom, and the bay became a flurry of activity as everyone cleaned different areas. Monica eventually led Tiffany through her new job, pointing out everything that needed to be done, but then left her alone to work, with only her thoughts as company.

The thing foremost on her mind was the revelation that Franklin wasn't what he appeared to be, but then again, she didn't know him in the first place. He may have been the worst mentor in the world. Nearly getting her killed by Bones proved that point, but that was partly her own fault. He did tell her to wait.

Corinne and her help! Blech. With Tiffany's luck, she'd get saddled to D.K. as her new mentor. *Wouldn't Corinne and her friends laugh about that?*

It didn't matter. Whether Franklin was a retired ghost hunter mentoring for the first time in years, or a reckless man who didn't care about her or anyone, working with either meant she had a chance to see her parents again. All that mattered to Tiffany right now was that Franklin was taking her up top again. The first time went by too quickly for her to even think straight. This time, she had a plan. Or an idea, at least. She had a chance to let her parents know she was still alive. Somehow.

"Lights out," was called through the bay and the main area went dark. Corinne came by to ask how Tiffany was doing. Tiffany acted strong to avoid seeming weak, even though she wished for someone's help, but her false bravado only resulted in Corinne shutting the bathroom door on her, leaving the room lit for Tiffany to clean the sinks alone. She scrubbed the showers last and dried them with a single towel, wringing it repeatedly even though the muscles in her hands burned. Her blistered hands were sore and worn, her fingers ached by the time she put everything away and dragged her wings out of the bathroom and into the hall.

Hedika's candle glowing by the door was the only source of light, so Tiffany leaned against the hallway wall while her eyes adjusted to the darkness. Eventually, she found her way to her locker and took out her training baton. She wasn't going up top again without a weapon.

The dark bay felt lonely. Even Hedika was too far away. She sat still as stone in a tall chair beside a shelf on which she'd propped her book and placed her candle, her eyes fixed on the pages, her dark blue wings arched over her like a shadow. She looked more like a gargoyle than a girl. Tiffany wanted to go straight to Hedika and ask for a hug, to help set things straight, but the blue-skinned girl seemed more like a statue than a vessel of comfort.

Tiffany sucked in a quivering breath to keep her tears at bay. She longed for the touch of her mother, a hug or kiss or any glancing embrace would do. Or her father's kiss on her forehead. Anything to set the world right, but that was a different world. She slid the baton under her bed and draped her wings over the sides as she lay on her back.

I'll get home somehow.

She squeezed her eyes shut, wanting only to sleep.

TWENTY-THREE

TIFFANY WOKE ABRUPTLY at Hedika's touch, lurching up, only to be held down by her own elbows pinning her wings. It was the middle of the night and darkness filled the bay except for a hint of light near the main door.

"You really need to stop sleeping on your wings," Hedika whispered into her ear.

"It feels good," Tiffany groaned softly.

"Well, get up. Your mentor's here."

Tiffany sighed and turned to her side slightly to haul in one wing, then turned to haul in the other before sitting up. She rubbed her eyes and focused on the candle glowing near the doorway. *Hedika kept it lit from this distance,* Tiffany thought, impressed by such a feat.

"Where are you off to?" Hedika asked, sitting down opposite Tiffany.

Tiffany listened to the other girls sleeping, wondering if any were quietly awake and eavesdropping on their conversation. "You didn't promise," Tiffany whispered softly. Even in the dark, Tiffany could see Hedika frowning. "But I trust you. Up top. To catch a ghost my mentor thinks knows what Bones is up to."

"That's what I thought," Hedika said as she held out a hand. "Here." Tiffany put her hand out and felt Hedika place something soft, like fur, into it. "Just in case."

"What is it?"

"A lock of hair. If you get into trouble, sprinkle it everywhere. It confuses ghosts. It's old school protection, but it works better than a pair of broken glasses."

"Those work pretty well, by the way."

"This is better," Hedika said, tapping a finger into Tiffany's palm.

Tiffany knelt beside her bed to make it in the dark. Hedika got up and went back to her perch by the door. Tiffany wished she could make a little more light to see by, but not at the risk of waking up Corinne or her friends. She pressed the sheets of her bed flat with her arm, then tucked the sides in, and did the same with her blanket, tucking the pillow into it as Hedika had shown her. Before getting up, she reached under her bed and felt for her training baton, pulling it out and gripping it tightly while taking a steadying breath. Her hands still ached from cleaning.

I have to do this, she told herself. *There's got to be a way to tell Mom and Dad I'm still alive.*

Hedika looked up from her book and climbed down from the stool as Tiffany reached the main door. "I know your mentor," Hedika whispered. "He didn't kill a cadet. His last charge got *himself* killed *after* he graduated. Your mentor was forced to retire early. He's one of those icons I told you about. He's supposed to be a little unorthodox, but no one has ever collected more chimera than him. Ever. Don't let Corinne get to you."

How did Hedika know about her conversation with Corinne, Tiffany wondered at first? Her second thought was that she wished Hedika had been there to say it in front of Corinne and the others.

"Did you hear us talking about it?" Tiffany asked.

"Cynth told me about it," Hedika said.

"Cynth?"

"Cynthia. The girl always perched on the wall. She hears everything."

"Oh," Tiffany said, smiling, imagining if Hedika had been at her bed how she would have called Corinne out on her story. Corinne would have been furious, but Hedika wouldn't have cared. She would have ignored the bay chief and gone on reading her book, confident in her knowledge and equally confident that her strong body would deter any physical confrontations. Tiffany's smile faded. Her own body wouldn't deter a gnat.

"Is it your hair?" Tiffany asked, putting her hand into her pocket to feel the lock of hair.

"It only works if it's gargoyle hair," Hedika said while showing where she'd cut it.

Tiffany wanted to hug Hedika, but only bounced on her toes, reminding herself that Hedika may not be as ready as Tiffany was for a friend, even if she did look out for Tiffany when she hardly cared about anyone else. They walked to the end of the hallway and Hedika paused. "Are you ready?"

"I suppose," Tiffany said nervously. "I have to be."

"You don't have to go," Hedika offered.

"I have to," Tiffany replied firmly. For her parents, she was determined to go.

The door clacked open and Hedika pushed Tiffany through, closing it behind her. As the door sealed shut, Tiffany heard Hedika's muted voice calling out to the bay, "False alarm."

TWENTY-FOUR

FRANKLIN PACED IN THE DARK CAVERN. He turned to Tiffany and held up a candle stick, which shined a soft blue-white glow. Tiffany squinted at the sudden light and put her hands up to see. Franklin seemed fierce in the light, or maybe it was her new perception of him. She wanted to believe Hedika, but the fact that one of Franklin's cadets died was still unsettling.

"Good, it's you. Come on. We need to get moving."

"Good morning to you, too," Tiffany said to his back as he walked toward the perch.

"It's hours 'till dawn."

Franklin led her around the crash pit until he put his toes to the ledge and looked out over the dark cavern. Tiffany stood beside him, a step back from the edge. All the lights were out everywhere except a few large caves Tiffany suspected led to the Endless See. Enough light came through those caves to wash the entire hollow mountain as though a quarter moon hung in the sky. One area on the ground was also lit up, a huge, empty city square. She didn't zoom her vision on it, though. Franklin coughed and she looked at him instead.

"If you go back inside—"

"I'm ready," Tiffany said, taking a step closer to the edge.

"Fair enough," Franklin said, diving off the ledge.

Tiffany followed Franklin as he circled to the ground inside the hollow mountain. Hardly another soul was awake, much less flying at this hour. The few that ventured into the air did so in a direct manner, cutting straight across the enormous cavern from one darkened landing to the other, like sentries checking their posts. Tiffany mostly concentrated her vision on the massive square below, all lit up and bustling with activity even at this hour. She couldn't focus on anything in particular in the square, though. She had to keep looking at Franklin and righting her angle or elevation to stay even with him as he glided effortlessly, hardly flapping the whole way down. She, on the other hand, flapped almost nonstop.

Franklin landed on a perch overlooking the wide-open square. Tiffany held her breath as she swooped in beside him. Her feet struck hard and she teetered, starting to fall backwards, stumbling sideways until Franklin grabbed her arm and tugged her upright.

"Thanks," Tiffany said.

"When we get back, we'll start working on your flying," Franklin grumbled. "And landing."

Franklin led her on foot down a series of stairways with long switchback landings. There was plenty of light to see their way, and plenty of light for Tiffany to notice Franklin hobbling on his injured leg.

"Does your leg still hurt?"

"A lot," Franklin said sourly.

"Then why didn't we fly all the—?"

"This is a no-fly zone. We don't have a whole lot of choice in the matter."

The echo of a big slab of stone hitting another rose from below. It sounded like bowling balls colliding. She looked down at the square to see where it came from, but sound echoed off the buildings, making specific noises hard to find in all the activity. The square was ringed with enormous rectangular buildings like the one they were climbing down the side of. In the square itself, slabs of stone were being moved about like rafts by wingless and tailless workers. They pushed the rafts using long poles that resembled the kind used by the Sentinels. Tiffany zoomed her vision in and thought for certain the stone slabs hovered. She didn't see any wheels, and yet they moved about as though on conveyor belts, fully loaded with crates and wooden containers.

"Where are we?" Tiffany was thoroughly lost now that she was on the ground. She looked up, trying to find the yellow perch of her barracks, but couldn't see it in the darkness of the night glow.

"This is the shipping yard."

Tiffany let her vision retract and held the stair rail until the dizziness wore off. "Why are we here?"

"To catch a lift topside," Franklin said.

"I thought we were going to go through the portal."

"We are. Just not the regular one."

"Wait a minute. I thought we were going to go up with someone else."

"I told you—"

"No, you said we were breaking some rules. Not this. Not going up there *alone*."

"You always go alone," Franklin said, suddenly turning to face her. She stopped quickly, almost walking into him. He wore a scowl that showed his irritation. "We're hunters. They're afraid of us, not the other way around. Even Bones won't take you on in a fair fight.

"Now, I told you I was going to be breaking rules. I told you not to come. I even told you not to get that," Franklin added, pointing at Tiffany's training baton.

Tiffany turned the baton in her hand slightly, looking at it to avoid Franklin's harsh gaze. She didn't like him picking on her choice of weapon. He'd never even seen *Star Wars*.

"Go back to the bay," Franklin added, pointing up the stairs.

"No," Tiffany replied. She lifted her chin. She wasn't going to be turned away this close to getting out again. She just needed a little time up top to figure things out. There had to be a way. "No, I'm ready. I want to go up top again."

"Why?" Franklin asked, glaring at her.

"Well, because," Tiffany shrugged, trying to think of an excuse that would sound legitimate. She never expected him to question her about t.

"You can't see them again," Franklin said sternly. "Besides, where we're going, your parents won't be born for another twenty years."

Tiffany shrugged, looking away from Franklin's stare.

"We're not going on a field trip. I can do this without you if I have to. If you come along, you need to promise me you won't be a liability. You need to focus and listen to me, and do as I say. Do you understand?"

Tiffany nodded.

"Look at me," Franklin growled. Tiffany faced him. "Do you understand me?"

"Yes," Tiffany said evenly.

"Once I know what Bones is up to, *then* I'll involve D.K. She does things by the book, and it's an old book that doesn't apply in this case. Now come on, we're running out of night."

Franklin moved down the stairs quickly, using the handrails to skip two, three, and four stairs at a time. He avoided using his injured leg whenever he could until they reached the wide, flat square. A line of slabs cruised like a train in front of them, pushed by a single, hulking wingless and tailless worker with skin the color of aged copper, replete with green blemishes that looked like he needed tarnish remover as much as a bath. Franklin cut in behind the huge worker and Tiffany darted through on his heels, avoiding another fleet of slabs passing by right behind the first.

Franklin crossed the large square, navigating around a length of hundreds of empty slabs standing on their sides, lined up in a single row. He led Tiffany toward a large red building near the center. A line of slabs was cruising out a large opening in its side and Franklin went in against the flow of traffic. Tiffany stayed close behind, worried she might get run over if she strayed too far.

Franklin climbed up a set of stairs to a perch overlooking the enormous warehouse. On the far end there was a giant square pillar rising to the ceiling, at its base a huge tunnel large enough for slabs to move through it. Like a conveyor belt, the empty slabs passed through from the other side, came to a halt, disappeared, and in a few minutes reappeared fully loaded only to be pushed out of the pillar to join the train leaving the warehouse.

"What is all this?" Tiffany asked.

"Food, mostly," Franklin replied over his shoulder, leading Tiffany along the second floor railing toward a tall wingless with a tail standing on a platform overlooking the pillar. "Supplies. Everything we need from up top."

"It's shipped in?"

"Every night."

Franklin pointed at the man ahead of them. "That guy is the gate warden. He opens the gate and sends the slabs through. Workers up top load the slabs and send them back."

"That fast?"

"Different slabs. They rotate."

Franklin stopped at the warden's platform. The gate warden stood beside a tall desk with a clipboard on it and several strange looking figurines being used as paper weights for what looked like cryptic order forms on different colored papers. In the center of the platform was a pedestal like the one in the obsidian dome that Kendall had placed Franklin's chimera on. This one had a cube on it with a grain silo beside it.

"Did you bring it?" the man asked, not looking at them.

"Right here," Franklin said, pulling the deformed figurine out of his coat pocket and holding it up.

"Who's she?"

"She's with me," Franklin said.

"Does she know the rules?"

"She won't try to return unless you give the signal," Franklin replied. Tiffany knew he was avoiding answering the question. It made her wonder what the rules even were.

"Get in line there," the tall gate warden said, pointing. "As soon as the next one comes back, I'll send you through. Wait for my signal top side."

"Got it," Franklin said, stepping close to the man and putting the figurine on the table beside him.

Franklin hurried Tiffany down another set of stairs to the ground floor. He hobbled quickly to the back side of the square pillar where the empty slabs were lined up to be pushed through. Several burly wingless and tailless workers glowered at them. They all had brutish faces and menacing physical characteristics. It even looked like one of them had horns, but it could have been his hair. Tiffany didn't dare take the time to see for sure, worried he might crush her with his bare hands over any such insult.

"What did he mean by rules?" Tiffany asked.

"On the other side," Franklin said. "The gate in the dome

hardly gets any traffic. This one has slabs of stone in it constantly. If we come back at the wrong time here, we'll materialize inside solid stone, so Cardinal will send a signal stone through when it's empty and then give us to the count of sixty to come back before switching gates."

"His name is Cardinal?"

"Yeah, so what?"

"Nothing. He just looks, I don't know. Not like a Cardinal. That's a bird, isn't it?"

Franklin stared at her dumbly.

"You two," one of the brutes roared. "Your turn!"

Franklin and Tiffany looked back at the enormous wingless and tailless worker who glowered at them as he pointed at the empty pillar. Franklin nodded and tugged Tiffany by the arm, leading her inside. He let her go when they reached the center.

"One more thing," Franklin said as he opened his wings. "You might want your wings open for this one."

"What? Why?"

"We'll be coming out the side of a building. It'll feel like being shot out of a cannon, then falling twenty or thirty feet."

Tiffany's eyes widened and she snapped her wings open, trying to avoid falling over. She gripped her baton tighter and took a deep breath as she heard a humming noise growing louder all around her. Her hair rose with the static and the light above stretched toward her.

Not again.

TWENTY-FIVE

TIFFANY COULDN'T SEE A THING, but she felt weightless and out of control, as though one of those large wingless and tailless workers had blindfolded her and thrown her into the sky. Air rushed by and she instinctively tried to right herself by facing it. She cupped her wings and flapped once, then slammed face first into the unforgiving branches of a tree. Thankfully, the fat leaves softened the stunning blow. Her wings flailed on the canopy above, keeping her from falling further as she swayed blindly amongst the inner branches.

Her vision caught up with her, but it was still dark. She hung in the air above an old asphalt road, looking down at a thirty foot drop. Behind her, across the narrow lane, was an old, eerily dark church.

There were no large branches beneath her feet to stand on. Her wings were the only thing keeping her from falling through, and the thin branches that supported her weight poked and scraped as she swayed with the mild breeze. She tried to flatten her wings, thinking it might lift her up out of the hole, but instead it pressed the leaves above and she sank lower while more branches scraped her face and neck. Thinking she might fall through, she eased her wings back the way they were before.

"Crap," she grumbled.

Where was her baton? She replayed her blind impact and remembered it whisking out of her hand when she tried to cover her already scratched and whipped face. Now she searched frantically, turning her head, eyes darting this way and that, trying to distinguish the gray shapes of interwoven branches in the scarce light of night, lit only by a sliver of a moon. *There!* A wave of relief settled her nerves, but the baton was still over three feet beyond her reach, stuck in a fork of the branch.

If I had it, maybe I could cut myself free.

Everyone warned her the light would cut her wings off, so it had to work on trees. She took a deep, calming breath and closed her eyes as she reached a hand toward the baton. *Come*, she commanded, imagining the warmth of the wood grains, the way they felt when she passed her light through to it. Her mind wandered to thoughts of *Star Wars* and Luke Skywalker using the *Force* to retrieve his light saber before the yeti monster got him. *Come*, she thought again, clearing her mind. She stretched her hand toward the baton, visualizing it floating to her, feeling the breeze as it poured over the tree above her like a surge of power.

"What are you doing?" Franklin asked from above.

Tiffany gasped and opened her eyes. The baton hadn't moved. Franklin hovered several wingspans above her, flapping his wings in deep, long strokes that pushed waves of wind over the tree, hissing through the leaves in a rhythmic chorus.

Tiffany's face felt flush with embarrassment. "I'm stuck."

"I can see that," Franklin replied.

"I was trying to get my baton," Tiffany admitted.

"Flatten your wings."

"I tried that—"

"Flatten 'em."

Tiffany groused to herself, but did as she was told. Nothing happened except the tree sagged a little lower again. "I'm flattening—"

Her words were cut off as Franklin suddenly swooped in and grabbed her by the armpits. Her whole body sagged as he lifted her up out of captivity. Her heart felt as though it had been left behind. He rose above the tree, ripping her from its grasp, and veered aside suddenly as his hands began to slip.

"Fly," he grunted just before he dropped her.

She flailed her wings, hardly catching enough air to keep from falling like a brick. She plummeted past the tree. Even in the dark she could see the spear-tipped, wrought iron fence surrounding the cemetery beneath her. The sharp ends looked as big as railroad spikes. Her wings caught a pocket of air and she angled just above the pointed finial tips, lifting her legs and throwing them forward to avoid being caught up by the iron rods. With her concentration so firmly on the tall fencing, she didn't see the crypt ahead of her. She slammed into it at the chest. Her eyes bulged and she felt dizzy again. As her body began to slip, she clawed the roof to hold on, trying to suck in a breath, wheezing for air.

"Are you alright?" Franklin asked as he swooped in beneath her.

Tiffany didn't answer. She didn't have enough air to even speak.

"Hang on," Franklin said, grabbing her legs to lift her a little. She looked down to make sure he had a good hold of her this time and let go of the roof of the crypt. He eased her to the ground and she sat down on the cold stone pavers, wheezing. "I'm sorry. You're wings were out and the wind pulled you right out of my hands."

"It's OK," Tiffany gasped, thinking it wasn't. She just didn't have the strength to be angry. She sucked in quick shallow breaths to try to catch her breath as she stewed over the fact he hadn't warned her about what he was going to do. "Baton," she added breathlessly, pointing at the tree. "My baton."

"In a second," Franklin said, kneeling beside her with his wings wrapping around them like a vulture. "I want to make sure no one heard us." Franklin turned an ear to listen to the breeze rolling past.

Tiffany slid to her side and leaned on an elbow as she tried to catch her breath again. She gently rubbed at the soreness in her ribs. Her heart throbbed painfully. Her face and neck and the backs of her hands burned with nicks and scratches, but not a scratch where her gown covered her. *At least it's not ripped again.*

Franklin closed his wings, allowing the dim moonlight to reach them again. The white fabric of her gown now stood out like a beacon.

"I think we're fine," Franklin said.

"Does that happen every time?" Tiffany asked in a whisper, her breath still ragged.

"What?"

"Blindness. I couldn't see when we came through."

"Oh, yeah, that. Once you've been through a few times your recovery time gets a little quicker and you hardly notice it. Mostly you get better at gauging the world with your eyes closed in the first place and you react to it faster. You'll learn as you get better at flying."

Franklin helped her to her feet and they walked back to the tree to knock her baton from the branches above. Franklin went to get it, flying over the fence and then climbing up underneath the tree branches to jab it out. She felt a little safer with it in her hand again, especially considering where they were.

The dark cemetery was shrouded by a wide ring of trees

growing just outside the iron fence. Across the road, an abandoned church sagged beneath the weight of an old, shingled roof. They stood near the locked lichgate, with its black chain hanging between the doors. The headstones were tightly packed, organized in paved lanes of stone that stretched end to end. Most of the more stately burials were near the middle with large crypts and above-ground tombs—sepulchers made of massive marble or alabaster slabs. A hazy shadow stretched under the crypt she had slammed into, and she thought maybe it was her own shadow still stuck there. The light from the tiny moon sank behind high clouds that meandered slowly through the night sky, but there was enough light to read the surname over the crypt door: VON CHARSSEN.

"Where is this guy we're looking for?"

"I don't know," Franklin said with a shrug. "We're going to have to look for him. Why don't you take that side, and I'll take this side? His name is Matthias B. Thorp."

A chilling breeze washed over the cemetery. She turned into the wind, gripping her baton, expecting to see a ghost materialize, but didn't sense a presence. She took a deep breath to calm her nerves. "Why don't we look together?" Tiffany suggested. The remnants of Bones' meddling with her mind rattled like old chains in her thoughts.

"I'll be able to see you the whole time," Franklin said, moving away as he scanned the headstones in front of him.

Tiffany swallowed hard.

"You'll be fine," he added confidently. "Go on, help me out."

Tiffany nodded, but didn't move.

She began to look at the names on the nearest headstones. Beatty, O'Brien, Northam, and Frost. She squinted to recognize the letters that tried to fool her in the darkness. Kennedy,

O'Farrell, and Jones. The rest of the names were hidden by other headstones. She had to start walking the length of graves to keep reading names. She followed the row of headstones toward the far fence, looking over her shoulder toward Franklin repeatedly. He didn't pay her nearly the attention she wanted, looking her way only every so often—enough time for a ghost to snatch her or for *something* bad to befall her without his notice, she was sure. She reached the end, McDaniel, and turned to follow the next row back to the center.

They zig-zagged their way deeper into the cemetery. Tiffany tried to keep up with Franklin so that he wouldn't get too far ahead, so he'd be able to get to her when something bad happened. The breeze kept washing through the cemetery, hissing through patches of overgrown grass near the fence and rustling through the leaves of the trees. Things brushed against her in the dark, fat leaves blown past her in the wind maybe, but not knowing for sure made her wonder. Her wings buffeted around when she turned the wrong direction, the wind always pushing her toward the center of the cemetery as though some dark being were sucking her in. She didn't feel the presence of any ghosts, though.

"Where are we, anyway?" Tiffany asked as she neared the center at the same time Franklin did, although he was a few rows ahead.

"A cemetery."

"No, I mean what state, or country, or city?" If she knew where she was, she could figure out how to get word to her parents.

"Liverpool, 1952 or '53."

"But that's *after* our run-in with Bones." *Were her parents even alive in 1952?*

"So?"

"So, how's this going to work? Did we come into the future so we could ask Matthias about the past or something?"

Franklin's shoulders slumped and he turned around to face Tiffany. "Ghosts are non-linear. This is a concentration point. Every time our ghost friend leaves his grave to haunt, he does so on this night in time. He goes to sleep every morning before dawn in this grave, and he wakes up each night at dusk, and it is always here, on this night. Does that make any sense?"

"Kind of," Tiffany said, a little confused by the notion. Matthias was stuck in some kind of time-loop. "So it's really today—our today—for him and us."

"Bingo," Franklin said, pointing at her. "Now keep looking."

Tiffany followed her row again. When they came together he was another two rows further.

"Do they know it's the same day?"

"Maybe." Franklin shrugged. "Maybe not."

He didn't stop, so Tiffany continued her vigil down one row, then another, and then more. When she looked back at the front of the cemetery, she was twenty rows deep and still had another thirty or forty to go. She yawned and stretched, her eyes tired from fighting the dim light to read.

"Found it," Franklin said. He was a dozen rows ahead of her. He waved for her to come to him and she jumped at the opportunity. When she caught up to him, he was on his hands and knees, pulling up several cobblestones in the path beneath the headstone.

"What are you doing?"

"When you earn enough stripes, you're going to start learning some really cool things," Franklin said, looking up at her with a grin. He put his hand on the dirt beneath where the cobblestones had been and turned his attention toward the earth.

She expected to feel some power or hear him chanting, or see some form of light erupt from the palm of his hand, but none of that happened. He just knelt there with his open hand on the dirt, unmoving as the breeze coursed through the cemetery, jostling their wings a little. She was about to ask him what was supposed to be happening when suddenly the dirt beneath his hand erupted and several bones lurched out with it.

"Ha! Here," Franklin said as he plucked a few bones from the clutch flowering out of the ground. "Three should do the trick," he added as he held the large rib bones out for her.

Tiffany gawked at them.

"Go on, take them. He'll be here any second."

Instead of taking them, Tiffany lifted her training baton in front of her expectantly. Franklin waved the bones at her again, grumbling something. She fumbled to take them from his hand, clutching the bones against her chest to avoid dropping them as she spun slowly, looking for signs of the ghost. "What am I supposed to—?"

An eerie screech came from a nearby tree. Tiffany faced it and felt a wave of cold air wash past her, buffeting her wings.

"Here he is," Franklin said coolly, brushing his knees as he stood.

The sound of children giggling behind one of the tombs drew her attention. A small, dark shadow dashed from one tomb wall to the next, growing longer as it stretched across the cemetery. The lichgate began to creak, the chain binding the two great doors of the front gate rattling. Behind them came a shrill scream of a woman.

Tiffany's heart pounded uneasily. Franklin hardly moved except to scratch at his sideburns.

A long, black shadow crept across the entire cemetery,

blotting out the moonlight as it blanketed the headstones and crypts. It enveloped everything in its path toward them.

Tiffany looked to the sky, expecting to see some enormous cloud or winged giant cloaking the moon, but the slight crescent shape shone unobscured. The shadow continued to roll over the headstones toward them. Tiffany held out her training baton and closed her eyes, trying desperately to think of something to make her happy. Thoughts of flying strayed to crashing into the tree, thoughts of Hedika were mired in their conversation about being disowned, and the warmth of her light seemed blanketed by memories of Bones invading her thoughts.

"Don't use your light," Franklin said softly.

"What?" Tiffany asked, opening her eyes again, startled by his command.

"These are parlor tricks," Franklin said dismissively, turning his back on the approaching shadow. He pointed in the other direction, over Tiffany's shoulder. "Besides, he's over there."

Tiffany spun, expecting a ghost like Bones to be towering above them, its white light glowing fiercely, but she only saw more cemetery, with a stand of crypts where Franklin pointed.

"How do you know he's over there?" Tiffany wondered aloud. She couldn't feel the ghost's presence at all. "Do you feel him?"

"Feel him?" Franklin regarded her with a queer look. "We don't—"

Franklin's eyes widened as he looked past her. Tiffany wanted to turn to see, but Franklin shoved her so hard she fell sideways. Franklin side-stepped out of the way of a dark maw rising from the ground. Tiffany only saw it a moment as it shot between them. Franklin leapt after it, diving through the air as though he were leaping on the back of a tiger.

Tiffany stopped her fall with her right wing pressing against the ground and the end of her training staff pointed out. For a split second she felt amazed at her agility, until she fell onto her knees, lacking the strength to do anything else. Imagining Hedika getting out of the same predicament by doing a karate spin in the air only disheartened her.

Franklin laid face-first on the ground a few feet away, both of his arms stretched out above his head, his hands together, clutching something stabbed into the ground.

"Got you," Franklin said triumphantly.

Beneath his hands the ground radiated a cackling light that sparked rhythmically, like a pulse. The strand of light burst out from under him, shooting off in a different direction each time to speed across the cemetery. The light brightened into a ball when it reached a certain distance—stretching its trapped skin to the limit, Tiffany realized—and in a frustrated rage, winked out only to try again in a different direction.

Franklin struggled to his knees, pressing his weight onto his hands to keep whatever he held from getting away as it shot around like a fish on a hook.

"Now comes the hard part," Franklin said, waving Tiffany over with nods of his head.

Tiffany stepped closer nervously, understanding now that Franklin had pinned the ghost to the ground. She worried it might lash out at her or strike her, or worse, get into her head.

"Come on, we haven't got all night," Franklin groused at her. The ghost stretched out away from them both and Tiffany side stepped behind Franklin, thinking she'd be safer out of the way.

"I need you to hold this down," Franklin said. Being this close, Tiffany now saw that what Franklin held in his hand was one of the rib bones like the ones he had given her. "Put all your weight on it. Don't let go, and don't let up. He's going to fight like a bucking bronco."

"Wha—"

"Drop your bones. Your baton too. Come on."

Tiffany dumped the things she carried onto the ground next to Franklin and crouched beside him. She put her hands over his and he slid his down the length of the bone to let her take the top.

"Don't let the bone come off the ground," he warned her, looking her straight in the eye.

Tiffany gulped then nodded, unsure if she had the strength, or the stomach, to do as told. She stared down at the seething ball of white, cackling lightning contained inside the skin of this amorphous black shadow, and watched it rocket away. The bone jerked in her hands as the light slammed into the limit of its stretched skin. Without Franklin, she probably would have lost it.

"*All* your weight," Franklin said.

She nodded again and leaned forward over the bone. Franklin let go with one hand and reached over to grab another bone from the pile Tiffany had made. He punched it into the ground next to the first bone and dragged it over the stone pavers of the path. Lightning shot between the two bones, ramming both in a frenzy to break free.

A howling sang behind Tiffany, so close she expected a wolf to be standing at her feet. She looked back but saw nothing.

"Ignore it," Franklin grunted. "It's not real. Here, hold this one too. All your weight on both. Don't let him up."

Tiffany nodded uncertainly as a deep growl rumbled all around her, rising up from the very earth beneath them. She slid a little sideways and was able to reach both bones and lean onto them at the same time, bearing all her weight.

Franklin seemed giddy now, clasping his hands together before scooping up the other two bones. He jammed one into the ground and dragged it away from Tiffany, closer to the headstones. The arc of lightning shot between the three points now, illuminating a triangle on the ground bound by an ethereal fabric that Tiffany realized was the ghost body of Matthias B. Thorp.

Franklin reached a headstone and pulled it down with apparent ease. The earth around it lifted and let the huge stone free. He eased it down over the bone he held and gently put all of the headstone's weight over it.

"Now then," Franklin said, catching his breath as he crouched down over the stretched-out form of darkness. He put the fourth bone on the ground, catching the translucent skin stretched between Tiffany and the headstone. "We just want a few answers."

The arcs of white light vanished, as did the noises all around. The giggling child, the growling wolf, the screeching owl, and even the cold wind. Everything went silent and still except for the grinding sound of the bone as Franklin dragged it across the paving stones. Franklin stretched him out six, eight, then ten feet.

"I know this hurts," Franklin said viciously, jerking the membrane a little.

The ghost cried out in pain, sending a shiver down Tiffany's spine.

Franklin eased up on how far he stretched the ghost, giving back an arm's length.

"You don't know pain," the ghost rumbled from beneath the stones along the path.

"I know how to dish it out," Franklin replied, inching the bone in his hand closer to where he knelt. The ghost hissed painfully and Franklin eased his torturous dragging again.

"You'll never be able to stretch me as far as he."

"Let's see about that." Franklin dragged the bone a little. Matthias moaned softly, his pain resonating between the headstones. Tiffany wanted to cover her ears and look away, to pretend none of this was happening. She never envisioned using torture to get information out of the ghost.

"Stop," Tiffany shouted, lifting one of her bones. The skewed square of darkness recoiled into a triangle and the agonizing wail dissipated.

"What are you doing?" Franklin growled.

Her mind raced. She didn't want to admit she couldn't torture Matthias, or any ghost for that matter. Her father used to say torture never worked, but she couldn't remember why—she only remembered him angry at a television report about some place in Cuba—and that wasn't going to be enough of an argument for Franklin. She closed her eyes and dug into her memories for that moment, begging to find it amidst the jumble of competing thoughts. *The worst you can do is control them.* That was what her father said. She remembered because he'd pointed at her when he said it, as though she had any part in what was transpiring on the television.

She sighed. What use was that?

"Stretch him back out," Franklin ordered fiercely.

Why, she wanted to scream. *You can't control him.*

Tiffany's eyes widened. "Wait," she told Franklin.

"For what? Stake him again or I'll do it myself."

She looked at the bone she still leaned on to wedge the ghost into the ground. She put the other bone beside it and dragged the empty membrane slightly, watching the fabric of the ghost stretch, knowing it probably hurt it, knowing she was in complete control of where it went. She lifted the second bone again.

"Stop playing," Franklin rumbled.

176

She ignored him, staring at the flashes of white light racing from stake to stake, rattling each in an attempt to break itself free of their hold. "Matthias, you said we'll never stretch you as far as he. Who is *he*?"

"The one you name Bones," the ghost replied hollowly.

"You're wasting time," Franklin said.

"Hang on for a second," Tiffany told Franklin, then looked down at the dark membrane beneath her. "He has your bones, doesn't he?"

The ghost didn't reply.

"What?" Franklin asked, glaring at her.

"At the boy's house the other day, I saw a pile of bones outside."

"He has your bones?" Franklin asked Matthias, giving the ghost a quick stretch.

"Yes," Matthias shrieked.

"Will you stop that?" Tiffany asked Franklin irritably. "Matthias," she said, her voice as firm and confident as she could muster. Her strength came from her anger at Franklin more than anything. She was mad at him for involving her in torture. "Let's make a deal. Bones for Bones. You tell him what he wants to know," Tiffany said, nodding toward Franklin. "And when we get Bones, we'll give you back *your* bones."

"What?" Franklin asked incredulously.

"That's pretty fair," Tiffany said. "He helps us, we help him."

"Your terms are reasonable," Matthias said deeply, his voice rising from beneath them. His answer seemed to surprise Franklin. He stared in disbelief at the shadow, his own features darkening beneath a scowl.

"Fine," Franklin said, glowering at Tiffany. "All I want to know is what Bones is up to. Why is he attacking our chimera?"

The ghost didn't answer. Franklin dragged the bone a little. A sparkle of light flittered from the point and washed over the dark form of the stretched out ghost.

"He seeks to break a dam," Matthias wailed hastily. "He said he cannot break it from the outside, so he will crack it from within. He talks endlessly about a flood from a never ending ocean. Please, I know nothing else. The times he has summoned to use me, he only talks again and again of his revenge, of the never ending flood."

"The Endless See?" Franklin asked, dragging the bone once more.

"Something like that. I don't know. It hurts, please."

"Think harder," Franklin snarled. "When is he planning to do all this? From where?"

"I don't know where. He summons me at his will."

"Then when?"

The ghost didn't answer.

"When?"

"Tomorrow. He said something about surprising you for the last time...to be ready tomorrow."

A rock clattered to the ground nearby as though thrown into the cemetery.

"More parlor tricks?" Tiffany asked.

"No, that's the signal stone," Franklin said dejectedly. He lifted the bone he held Matthias with and dropped it to the ground as he stood. "Come on," he added, waving for Tiffany to get up. He stepped past Tiffany as she let Matthias go with her two bones. The black shadow recoiled into a small, wavering shroud of darkness surrounding the headstone Franklin had set on the other bone stake. Franklin lifted the headstone and kicked the bone out from underneath. The dark shape of the ghost shot away. Tiffany dropped her bones and picked up her training baton.

"I should leave you here," Franklin snarled as he took Tiffany by the arm. He drew what looked like a sword hilt from inside his overcoat. A five-foot-long blue-white light erupted from it. She held a hand up to shield her eyes. Franklin reached it out and tapped one of the headstones and everything went cold, dark, and quiet.

TWENTY-SIX

FRANKLIN TUGGED HER BY THE ARM, leading her even though she couldn't see. She knew by the echo of a deep voice shouting "they're here" that they were back in the gargoyle world, in the shipping pillar. She didn't need her vision to know Franklin was angry with her, either. His iron grip dug painfully into her arm.

"The next time I tell you to do something, you do it," Franklin barked as he spun her to face him.

Her vision partially returned and she blinked at spots and the brightness of the warehouse. They stood outside of the pillar next to the line of empty pallets stretching out behind Franklin like a train. The same burly, menacing wingless and tailless worker glared at them, making her feel even smaller than Franklin's admonishment.

"I'm sorry—"

"I didn't bring you to stick your nose into things. All you needed to do was hold that damned ghost down so I could interrogate him."

Her eyes flared. She bit back an angry reply, thinking, *you mean torture him.*

"Come on," Franklin snarled, walking toward the stairs leading up to the gate warden's platform.

Tiffany didn't budge. She fumed over being yelled at in front of others. She defiantly folded her arms over her training baton, hugging it to her chest as she leaned against the outside of the pillar. The huge worker stood close by, pushing one of the empty slabs inside the pillar with his long staff. She watched it slide, hovering inches above the ground, until it came to a halt inside the pillar. A humming noise rose around them and, in a flash of blue-white light, the slab disappeared. She blinked at new spots in her vision caused by the flash, thinking that it wasn't just the other side that could blind her.

Franklin hobbled up the stairs without her, not even looking back. *He doesn't care about me. All he cares about is getting Bones.* She glared at his back.

"Are you coming or not?" Franklin shouted, not looking her way.

She blew out a frustrated breath and pushed herself off the pillar to follow him. What else could she do? As she climbed up the stairs to the walkway, Franklin reached Cardinal's desk and retrieved the figurine of Matthias, clapping the warden on the shoulder and shaking his hand. Tiffany saw them talking, but there was too much of an echo all around to hear their conversation. She knew if she cared she could have zoomed in her vision to read their lips, but right now she was angrier at Franklin than curious about what he was saying. Probably lamenting his disappointment in her, not being strong enough to dish out a little torture. Was that the kind of mindset a ghost hunter needed to be able to kill?

No wonder Hedika hadn't made the cut. She hoped anyone else she'd ever call friend couldn't do it, either.

Franklin shook Cardinal's hand again and stuffed the figurine into his coat pocket. He started along the platform, looking back this time, donning a sour expression after seeing how far Tiffany lagged behind.

"Come on," Franklin called, waving his arm for her to catch up.

She walked past the gate warden's desk quickly, falling in line behind Franklin, but keeping a full wingspan between them the whole way out of the red building. They climbed out of the vast square by a different set of stairs that had only a few switchbacks and seemed to go straight up for hundreds of steps at a time. Franklin climbed ahead of her the same way he flew better than she did, which only irritated her more. Even with a wounded leg his body was stronger than hers.

He glowered down at her as she ascended the last fifty stairs. Her legs felt like Jell-O, her breathing ragged, and her wings felt like a thousand pounds strapped to her back. Her little body, as usual, was letting her down.

She finally reached the top, breathless, and hunched over the rail overlooking the enormous shipping yard. The trains of empty and loaded slabs circled and wove their way around and through buildings under the direction of scores of wingless and tailless men. Tiffany was too tired to even zoom her vision over them to get one last look.

"I'm going to find D.K. You should fly home. If she knew you'd came with me...well, you've seen her when she's angry."

Tiffany didn't say anything, still breathing too hard to talk. And she doubted if she had the strength to fly ten feet, much less all the way back to her barracks. She craned her neck and looked up. While they were gone, the interior of the mountain had shifted from nearly pitch black to a dull gray, like the first inkling of morning. Hundreds of cave lights were lit, although the sky still lacked any substantial activity.

"I don't need to remind you not to tell anyone what happened, right?"

Tiffany nodded, wondering if in his mind he meant the torture, or just going up top in the first place. She was sure he meant both. The worst thing about the whole trip wasn't even that he'd used her to torture a ghost. That was bad, but the guilt of it didn't compare to the anguish she felt over squandering another opportunity to find a way to contact her parents, to let them know she was alive. When was the next time she was ever going up top again? How long had Hedika been here? Hedika had never even gone through a portal, and here Tiffany had been through twice!

"Can you make it back on your own?" Franklin asked.

Tiffany nodded. Her feeling of overall weakness lessened considerably after catching her breath. Even though her legs were tired, she knew she didn't need them much to fly, and at worst she could just sit here a while to rest.

"I'll let you know what D.K. thinks of all this."

Franklin jumped off the other side of the building top, diving a little, then flapped his large black wings to swoop upward. He banked toward the central dome and rose over the building tops to glide out of sight.

"Don't do me any favors," Tiffany grumbled.

TWENTY-SEVEN

LEAVING THE SHIPPING YARD, she tried a direct ascent, which wore her out faster than she realized. After climbing about half of the way up the interior of the mountain she found herself nearly breathless and wingworn. Forced to glide to catch her breath, she began losing altitude fast. She flapped occasionally to keep from falling out of the sky entirely, but it wasn't until she'd lost half of her gains when she was able to circle and climb normally. She cruised slowly for a while, rising until she was three-quarters of the way there, then started her aggressive angle again.

It left her completely exhausted when she swooped onto the yellow ledge of the landing bay. She didn't even come close to touching down, sweeping past it and careening sideways into the pit of sponges.

Argh! She lay on her side, breathing heavily, angry at herself for still being such a lousy flier. What good was having wings if she couldn't use them properly? She expected Priya to step up at any moment and make some snide comment. And a lot of help Franklin had been so far. At least D.K. told her some of the basics. Hedika actually *tried* to talk her through it. Franklin just cringed every time she crashed, more worried about being embarrassed by her than willing to help.

What kind of lousy mentor was he, anyway? Torturing ghosts. Going up top through the shipping yard so D.K. wouldn't find out. Doing things in the middle of the night like thieves. Breaking rules in the first place and almost getting her killed.

Maybe Corinne was right, that she needed a different mentor. It wouldn't be so bad, being like Hedika for a while. Except, then they'd give *her* the night watch duty! *Ugh.*

Tiffany crawled over a few sponges and stopped, too tired to make it all the way in a single go. She looked at the rope ladders at the edge of the pit. They seemed so far away. Another three lengths of sponges and she collapsed. If she slept here, would anyone care? Priya would start calling it her home if she found her. No, she had to get out. She crawled to the edge and grabbed onto the rope ladder, pressing her head against the cold stone and closing her eyes. Just a second to rest.

She envisioned her mother, so elegant and graceful, and yet so scrawny. She always knew she'd grow up no bigger than that. Even her father, as fit as he was, was small compared with other men. Those were the bodies she'd inherited. Not like the tall girls, or the athletic ones. Scrawny Tiffany Noboru, stuck in a pit of sponges.

It infuriated her enough that she growled and hoisted herself up, pulling herself and climbing out of the sponges even though her arms and legs burned. She rolled over the ledge at the top and lay on her back, smiling and panting, letting her wings sprawl with her baton resting on her chest.

If Priya found her here, it wouldn't be so bad. She closed her eyes until her heart stopped beating hard, then forced herself to roll on her side and get up. The stone ground wasn't very comfortable and it wasn't *that* far to her bed.

Tiffany pulled at the door, but it didn't budge. It was still dark out. She berated herself for forgetting, and started knocking gently. She hoped it was only loud enough for Hedika to hear, and not so loud to wake up the whole barracks. She knocked four times and waited, but no one came.

"Come on, Hedika," Tiffany whispered, knocking a little louder this time.

She waited. Again, no answer. What if Hedika had gone to bed? She didn't know when night watch ended. How long would she be stuck out here before someone would open up? She knocked again, one thump she hoped was loud enough—

The door flung open. Tiffany stepped back with a start. A tall man, at least two feet taller than her, stood in the doorway, glaring at her. He had pink skin the color and complexion of worn river stone. He wore a dark green shirt with several white lines on the sleeve, a rank Tiffany didn't recognize yet.

"I'm sorry," Tiffany said, looking toward the other barracks doors. She saw the 1 and 2 to her left. "Is this barracks 3?" Had she landed in the wrong place?

"It is," the man said, staring at her with a furrowed brow. "Who might you be?"

"I'm Tiffany. I'm—" She pointed past him.

"Oh, you're one of my charges," he said, allowing the door to open all the way. He stepped aside politely, waving for her to come in.

Tiffany didn't feel comfortable with the way he looked down at her. He seemed disingenuous, a lot like Corinne in that regard. She knew something was wrong the moment she stepped past him and the door slid shut behind her. The hallway was lit, as were the barracks ahead of her. She took several steps down the hall to move away from him, then slowed as she realized all the girls stood at attention at the ends of their beds, wearing night gowns or

sports bras and shorts. Even Hedika, the only girl in uniform, stood at the end of her bed. Tiffany stopped.

"Go on," the man said softly. "They won't bite."

"I'm sorry," she said. He stood too close. Her wings nearly touched his face as she turned around. "What's happening?" she asked as innocently as she could.

"Well, young lady, this is an inspection," he said, clasping his hands together in front of him, interlocking his fingers as though praying. He wore a wicked smile that made Tiffany back into the room. He followed, matching her step for step. "In an inspection like this, during curfew hours, you're *required* to be at your bedside and in either approved sleeping attire or a *clean, dry, and serviceable* uniform. Yours is none of these things," he said, extending his index fingers together, hands still clasped, to point at her arm.

Tiffany looked at her flight gown and sighed in disgust. Her sleeves were dirt and blood stained, probably from when she crashed into the tree, and her dress was caked with dried mud from the knees down.

"You've earned the bay two demerits," he went on, pointing his index fingers at his own chin. "One for each infraction of said rules. I would be inclined to give you a third for the blood stain and cut on your chin if you were in the boy's barracks, but today I'm feeling exceptionally gracious. Now, why don't you lead me over to your locker so we can find out what other rules you've been busy breaking since your arrival to my bay, shall we?" He pointed his two index fingers at the far end of the barracks.

Tiffany turned to lead him, feeling the full weight and scrutiny of every girl's stare as she passed. She didn't look to any of them, not even Hedika. Not only was she afraid of their scorn, but also of what the man might say or do if he caught her eyes wandering.

She felt him just behind her and a stride to her right, and she knew he watched her closely, expecting her to mess up somehow. The irritating thing about all of this, though, was she didn't know how she should have been acting except by the way she remembered the girls reacted to D.K. on her first night.

"Bay chief," the man said sharply, startling Tiffany. She didn't stop, though, afraid he would yell at her if she did, afraid he was going to yell at her anyway.

"Yes, sir," Corinne called out from behind them.

"Your eyes, please."

"Yes, sir."

Tiffany reached her locker and tried to open it.

"Wait," he said.

Tiffany let go of the locker handle and stepped aside, unsure why he didn't want her to open it. Corinne arrived and stood a few paces away.

"May I have your baton, please?" the man asked, holding a hand out. Tiffany looked at her baton, surprised that she still carried it. She reluctantly gave him her training baton, knowing something bad would probably come of it. He appraised it a moment and gave it to Corinne, saying, "You do realize you have wings, right?"

"I'm sorry?" Tiffany asked, confused by the statement.

"Your baton is for wingless and tailless, used for close-quarters strikes."

Tiffany said nothing. He stared at her, making her feel uncomfortable and worried that she had no answer for him, unsure if there was even still a question.

"Bay chief, open it up," he said at last and Corinne stepped between them, opening Tiffany's locker. She stepped back to let the man examine her meager belongings.

"Ah, another gown in similarly ruinous condition," the man said, pulling out Tiffany's first gown.

Corinne let out a soft groan and Tiffany winced, remembering what Corinne said about putting it in her laundry bag.

"Well, I've seen enough, young lady," the man said, dropping the gown and hanger onto the floor with a clatter. He held a hand out for Tiffany's baton and Corinne gave it to him. He dropped it into Tiffany's locker, making another loud bang. Tiffany winced. "One more demerit for improper storage of dirty clothes. Bay chief, do you concur with the findings?"

"Yes, sir," Corinne said flatly, her ire apparent.

"I have to say, I'm quite disappointed…in everyone," he said, leaving Corinne to glare at Tiffany. He walked the length of the barracks as he spoke loudly and slowly for everyone to hear. "Each of you is a mighty stone, but what good is a single stone where a wall is needed? And strong walls need mortar. Mortar is what we all share. It binds us together because we live for the same cause.

"I don't hold that young girl responsible for your failure today. I hold you *all* responsible." He stopped at the far end of the barracks and looked down the line of beds. "Ladies," he said, bowing, then turned and walked into the hallway. Tiffany didn't know if that meant he was leaving or not. None of the other girls moved. A few long seconds later they all heard the main door close, its thump echoing through the silent barracks.

"At ease," Corinne called out. There came a unified groan from the girls as they retreated to their beds, except for Karla, who glared at Tiffany.

Corinne stepped closer, leaning over Tiffany to make her feel even smaller. "What were you doing out of bed? Where were you?"

"I…my mentor came for me…I—"

"And what is all this?" Corinne pinched the fabric of Tiffany's sleeve, holding her arm up to inspect the stains on her forearm.

"I was…training."

Corinne reached down, batting Tiffany in the face with her wing, snatching Tiffany's gown from the floor. She crumpled it between her hands in front of Tiffany's face. "I thought I told you to throw this away."

"I…."

"Do what I tell you," Corinne snapped. "This isn't high school."

"But I didn't mean to," Tiffany tried to explain regretfully. "I just forgot."

"Well, I'm going to make sure you remember. You just earned laundry detail for two weeks—in *addition* to bathrooms—starting with what you're wearing," Corinne said, flicking her eyes down Tiffany's gown, sneering.

Corinne turned, her wings batting Tiffany again before the bay chief stormed away.

"What about my dress?" Tiffany asked. Corinne still carried it in her hands.

Corinne didn't answer. She walked to the trash can and threw the dress into it. "Get another," she said loudly over her shoulder.

Tiffany felt a lump in her throat. She wanted to go get her gown out of the trash, but all the girls were still watching her, their contempt and disappointment apparent by their weary looks of disgust. Even Hedika turned a cold shoulder to her, walking back to her post by the hallway.

"Lights out, girls," Corinne shouted. "Let's try to get that hour of sleep back."

Hedika placed a hand on the wall. The white glow emanating

from the stone went gray, then dimmed quickly to black. The girls climbed into their beds in the waning light, leaving Tiffany standing by herself next to her open locker.

The hall light went out and Tiffany waited in the dark, but Hedika didn't light a candle. It didn't matter. Her eyes adjusted soon enough and she quietly closed her locker and avoided knocking into anything on her way back to her bed. She lay down on top of her sheets and covered her face with her hands, fighting back tears. *Don't cry!* Her whole body was so tired. When was this ever going to end?

TWENTY-EIGHT

TIFFANY WOKE WITH A START. A sharp pain resonated on her forehead. The barracks were brightly lit except for a dark shadow in front of her eyes. Tiffany threw her hands up instinctively to protect her face from the large hand hovering there. It retreated and Tiffany squinted, blinking to wash the bleary haze from her vision.

"Ow," Tiffany said, rubbing her forehead, distinguishing the large figure standing over her. Karla. Tiffany looked around, a little worried about an encounter with the big girl. The barracks were empty except for two other girls changing at their lockers. "Why'd you hit me?"

"You sleep too hard," Karla said.

You hit too hard.

She held her tongue, wondering if her forehead was going to bruise.

Tiffany tried to roll so she could retract her wings, which were draped out onto the ground, but Karla put a hand on her shoulder.

"Hey—"

"Don't forget to do the sinks and stalls before you go anywhere today," Karla said menacingly. Her fingers dug into Tiffany's shoulder. "And you've got laundry detail tonight."

Tiffany felt Karla's foot step lightly onto her wing's forearm.

She eased her weight onto it and Tiffany sucked in her breath at the pain.

"Don't screw up again," Karla added with a sneer, turning her foot.

"Alright!" Tiffany cried out, wincing, trying to turn and retract her wing.

Karla let up on her wing, but not her shoulder. She glared at Tiffany a moment, then slapped Tiffany on the face before marching off. Tiffany looked at the two girls at the lockers, but both turned their backs in tacit agreement.

Tiffany swallowed hard and began rolling side to side, retracting her wings slowly so she could sit up.

Where was Hedika?

It didn't matter. Not this time. Hedika was no match for Karla. Tiffany needed a Sentinel to take Karla on, pound for pound. It was a losing battle. The only thing to do was obey.

Tiffany's body ached. Every muscle felt sore and tight, resisting her attempt to stand. She shuffled, slightly hunched forward, toward the hallway to the bathroom. She went straight to the trashcan Corinne had thrown her gown into and looked inside. The trash was empty.

"No," she whispered. Both her hands dropped to the rim of the trashcan. She felt numb inside even as she wanted to shake it or pick it up and hurl it across the room. Instead, she stared into its emptiness long enough for the realization that the only thing left to connect her with her past life was gone. She let go of the trashcan and shuffled to the bathroom.

Luckily none of the girls used the showers in the mornings. The toilets and sinks were all that Tiffany needed to clean, but even that took what felt like an eternity. When she came out, the barracks were eerily empty. She changed all of her clothes, stuffing her dirty gown and underwear into her laundry bag, then left for the perch, her mind only on food.

She dove off the ledge without thinking and flapped to stay level. Her clumsy meandering drove her toward the chow hall landing, but not without effort. Her wings were as tired as the rest of her body.

The place she wanted to land, a deep spot at the far end of the landing perch, was occupied by several boys and girls talking in a group. She veered to the narrower part and dove in to land. Her feet touched down, but she had too much momentum and arced sideways, falling flat on her face. She slapped her hands out to stop herself from real harm, but felt a sting on her nose and forehead. The boys and girls burst out laughing.

She looked up at them, red faced and angry, not only with herself, but at them. The boys wore their silver-shirted uniforms and pants—*why did they get to wear pants!?* Tiffany rolled to sit with her feet dangling over the lip of the ledge. She tried to hide her face by looking at her hands as she rubbed the sting out of them.

"Nice landing, newbie," one of the girls said, laughing as she dove off the ledge next to Tiffany. The end of the girl's wing brushed against the back of Tiffany's wings and head, pushing her forward precariously. The other boys and girls dove off after her, some of their wings swatting Tiffany as well as each stepped off, their laughter echoing lightly as they banked away.

Tiffany sniffled and wiped her nose with the sleeve of her gown.

Argh! A stain of fresh blood now streaked her sleeve. Her one clean gown. She pinched the bridge of her nose and felt tears welling in her eyes.

Don't cry! She winced hard, trying to fight back the tears.

196

Everyone will laugh at you.

Everyone always laughs at me. I'm a joke. Look at me! A stick with a head. I can't even fly.

I'll never get home. They'll never let me go up top again. Not after yesterday. Too afraid to torture a ghost.

I should have just flown away yesterday. Why didn't I just fly away?

Why don't I just fly away?

Tiffany opened her eyes and stared down the chasm. *Why not just leave?* She looked for the shipping yard, but couldn't place it now that it was light. There were so many squares below, all similar in size and shape. If only it was still nighttime.

I'll just hide until nightfall! It seemed like the best option to Tiffany. *If I don't go back to the barracks, then no one will be able to stop me. I just need to go someplace no one will look for me. Then tonight, when they push in an empty slab, I'll rush in with it and poof! I'm topside flying away.*

Tiffany ran away once because Beth Ericson wouldn't stop bullying her in school. It had been going on for several months, and even though teachers and her parents knew about it, nothing ever seemed to get done to stop it. Not until Tiffany actually ran away. Her mom found her, of course. Tiffany went to a friend's house to spend the night—to hide out before getting on a bus—and her friend's mother tattled. Tiffany's mom yelled at the principal over the phone in two languages, then changed schools.

But this time she wasn't running away. This was an escape attempt.

She let go of her nose, hoping it wouldn't bleed more. She felt a drop of blood on the tip of her nose so she leaned forward and let it fall. She watched it drop straight down the chasm until it almost disappeared from sight, but then she zoomed her vision in on it, and as it fell, she followed it with her eyes. It felt as though she were falling with it, free-falling but without the wind rushing through her hair. Eventually it slammed into the stone of a small court wedged between several tall buildings. A fountain bubbled with water in its center, and a large, empty bench lay quietly beside it, inviting her to join it. She slowly retracted her vision until she was able to recognize the spot.

That'll do nicely.

TWENTY-NINE

THE COURTYARD WAS LARGER THAN IT APPEARED from above, but harder to get into. She couldn't land in it because of how narrow the opening between the buildings was, so she flew around to the main street and landed outside. For once, she managed to stay on her feet, but it felt like she'd jumped out of a moving train and hit the ground running. She jogged to a halt and caught her breath, looking for a way in.

She curled her wings in tightly to get through an alleyway, and she knew she was going in the right direction because the echo of trickling water grew louder. The scent of flowers—real flowers— swam in the air. She expected birdsongs, but the only other sound aside from the ever present reverberating noises of the hollow mountain was a woman humming.

The alley widened and Tiffany emerged to a courtyard flower garden. Long alabaster planter boxes stood alongside the building walls, each filled with thick rows of bushes in full bloom. There seemed no discernible pattern to their arrangement, leaving a mish-mash of color like paint thrown randomly in every direction.

The buildings above were shaped more like trees than tall apartments. The bases were narrow, but the tops wide as though attempting to create shade. Tiffany hadn't seen the planters from above because there was no way to. They were tucked too far under the overhangs.

In front of the planter boxes were stone benches. To each side stood statues of men—human men, without tails or wings—in various guarding poses. Some held shields and swords, others stood with spears, and others with empty hands. A few were completely naked.

The humming came from an older woman leaning on a staff as she tended one of the long planters. Her skin was the same color as a weather-worn brownstone building Tiffany once saw in a picture of a Chicago neighborhood, replete with pock marks and blackened stains. The woman picked dried leaves from the dirt one by one, placing each into a basket beside her on the marble bench, one by one. Tiffany took several steps into the courtyard, marveling at the colorful display.

The woman suddenly gripped her staff and turned, pointing it toward Tiffany. Tiffany stiffened, staring at the end of the staff, expecting it to ignite in a blue-white ball of lightning or into a spearhead.

"Oh, you startled me," the woman said as she eased the staff back down and once again leaned forward onto it. She smiled at Tiffany and raised an eyebrow. Tiffany took a deep breath to relax her shoulders. "Not many find my garden."

"It's beautiful," Tiffany said, her voice shaky.

"It's a start."

"What is this place?"

"My light," the woman replied, nodding appreciably as she looked around the courtyard. Tiffany spun, taking it all in. The bubbling fountain in the center had just a small trickle of water, not enough to bathe with, but enough to water the plants, if needed.

Tiffany felt keenly aware that the woman stared at her

intently.

"What is a girl with wings doing down here?"

"Oh, I'm just…." Tiffany shrugged.

"You're new, aren't you?"

"Do you mind if I eat here?" Tiffany asked, evading the question while holding up the sack she got from the chow hall before flying down.

"I suppose not," the woman said.

"I'm Tiffany, by the way."

"You *are* new," the woman said with a grin. She turned slowly and leaned with her staff over the bench to again tend the planters.

Tiffany sighed and sat down at the nearest bench and opened her bag. She ate and watched the woman slowly pick dead leaves from the topsoil. The woman hummed, picking up leaves one by one, content to place them in her basket in the same, achingly slow manner. She moved slowly along the planter box, as though she had all the time in the world. Tiffany supposed she did. After all, what else was there to do?

Tiffany folded the bag and wrappers beside her when she finished eating. She felt better for having a full stomach, but her body was still sore everywhere and her eyelids had become heavy.

The woman picked up her basket and turned around to face Tiffany. "It's been nice chatting with you, young lady, but my shift on the wall is about to begin."

Chatting? The woman hardly said two words the whole time.

"Are you a Sentinel?"

"You really *are* new around here, aren't you, dear?"

"A little," Tiffany admitted. "I've been wondering, though. Why do Sentinels stand on the walls?"

"Our light holds back the Endless See. They fear it."

"They?"

"The dead." The woman sat on the bench beside Tiffany with a heavy sigh. "I remember a time when the dome wasn't needed to keep them at bay, but there are so many now. I feel sorry for them sometimes; the poor, lost souls. Their light is just so dark."

"They have light too?"

"Oh, of course they do, dear. But theirs is focused inward and it shines so little. You see, the things that give *us* light are the things we *want* to live for, not the things we cling to. Simply wanting to live isn't enough, and that's really the difference between us, and them." She leaned her staff toward the Endless See. "They only focus on the life they lost."

Tiffany nodded, afraid to admit she was no better.

"This place," the woman said, leaning her staff toward the fountain. "This place is why I want to live. To see it cared for." The woman stood and picked up her basket again. "It's time for me to go."

"Do you mind if I stay here a while?"

"As long as you leave things as you found them."

Before Tiffany could say anything there was a quick flash of blue-white light from the base of the woman's staff. The ground around her feet crumbled and bubbled, forming a pit. The woman fell into it swiftly, as though the ground sucked her in. The light vanished and the ground settled. It looked solid again, like nothing had happened. Two dried leaves flittered to the ground.

"Now that's got to be harder to learn how to do than flying," Tiffany thought aloud.

Tiffany cautiously walked over to the spot where the woman vanished, tapping it with her foot to make sure it was solid. She bent over to pick up the dried leaves. They were real, just like the flowers themselves appeared to be. She retreated to the bench and touched the petals of one of the flowers, then another. They were all real.

Tiffany smiled as she lay down on the bench, facing the flowers, with one of her wings dangling to the ground, the other folded over her shoulder like a blanket. It wouldn't hurt to catch a few hours of sleep.

THIRTY

TIFFANY ROUSED to the sound of Franklin's voice. "Come on, wake up," he said softly. At first she thought it a dream and that she was in prison again, until she felt him shake her gently on the shoulder. She opened her eyes to a dark courtyard under a gray evening sky. Franklin sat on the bench by her head. "There you are."

"What?!" Tiffany asked. She lurched up abruptly, dragging her one wing off the ground, pushing her other wing off her shoulder. She spun onto her hands and knees, facing him like a feral cat.

No! How did he find me?

"You really shouldn't drape your wings like that."

"It feels good," Tiffany replied irritably. *Why does everyone care about my wings?* After her run-in with Karla this morning, though, she had to agree that it left her a little vulnerable.

The trickling water in the fountain still burbled softly, but in the dim light the flowers lost their luster, and the statues looked more like shadows, each one tricking her into thinking they weren't alone.

"I had a heck of a time finding you," Franklin went on. He sounded less abrasive than normal, almost humble. He didn't look at her. Instead, he sat forward, his elbows on his knees, hands

206

clasped together as he stared at the fountain. "After I ran into Hayes at the dome, I figured you needed some cheering up."

"Who?"

"Lieutenant Hayes."

Tiffany didn't stir.

"Your squad commander."

"Oh, him. He didn't say his name."

"Yeah, well, he was acting smug when he found me, and he told me about your appearance in the middle of inspection, thinking I'd reprimand you or something. He's kind of a jerk. I set him straight, though. I told him I was training you hard and ruined your uniform. He already thinks I'm weird anyway, so telling him I train you at night didn't sound out of the ordinary."

You hardly train me at all, she wanted to say. Why was he here? How was she supposed to run away with him around? She sighed and climbed off the bench to sit on it, avoiding looking at Franklin. She stared at the building where she'd come in earlier, to where she thought there was an alley. Had it vanished in her sleep? She stood and walked toward the space between the buildings and found it somehow shrank, now far too narrow to get through unless she was a cat.

"Where are you going?"

"This alleyway," she said, pointing at it. "It was...I came through it earlier."

"Oh, well, whoever owns this place probably locked it up when it started getting dark," Franklin said, standing as well. He walked closer to the fountain and looked down at the water. Tiffany looked up to the sky, wondering how she was going to fly out of such a small space, wondering how Franklin had flown in.

"Are you alright?" Franklin asked, his concern evident in his tone. "I mean, how are you feeling?"

"I don't know," Tiffany replied tersely, folding her arms.

Franklin spun around to face her, his usual gruff appearance rising. The irritation in his eyes faltered, though, and he sighed. His shoulders sagged as he shook his head.

"I—" He coughed to clear his throat. "I just figured you might need some cheering up. You know, I'm...I'm here...you know, if...you need me."

Why was he being accommodating now, when she still wanted to be angry at him? It made it a thousand times harder to run away—to escape.

"Hey, I, um—" He coughed again. "I talked with D.K. this morning. We've got a team assembled and we're going after Bones tonight. Duke helped track that ghost again, and he's sniffed out a few others. They're all hiding out near one of our shipping lanes. Based on what that ghost told us—"

"Matthias?" Tiffany asked. She didn't like the way Franklin disregarded the ghost.

"What?"

"His name is Matthias," Tiffany said sourly.

"Oh, yeah, that's right. Well, we think Bones is going to try to get in through our supply convoy at the shipping yard, so we're going to set a trap for him this time. He's not going to use our shipping lanes!"

Of course, the shipping yard. Tiffany sighed in annoyance. Another one of her plans dashed.

"We're taking a dozen hunters up there tonight, and we'll have a dozen more on this side waiting."

"Great," Tiffany said unenthusiastically.

"We're going to get him," Franklin went on, stepping closer, his tone rising with the excitement she knew he felt in his heart. "You won't have to worry about Bones ever again."

208

"I don't worry about him, Franklin," Tiffany snapped. He looked perplexed and stunned simultaneously. "You're the one obsessed with him. I mean, I'm pissed off that he killed me, but all I really want to do is go home. I want to see my mom and dad. I don't want to be a gargoyle. I didn't ask for any of this. I don't fit in. I can't fly. No one likes me. I'm never going to be strong enough—"

She threw her hands in the air in frustration. "Argh!" Tiffany spun and stomped her feet as she marched toward the marble bench. "I'm useless. I can't even run away in this place. There's nowhere to go!" She slumped onto the bench, thumping the heel of her fists onto the cold stone. It hurt. *Stupid, wimpy body.*

Franklin was still as stone.

"Why am I here?" Tiffany moaned, struggling to hold back her tears. "I mean, why would anyone choose *me* to be a gargoyle?"

"I don't know the answer to how or why we're here," Franklin said softly. "But I do know everyone has a purpose."

A tear rolled down her cheek. She sniffled and wiped her nose with her sleeve, frustrated again, knowing there was already a bloodstain there. Another example of how unqualified she was to do anything remotely important.

"I let everyone down," Tiffany said, holding up her arm to show the stain to Franklin.

"No you didn't," Franklin said somberly. "It's the other way around. And you can point me out as the first to blame."

She looked up at him through tear-bleary eyes. He was a glimmering mass moving to sit at the opposite end of the bench, sweeping his wings out behind him with his long trench coat. Although Tiffany sat on part of her wings, they still splayed out behind her, pressed against the tall planters. Franklin's wing slid

against hers, dragging gently. It felt like static on the hairs of her arms.

"I've been a lousy mentor to you from the very start. I wasn't there for you. D.K. had to show up in my place on your arrival."

Tiffany sucked in a deep, quaking breath. Tears dripped from her eyes onto her lap.

"And the girls in your bay; it's not fair to you there, either. You've got no one your own age or color."

"Corinne is flesh-toned," Tiffany said with a breaking voice.

"Your gown color. You're the only white they've seen in forever. Most of their humanity has been trained out of them, and here you come along chock full of it.

"And then you've got me taking you to places you have no right being, endangering you all because of—" Franklin sighed and looked down between his legs. "Because I'm obsessed with Bones, just like you said. And I know why you're mad at me. I shouldn't have yelled at you. You were right. I thought I could muscle the truth out of that ghost—"

"Matthias," Tiffany said and sniffled.

"Right, Matthias. Truth is, I probably wouldn't have gotten anything from him. You…well…you did right and I…I'm not good with admitting when I'm wrong. I haven't had to do it much, you know?" He took a deep breath and straightened, turning slightly to face her. "I'm hoping you'll stick with me and keep me straight when you think I'm wrong. OK?"

"Is that some kind of apology?" Tiffany asked, laughing painfully through her tears.

"Yeah, lousy, huh?"

Franklin stood abruptly and spun around to face her, crouching down on one knee. He leaned forward so they were eye to eye.

"I'm sorry," he said evenly.

His words dug to her core. More tears began to form, obscuring his form in the dim light, giving him an angelic appearance. He leaned closer and kissed her forehead. A warmth radiated inside that she didn't expect. It felt like her father's kiss each night before bed, the kind of assurance and love that came with all night vigils by the window, or when he held her hand near traffic, or his hugs when she fell down and scraped a knee.

Tiffany threw her arms around Franklin's neck and cinched tightly as she began to cry. His whole body stiffened. She was sure he'd never known the warmth or caring of an embrace, but to her astonishment, his rough and calloused hands touched her shoulder blades just behind her wings. He pressed her gently closer to him.

"I'm so sorry," he whispered into her ear. "For everything that's happened to you."

Tiffany sobbed into his shoulder, weeping great tears that nearly drowned her. She coughed and sniffled and bawled until the wave of crushing emotion finally receded. Eventually, she let his neck go and eased back. With two soft pats on her shoulder he backed away, giving her room to breathe again. Her face felt flush and raw, stinging from the drying tears.

"I was one of yours, wasn't I?" Tiffany managed to ask. It had been gnawing at her since she first met him, when she nearly crashed. *Don't go dying on me twice,* he'd said.

"You still are, kid," Franklin replied, putting his hand to her chin to hold her face up. He looked her in the eyes as he said, "And I'll always be here for you."

She wanted to cry again, but all her tears were spent. And even though it pained her to smile, she forced one for him to hide the guilt that clawed at her insides. She was the one who threw away the figurine her father had given her for protection. Just like that boy Bones was after. She let Bones into her room. She let him kill her, and Franklin never had a chance to stop it.

But she could make amends.

"Let's go get Bones," Tiffany said softly.

THIRTY-ONE

FRANKLIN CARRIED TIFFANY out of the courtyard. He leapt with her clutched in his arms in the same manner as their freefall, but this time his strong wings surged them into the sky. She had no idea how much power wings could deliver, but after feeling the force of his velocity, she knew her attempts at flight were childish by comparison, like an infant learning to walk versus a sprinter racing down a field.

Franklin landed them on the roof and set her down gently.

"How did you find me?" Tiffany asked him as she straightened her wings.

"Come on, now. I'm a pretty good hunter, you know."

"How?" she asked skeptically.

Franklin shrugged. "I asked Duke to sniff you out."

"He's got a good nose," Tiffany agreed. If she ever ran away again, she figured she'd need to bribe Duke into giving her a head start at the least.

"How'd you find this place anyway?" Franklin asked.

Tiffany shrugged. She didn't want to admit it was just random luck. She peered down into the courtyard to where she thought her splattered drop of blood should be, but couldn't see it. Maybe it was too dark already. She looked up at the looming gray of approaching evening inside the mountain.

"I'll fly up with you," Franklin said, looking toward the yellow landing perch of her barracks.

"I can make it," Tiffany replied solemnly. "You have to go get Bones."

"It's just safer for you to stay behind this time. Besides, D.K. won't—"

"I'm fine," Tiffany told him. Franklin already explained that D.K. wasn't going to allow Tiffany anywhere near the shipping yard tonight. "I'd rather not go anyway. I'd just be in the way."

Franklin shrugged and raised an eyebrow in agreement. She wanted to punch his arm, but instead she smiled.

Her smile faded as she thought about what Franklin faced. Bones was more than just a frightening apparition, he was a murderer. Even worse than that, he enjoyed killing.

"I want you to get him for me," Tiffany said seriously. "I want you to put an end to his terrorizing. He has no respect for life and he doesn't deserve to live."

Franklin nodded grimly.

"And remember our deal with Matthias. Bones for Bones."

"No promises," Franklin said, but nodded agreeably, adding, "But I'll try."

Tiffany snapped open her wings, leaning forward to compensate for the additional weight, and turned slightly as D.K. had her do the first night. It helped steady her as she crouched low to jump. Franklin took several steps back to give her room and waved. She leapt into the air and thrust her wings down, surging upward. It felt as exhilarating and fresh as the first time and as she looked ahead, she grinned ear to ear. The air whisked by, combing her hair straight back. She banked and began the long, gradual circular climb up the interior of the mountain.

When she looked back to try to find Franklin, she couldn't

distinguish the rooftop she just left from any other. Franklin was already gone. Searching for him caused her to wobble unsteadily too, so she tried to focus on the flight ahead, looking down occasionally, hoping that he would be alright. It was silly. Franklin wasn't afraid of Bones, and he was going to be with a dozen hunters, and D.K. herself! But just thinking of the ghost ran a shiver down her spine. What if it was another trap?

"Watch out!" yelled a man.

Tiffany looked up and her eyes nearly bulged out of their sockets. She was flying headlong into someone. His wings flared suddenly. Tiffany threw her hands up in front of her, thinking she was about to collide with him. He flapped his wings hard and dove sidelong. Tiffany banked the other way, but felt the gust of his beating wings push her further sideways.

Her heart pounded quickly as she started to fall. She splayed out her legs and brought her wings in tight. It straightened her out like a skydiver so she flared her wings once more to stop her freefall. She caught air and arced hard to level out. Her breaths came in ragged fits.

Concentrate on flying, dummy.

She took a deep breath to settle her nerves then started flapping her wings to gain altitude.

By the time she reached the barracks, she was famished. Instead of landing, she passed by the yellow perch and angled toward the chow hall. Luckily, the wider and deeper perch area outside was vacant this time, so she swooped in and aimed for its center. She had a little too much momentum when her feet touched down. She staggered forward several steps, slowing herself just before she slapped her hands into the wall. Her palms stung and she rubbed them as she hurried away from the scene, hoping no one saw her.

The chow hall was packed with girls and boys, most of them of yellow and blue colors—the higher ranked cadets who didn't need to be doing any chores right now. She looked for Hedika while getting her food, but didn't see the blue skin and yellow gown of her friend. A contingent of silver-gowned girls were seated together on a long bench, among them the girls from her own barracks all clustered together. With a full tray, she took a deep breath and walked toward them. She had to start fitting in sooner or later, but as Tiffany neared the table, she noticed Karla's back amongst them, and the only space left was right beside her. If Tiffany turned away now, the other girls would notice. Some of them were already glaring at her, still obviously angry about the inspection.

Tiffany gulped down her fear and kept her course. The section of the table went silent and one of the girls nodded toward Tiffany. Karla turned, her wings moving aside like a curtain, and the big girl's brutish features darkened.

"What are you doing here?" Karla growled.

Tiffany stepped up beside her and put her tray down. "A girl's got to eat," she said. She heard the tension in her own voice, but at least it didn't break altogether. She sat down. She'd come this far. There was no backing down now.

Karla stared dumbfounded by Tiffany's stubborn bravery. The other girls were equally stunned.

"Oh," Tiffany said, digging into her pocket. "Look at what I found today." She pulled out the dead leaves she picked up when the Sentinel woman vanished. She put them in front of Karla. "They're dried leaves, from a flower bush."

"So what?" Karla asked, but she picked one up and twirled it in her fingers as she gazed at it absently.

One of the other girls reached across the table and picked up the other. "Where'd you get it?"

"A hidden garden," Tiffany said softly.

The mention of it aroused all kinds of curiosity. Tiffany stabbed several boiled carrots and stuffed them into her mouth, partly because she was hungry, but also to avoid having to talk. All she really wanted was a distraction, to keep Karla from breaking her wings.

"Can I see?" another girl asked the second, and the leaf started to be passed around.

Tiffany nodded and stuffed more food into her partly full mouth.

Questions worked their way around the table, directed every which way. *Flowers? Did you see them?* Tiffany didn't need to answer. Others filled in her silence with more questions or answers. *Of course she saw them. She brought the leaves back. Yeah, but how do you know they're not from a tree or something? Trees are part of a garden, too. Sure, but how do they grow without the sun? Why wouldn't the mountain light work? Because no one ever gets a tan in the mountain. I do. You're always copper-tone.*

The girls giggled. Even Tiffany smiled.

Karla finally put the dried leaf on the table again. "Don't forget, you've got laundry detail tonight." It wasn't said threateningly or menacingly, just a statement.

Karla stood up abruptly and picked up her tray. The other girls followed her lead, abandoning Tiffany in one fell swoop. Tiffany watched them put their trays away and walk out the hall to the flight perch.

"Well, that could have gone better," Tiffany muttered to herself. "Or worse."

The bright side was that she didn't have to fly back to the

barracks with the other girls. When she did leave, thankfully alone, she flew across the interior of the mountain, and in the waning light, once again misjudged her speed. When she threw out her wings to land, she was already too high over the yellow perch altogether. She fell feet first into the pit of sponges, sinking to her wings.

"Argh!" she growled and fought to get her legs out so she could crawl to the rope ladders. She had to stop halfway again, her body still harboring those deep body aches of overexertion. She wondered how she was going to hold the scrub brush again tonight with such swollen fingers.

She reached the top as a girl landed on the ledge behind her. Tiffany hoped it wasn't Priya. She crawled away from the ledge of the pit and struggled to her feet under the awkward weight of her wings. It was like trying to stand with a pack full of books on her back.

"Are you alright?" It wasn't Priya's voice, but Tiffany recognized it just the same.

"I'm fine," Tiffany said, flustered. She turned to face the girl who had told Tiffany how to dry her wings. She was one of the nice ones, or at least Tiffany hoped she was. "I'm fine. I just missed the ledge."

"You know you should have started laundry hours ago."

"Yeah," Tiffany said, swatting at her knees, hoping she hadn't just made her gown even filthier by crawling. *Thanks for the reminder.*

The girl walked around the pit and stepped up next to Tiffany. The yellow stone of the landing ledge highlighted her warm gray skin, making her lighter veins nearly white against her darker colors. She was taller than Tiffany by at least a foot, and much older too.

"You're going to be up all night waiting for it to dry."

"What do you mean?"

"It takes hours. Most girls do the laundry at lunchtime and leave it to dry in the vents."

"Huh?"

"No one showed you, did they?"

"Showed me what?"

"I swear, how do they expect you to learn anything? Come on."

Tiffany followed the girl toward the door with the large number 5 on it.

"I'm Em, by the way."

"Tiffany."

"Yeah, I know," the girl said with a partial smile. Tiffany rolled her eyes at herself for being so stupid.

"M? Is that like James Bond, or more like D.K. You know, she wouldn't tell me what her initials mean."

"It's Em, short for Emily."

"Oh, *Em*. Sorry." Tiffany felt stupid again. She should have looked at Emily's collar, at her embroidered initials "EM." It's probably where the nick-name came from.

Emily sighed and put a hand on the wall. The number 5 door clacked to unlock. "It's hot in there, so you'll want to change to a sports bra and shorts." Emily pulled the door open. A wave of heat poured out with it. Beyond the door was a large room with stone fountains and an enormous open area as deep as the barracks with rows of ropes stretched across to act as clothes lines. "This is the laundry room. All you do is bring in everyone's bags, wash them and hang them to dry. Everyone's clothes should have their initials."

"I've got Hedika's old things," Tiffany said, lifting her collar to show the initials.

"I don't think she minds," Emily said with a smile. "Come on in. I'll show you where everything is."

Tiffany was grateful to have someone show her what to do for once. She took careful note of everything the girl said and then followed her back to Bay 3. The main door was wide open and Hedika was coming out, stretching and yawning.

Emily didn't say anything to Hedika, but stepped out of her way to let her pass.

"Hi, Hedika," Tiffany said. She grinned widely at seeing her friend, unable to stop from blushing.

Hedika grumbled something and partially smiled at Tiffany, rubbing her bleary eyes as she staggered past. She stopped suddenly and turned back around. "Sorry. I just woke up," she said, purposefully making eye contact with Tiffany. "Hi." She smiled weakly and began shuffling off toward the landing perch. Tiffany felt a rush of pride. At least Hedika wasn't mad at her.

Emily led Tiffany into the bay and looked back down the hall, obviously shocked, whispering, "I don't think I've ever seen Hedika that nice to anyone."

"She's a nice girl, actually," Tiffany said. "But don't tell anyone. It'll ruin her image."

Emily chuckled. "Alright," she said. "You'd better go start the laundry."

"Thanks, Em," Tiffany said.

"Any time."

THIRTY-TWO

TIFFANY TOOK HER ONLY SPORTS BRA and shorts into the bathroom to change. She didn't feel comfortable changing in front of the other girls. Most of them didn't seem to have any hang ups about their bodies, and the more vivid their color, the more they showed off their skin. They strutted around shamelessly in just their bras and panties, carrying their night gowns or uniforms in hand or thrown over a shoulder rather than covering up their exotic skin.

Her mother taught her to act with modesty, but it was more of a protective barrier than cultural tradition, class, or social grace. The fact that she trained Tiffany to bury herself underneath layers of clothes just proved her mother knew Tiffany's body was irregularly small. It came down to insecurities. Stick thin and shapeless—that's what Tiffany saw in the mirror, and that's what the other girls would make fun of if she pranced around in front of them in just a bra and shorts.

Hiding in a bathroom stall, she tried to tug the sports bra over her head, but soon realized her folly. With her wings sprouting from her shoulders, she couldn't get the bra strap low enough to cover her breasts. Instead, she had to step into the bra and pull it up over her waist, tugging it into place, then wrestle her arms through the shoulder straps. *Why couldn't they just make the thing with hooks?* She slid on the tight spandex shorts and then put her flight gown back on. She didn't want to walk through the bay nearly naked in front of the other girls.

Rounding up the laundry was easy enough. She just opened each locker and dug out the sack at the bottom. Every locker's sack had the girl's initials on it and the locker number, except Tiffany's bag only had her locker number. She didn't mind the anonymity. It wasn't like anyone would mix up her white gowns with the other girl's clothes.

She lugged the bags six or eight at a time from the bay out to the laundry room. They weren't heavy, but they were bulky and hard to carry. She knew other girls probably took twice as many. *Stupid, little body!* It took five trips, leaving her arms and hands tired. When she had all the bags in the laundry room, she immediately tore off her flight gown and tried to cool off, but warm air rose from small holes in the ground, making the whole room insufferably hot.

She went straight to washing the clothes, one bag at a time. Thankfully only two or three items were in each bag. A gown and underwear mostly. Two pair of underwear and a sports bra. Little things that were quick to wash in the huge fountain's washing stones. The cold water soothed her hands and arms, a nice contrast to the warm air that made her sweat. She arranged the clean clothes on the lines over the vents, and placed the bags beneath them so she'd be able to return everything later without mixing everyone's clothes up.

When she finished the laundry, she slipped back into her gown and dragged her tired wings all the way back to the bay. Her back and arms were so sore, but her night wasn't over yet. She still had bathroom duty. As she walked into the bay, the cooler air began to reinvigorate her and the work ahead didn't feel so daunting. The girls were all still awake and getting ready for bed.

Hedika sat on her bed with a book propped against her legs.

"Will you wake me up in a few hours so I can put away the laundry?" Tiffany asked.

"No problem," Hedika said, not looking up from her book. "I'll even leave the bay door open so you don't wake everyone."

"Great," Tiffany said sarcastically, rolling her eyes. *I wouldn't want to disturb anyone's sleep!*

Hedika looked up and smirked as though she read Tiffany's mind. It made her worry. What if they could read each other's minds? She'd be in a lot of trouble, especially with D.K. Hedika didn't say anything, though, and returned to reading her book, leaving Tiffany nothing to do but shuffle to the bathroom.

Cleaning the bathroom seemed impossible at first. Several girls had used the shower. Water pooled everywhere. *Just do the sinks and get that over with.* The floors were the last thing anyway, she reminded herself. By the time she dug out all the cleaning supplies from a closet, she felt hot again, so she slipped out of her flight gown and hung it on a peg.

She worked without pause even as the lights to the bay were dimmed and Corinne called out the first of three warnings. Tiffany scrubbed and dried the sinks and mirrors quickly and started in on the toilets before Corinne called the second warning for lights-out.

Tiffany wedged herself and her wings into one stall after the other, scrubbing and wiping down the toilets, replacing the paper that was low. She made it to the last stall by the time Corinne called out the last warning for lights-out.

Finally Corinne stepped inside the bathroom through the open door. Tiffany had been expecting it all evening. She hoped Corinne was just going to close the door for lights-out, so Tiffany could work and not bother the girls in the bay, but Corinne walked halfway in to the bathroom. "Hey," she said to get Tiffany's attention.

Tiffany backed out of the stall so her wings had room to drape. She turned around to face the bay chief, wiping a bead of sweat from her forehead with her bare arm. She crossed her arms in front of herself and curled her wings closer to her shoulder to help hide her exposed body.

"I talked to my mentor today," Corinne said. "I didn't know Craft was an active hunter again. I don't think there's anything I can do to get you transferred or—"

"I don't want a transfer," Tiffany interrupted. "I like him. I'm going to stick with him."

Corinne cocked her head as though Tiffany made no sense. "Alright," Corinne said. "But if you change your mind."

I won't. Tiffany nodded graciously, biting her words. "Thanks for looking out for me."

"Yeah, well," Corinne said, looking a little uncomfortable. "That's why I'm Bay Chief."

Tiffany nodded again. *Was Corinne ever going to apologize,* she wondered? That's why she was here, after all. To try to make things easier or better for Tiffany.

"Do a good job cleaning tonight," Corinne said. "They usually inspect us again right after we fail one." She looked around the bathroom, nodding appreciably then retreated for the door and left without saying anything; not about the way she acted or throwing away her gown or anything. Tiffany stood unmoving as Corinne called for lights out in the bay. The hallway outside began to dim. When she realized Corinne wasn't coming back, Tiffany walked over and slid the door shut, closing herself in, alone. She hated being alone. She hated being here worse. She wanted to go home, but more distressing was the thought of Franklin being alone too, and facing Bones.

Right now, at this very moment, he might be up top fighting Bones in mortal combat. *What did that even look like? How did they fight ghosts?* She knew it had something to do with their light, but was she supposed to chop them in half, or stab them in the heart, or stake them to the ground, or what? How gruesome was it?

She shivered, shaking her wings off her shoulders so that they draped straight behind her.

One stall left, she told herself. *Then the floors. Franklin will be fine. He'll be back in the morning.*

As she scrubbed the last toilet, she became acutely aware that she was the only one making any noise in the whole of the bay. Every tap, click, clack, or scratch echoed throughout the bathroom. It irritated her more than it frightened her. She didn't want the girls angry at her yet again for keeping them up all night.

Mopping the floors was probably the hardest task. Her tired body wanted her to just drop the mop and go to bed, but she refused. The broken blisters on her hands screamed for her to stop, but she wrapped her hands in a towel and pressed on. She finished the floors in a daze and put everything away, banging the bucket into a wall, and clattering the mop onto the ground when it fell, wincing at the racket she made. She collected her gown and dimmed the lights in the bathroom, then waited in the dark hall for her vision to adjust before returning to the quiet bay. As usual, only Hedika was awake, sitting by the door, hunched in front of a book on a shelf with only her candle for comfort. Tiffany wanted to tell her good night, but it would mean she had to walk over to her, and she was so tired already. She lamented the idea of being awakened in an hour just to finish laundry, but even an hour's rest seemed like bliss right now. She collapsed onto her bed, draping her wings out to either side, and fell fast asleep.

THIRTY-THREE

TIFFANY'S DREAMS EBBED AND FLOWED like the tide. In one moment, she fell from the sky without wings, unable to stop, only to land in a sea of flowers, the soft petals catching her like a warm blanket. Thorns stabbed through the fabric as she tried to pick them, and when she pulled away, she hit herself in the face and blood dripped to cover her bare arms. She heard a soft voice asking her to get up, but she didn't want to. Not with so much blood. She tried to scrub it off, but she couldn't rub it from her skin. Then something touched her and she woke gasping. She lurched up, but with her wings trapped under her elbows, she fell back onto the bed.

"Hey," Hedika whispered. "You're going to wake the whole bay."

"Huh?" Tiffany asked groggily.

"You're talking in your sleep."

Tiffany nodded, not liking the sound of that. Yet another thing the other girls would make fun of her over. "Has it been an hour yet?"

"No. I let you sleep."

"Huh?"

"It's almost morning. I was going to wake you in a little bit, but then you started mumbling."

"Why didn't you wake me earlier?"

"I tried, but you were dead to the world."

Tiffany nodded. It was a good description of how she felt. Numb head to toe, except for her abdomen. Those muscles sharply protested her startled awakening.

"I'd better get everyone's things."

"Here," Hedika said, handing Tiffany a candle stick.

Hedika retreated to her perch by the hall where another candlestick flickered its blue-white glow. Tiffany rolled side to side to pull in her wings and stretched her aching muscles. She managed to stand without falling over and shuffled out the open door. She shook her candle alight as she walked through the dark, empty cave. It didn't scare her. She was too fatigued to realize she was alone, dressed only in her sports bra and shorts, with just a candle. And her thoughts had been on Hedika. Someone who brought her happiness. She needed good thoughts to produce her light. The notion that anything bad might happen to her here was far from her mind, although one thing did bother her. Franklin hadn't come back yet. It made her worry.

The heat from Bay 5 poured over her as she opened its door, her candle the only light to fill the long room. The hanging gowns looked a lot like the nightmare of her closet, the images Bones etched into her mind with his hauntings. Her light wavered as her concentration faltered. *No!* She glared into the darkness and stepped boldly into the laundry bay. She slapped her hand to the wall. The room grew brighter even as her candle died out, and the gowns lost their horrific forms.

She had no pockets, but her shorts were tight, so she stuffed the candle down the side of her shorts and started collecting the dried clothes and putting them in their bags so she wouldn't mix up everyone's things. She could only carry a few bags at a time, so the first bags she brought back to Bay 3 were important. Hedika's because she liked her most. Corinne because she was in charge. Karla because she was afraid of her. And her own because she deserved it.

As she opened her locker to put her things away, she found a gown hanging inside. She closed the locker door and checked the number. It was her locker. She opened it and looked at the white gown. The only gowns she had left were in her bag or by her bed. What was this one? She turned the gown on the hanger and saw the initials T.N. on the collar. She looked at the mended sleeve. It was her gown!

She turned around to look at Hedika. Her friend sat at her perch, her smile beaming across the long bay, her eyes squinting to zoom her vision in on Tiffany. Tiffany tossed her laundry bag into her locker and crossed the room to where Hedika sat.

"Did you?"

"Yeah." Hedika shrugged.

Tiffany dove forward, hugging Hedika around the neck, gripping her so hard that if she had any strength, she would have been strangling her friend. Hedika stiffened in her seat, nearly picking Tiffany off the ground.

"Thank you," Tiffany whispered as she let Hedika go. She could tell Hedika wasn't accustomed to hugs or embraces. Maybe she'd been here too long, like Franklin said. Maybe Tiffany could break her down and make her more human again, too.

"I still have my first gown," Hedika replied, looking at her book instead of Tiffany. She seemed embarrassed. "You want some help with the rest of—?"

Tiffany ducked swiftly, audibly sucking in her breath. She felt a dark presence rush by overhead, so close that her wings shivered. It surged outward, spreading in every direction as though completely engulfing the mountain. Hedika stared at her like she was crazy.

"Did you feel that?" Tiffany asked.

A boom echoed in the distance.

Hedika jumped off her stool, crouching and looking toward the ceiling. "What was that?"

Tiffany blanched, feeling a wave of terror strike her at the core. She sensed it in every direction, that distinctive presence she knew to be Bones. It flared, a raging explosion of his fury and hate bombarding her, sending a tingling shiver through her wings. She ducked lower.

"Tiffany?" Hedika asked, her voice carrying a sharp edge.

Again, there was a distant boom. It woke some of the girls.

"What was that?" one of the girls whispered.

"Did you hear that?" another said.

The presence retreated from its all-encompassing range and nearly vanished. Tiffany's heart slowed and she stood straighter. The presence lingered, though, like the soreness of her muscles at rest. Just a weak reminder that it was still out there, waiting. She closed her eyes to calm her frazzled nerves.

"What do you think that was?" Hedika whispered.

"What's going on?" Corinne asked from her bed.

Tiffany felt the presence stir again, however. She could feel him down below, somewhere in the interior of the mountain, down on the ground where the Sentinels lived.

"He got through," Tiffany gasped.

THIRTY-FOUR

TIFFANY RAN TO HER LOCKER as the other girls stood beside their beds, frozen in the rising light Hedika created by pressing her hand against the wall. They looked like true gargoyles, statues with their heads turned skyward, listening.

Tiffany swung open the door of her locker and pushed aside her clean and mended original gown. As much as she loved it, the thing she cared most about right now was her training baton.

Something must have happened to Franklin. Bones must have laid another trap for them and somehow gotten through this time. She worried that Franklin was still up top, or worse. She had to find him.

On a shelf in her locker was Hedika's lock of hair. She had no pockets so she grabbed it and stuffed it into her bra.

"What are you doing?" Hedika asked as she stepped up beside Tiffany. "Who got through?"

"Bones," Tiffany said. She yanked her baton out of the locker. "They were going out tonight to stop him, but I feel him. He's here. Something must have gone wrong."

The awful sensation of Bones' presence erupted all around, like a sphere of darkness bursting and raining down over her. Tiffany ducked. Her wings tingled again as though fiery ash sprinkled over her. Another boom followed and Hedika ducked as well.

An alarm began to wail from somewhere nearby.

The few girls who weren't already standing sat up in bed hugging their knees to their chests. Others moved to the bathroom hallway as though it was some kind of earthquake. Corinne marched toward the main entry hall.

"Everyone on your feet," Corinne shouted. "We need to go to our emergency assembly point."

The bay erupted with the frenzied noise of more than thirty girls rushing for the door, all excited with worry, chattering and blurting out whatever came to mind. *Don't shove. Is it a drill? Ow, my foot! Where's your gown? I'm not scared.* This last statement came from Karla, of course. She growled the words loud enough for all to hear. "Let them come. We can take 'em."

"I have to go help Franklin," Tiffany told Hedika.

Hedika stepped closer to Tiffany. "We have to go."

"No. Something's wrong. Franklin never would have let Bones through."

Tiffany ducked again, her wings twitching ahead of a resounding boom. All the girls in the bay flinched and cowered at the echoing thunder. Dust drizzled from the ceiling, falling like fine mist.

"How do you know it's coming like that?" Hedika asked, appearing rattled for the first time Tiffany had known her.

"Don't you feel it? That surge before the thunder?" Tiffany asked in amazement. "Can't you feel him? He's everywhere!"

"Who?"

"Bones!"

"That's impossible. Nobody *feels* ghosts!"

"What do you mean?"

"What do *you* mean?" Hedika snapped.

Tiffany felt the all-encompassing presence dissipate again and slowly reform far, far below.

"I think he's at the shipping yards. Franklin said they were going to trap him in one of the shipping lanes, whatever those are."

Hedika looked over her shoulder at the other girls still frantically trying to fit through the narrow hallway all at once. Corinne stood to the side, counting heads and pushing girls into a semblance of order. She looked down the bay and spotted Tiffany and Hedika. "Come on," Corinne shouted at them.

Hedika set her jaw in grim determination. "You're not going alone," she said as she stepped past Tiffany to yank open her own locker. She grabbed a bracelet from a shelf and stuffed her hand through it, then yanked out her staff. It was a thick piece of wood, slightly curved like a bow, but sharpened on the arc, except in the middle where she held it.

"Come on girls," Corinne shouted to them. All but a few of the other girls had already pushed their way through the narrow hallway. Tiffany and Hedika got in line behind the last three girls and Corinne followed them out, last to leave. Everyone fanned out as they ran for the yellow perch. Tiffany saw the girls ahead diving off one by one in front of her. The sky was filled with fliers going every which way.

"Go," Corinne yelled as Tiffany slowed.

Tiffany felt apprehensive about getting into the sky with so many others. She was sure to plow into someone. The thought of falling thousands of feet to her death wasn't appealing.

"This way," Hedika said, taking Tiffany's hand and leading her to the side. "I'll get her down," Hedika shouted to Corinne so she could be heard over the echoing alarms and indecipherable voices in the air. Corinne nodded as she followed the remaining girls off the ledge. Hedika lead Tiffany to the edge and they looked down the cavern. The interior was lit bright red, an indication of the danger. Alarms roared, echoing up from the ground, reminding Tiffany of World War II air raid signals she'd heard in history class.

"Everyone is going to the outer gates," Hedika said, pointing toward several of the enormous tunnels. She then pointed to a spot on the ground. "That's the shipping yard there."

Tiffany zoomed her vision down on the space. It was eerily dark, unlit. The bright red of the mountain cast huge shadows from hundreds of fliers circling their way down to the exit caverns. Fliers cut through her field of vision, startling her. She could hardly see through them there were so many. She retracted her vision, feeling light headed.

"How are we going to get down there?"

"Most everyone is circling, waiting for an opening to land. I'm thinking we can do a slow free-fall down the center."

"OK," Tiffany said, gulping. The last time she did a free fall, it was daylight and there was hardly anybody in the air with them. Right now a hundred fliers jumped into the sky every minute. She wondered how they could fly in so much chaos, and with a little trepidation she admitted, "I've done that before."

"What?!" Hedika asked in surprise.

"Well, yeah, I did a free fall with Franklin the first day. No, the second day. Wait. I don't remember."

"With the way *you* fly? Your mentor *is* crazy."

Tiffany frowned. "He *held* me. He did all the flying."

"That may actually be a good idea," Hedika said. "Turn around." Hedika reached around Tiffany's middle and lifted her in the air, using her staff like a seatbelt to hold her. "You're pretty light."

Tiffany rolled her eyes.

"Keep your feet together when I let you go."

"Right," Tiffany said, nodding, then thought, *wait, I'm not wearing a gown.*

Hedika took two steps and leapt off the ledge. Tiffany tried to open her wings instinctively, but Hedika's grip kept them pinned between them. Hedika banked them so they were falling head-first down the center of the mountain.

Hundreds of blurry fliers rushed by to their sides. The circling mass gave her the impression of being in the middle of a tornado, diving for the ground without a parachute. A shadow passed by in front of them. Hedika banked, just missing the winged figure. Tiffany screamed, and kept screaming the further they fell. More shadows cut across their path, some far ahead, others so close Tiffany thought she felt Hedika stagger from their wings colliding.

What if Hedika got hurt? She'd never forgive herself.

"Let me go," Tiffany shouted. "We have to slow down."

"Just a little further," Hedika shouted in her ear.

"We're going to hit someone!"

But suddenly there were no more shadows, either in front of them or swimming in her periphery. The sky opened up and the dark buildings below started hurtling up at them. Hedika's wings fanned out and their angle changed. She began to swoop them toward the mountain wall.

"Ready?" Hedika called out.

Tiffany nodded. Hedika dropped her, whipping her staff out of the way and banking sideways to fall past Tiffany. Tiffany's wings flared out and she began to spin. *What's happening?* She'd kept her legs together just as Hedika said, but she didn't have enough of a tail to stabilize her fall.

"Throw out your left leg," Hedika yelled. "Just your left!"

Tiffany followed Hedika's instruction. Her spinning slowed and she began to glide in a straighter line, banking slowly. She caught her breath and put out her arms to try to adjust her course, flapping her wings to slow her descent. As much as she tried to adjust her legs, she continued to bank, like a car that wouldn't drive straight. She just had to keep steering into the turn.

Hedika pointed at the shipping yard and they flew toward it.

"Look," Hedika said as they cruised over the top of it. "There's someone there."

Tiffany only caught a glimpse of where Hedika pointed. She was having too much trouble staying aloft, and the chilling feeling that the presence of Bones gave her seemed to have leached into the very air itself. Her skin prickled against the freezing air.

Tiffany was a little scared to fly into the shipping yard. She knew the area was supposed to be a no fly zone. She hoped they didn't have surface to air missiles or something like it. Hedika didn't seem concerned as she sank into the open courtyard, curling her wings to slow her speed. Tiffany did likewise and the two landed side by side.

Hedika brought in her wings. Tiffany stumbled to the ground, dropping her training baton as she threw out her hands to stop her fall.

"Damn it," Tiffany hissed.

"It's cold," Hedika said, picking up Tiffany's baton and handing it back to her. "Where is everyone?"

"I thought you said you saw someone," Tiffany said.

"Right over there," Hedika said, pointing toward rows of tall containers.

Tiffany squinted and her vision zoomed in on the area. She scanned quickly until she saw someone on the ground, wings spread flat, an arm over his head. She could tell it was a man by his trousers. In his hand he still gripped a wooden staff, and by the way his head was turned, he seemed to be listening to the ground.

"What's he doing?" Tiffany asked.

"He's dead," Hedika said despondently.

Tiffany retracted her vision. The usual wave of dizziness felt more like nausea.

"Was that your mentor?"

"No," Tiffany whispered, thankful that it hadn't been, but frightened even more thinking of finding him in the same way. She hugged herself, holding her arms across her chest. The air was so cold.

"Look. Who's that?" Hedika said, pointing toward the body.

Another figure shuffled out from the shadows between the long rectangular storage containers. He led with a long wooden staff before him, swinging it silently and slowly. It struck the body and the large man stepped closer to it, leaning down over the body with an arm out to feel the dead man's wing. He stood again and tapped the ground with his staff. A white light flashed like a camera taking a picture. Tiffany squinted against it and blinked at the spots left behind. The body under the man was gone.

There was something familiar about him, though. Tiffany zoomed in her vision again. She recognized the face at once, a sideways oval with deep cavernous eyes.

"I know him," Tiffany blurted as she retracted her vision. She started running toward Duke, listing from dizziness, her legs straining against the soreness from days of labor, but she refused to give in to a tired body. Not now. Not in this cold. If she stopped, she knew she would end up dead.

"Duke," she called.

He turned and craned his head toward her voice.

She stopped suddenly and crouched low. The presence of Bones burst out, exploding in every direction all at once. Hedika came to a stop beside her, igniting her staff in a blue-white light. A distant boom echoed from somewhere outside the mountain.

Hedika's light shone along the sharpened tip of her curved weapon, forming a long, menacing arc-blade of blue-white light.

"Put it away," Tiffany said urgently. "Put away your light."

Hedika extinguished her baton, crouching low beside Tiffany.

She felt the presence form again ahead of them, just beyond the containers, in the hangar-like building she knew held the shipping pillar.

"Bones is in there," Tiffany said, pointing at the building. She stood again and continued jogging toward Duke. As they approached, he held his staff in her direction, but with his nose bent toward the sky. She slowed in front of him. He sniffed the air and raised his staff.

"I thought I smelled you nearby," he said. "Who's your friend?"

"Hedika, this is Duke," Tiffany said. "He's a friend."

Duke smiled. Hedika nodded toward him, her eyes expressing only a little revulsion by his disfigurement. To avoid looking at him, she immediately took a position at the edge of the storage container and watched the building Bones was in.

"Where's Franklin?" Tiffany asked. "What happened?"

Duke shook his head in regret. "Nothing happened. They went through and waited for hours and nothing happened. When they came back, they disbanded and left only a few hunters here just in case. Franklin walked me home, irritated at being tricked again by Bones. After that first quake, though, we knew something was wrong. I brought him back here through the stoneway. We found one of the hunters still alive. She told us a hundred ghosts came through the portal somehow. They tried to stop them, but there were too many. Franklin took her to the infirmary and I've been finding and burying the dead."

"Aren't you afraid?" Tiffany asked.

"Of what, my dear?" Duke asked.

"Being alone. The ghosts."

Duke chuckled.

"Of Bones?"

Duke's laughter faded to a weak smile.

"He's inside the shipping yard," Tiffany said.

Duke frowned. His whole body rose and he stiffened. "What?"

"He's in there now. Where the gate is. I can feel him."

"*Feel* him?"

"I felt him before, when I went up top with Franklin. His scent was all over me, remember?"

"We always feel ghosts when they touch us."

"No, I felt him before he got near me. I knew where he was in the room, just like I know he's in there now," Tiffany said while pointing. She put her hand down, realizing Duke couldn't see her gesture. "Can you find Franklin?"

"Wait here," Duke said. "Most of the hunters were massing along the lookout stations."

Duke tapped his staff on the ground twice and it swallowed him up with a flash of light.

"Who was that?" Hedika hissed.

"It's a long story."

"Look here," Hedika whispered urgently. "Look, ghosts!"

Tiffany stepped beside Hedika, blinking away more spots in her eyes. She looked toward the gate building. At first she wasn't sure if her eyes were fooling her, but then she was able to make out a dark shadow spreading across the ground outside of the entrance, moving slowly over the contents of one of the abandoned transport slabs.

"Is that him? Is it Bones?"

"No," Tiffany said. "I don't feel this one."

"We should get out of—"

Tiffany ducked again. Hedika winced. A boom echoed in the distance.

"I don't like this," Hedika said, nervously fingering her bracelet.

"Duke told us to wait."

"Yeah, but he meant 'don't go in there,' not 'don't go flying someplace safer.'"

"He'll be back," Tiffany said. "Wait, look at that."

The ghost at the front of the building began to swim across the shipping yard, followed by a score or more shadows. Tiffany and Hedika leaned their backs against the storage container, flattening their wings, hoping not to be seen by the procession of spirits. The dark forms rolled like the shadows of quick moving clouds cruising over the landscape.

The air grew colder and Tiffany began to shiver.

THIRTY-FIVE

THE SHADOWS POURED OVER THE CONTAINERS, fanning out as they slithered toward the buildings surrounding the shipping yard. Tiffany held her breath as they passed. One came over the other end of the container she and Hedika leaned against. It dipped into the trough between the rows of containers and turned toward them, pausing, undulating like an uneven pool of black water. Hedika put her hand on Tiffany's arm, gripping her.

"A deal's a deal," the ghost whispered.

Hedika stepped in front of Tiffany suddenly, lifting her arc staff.

"Wait," Tiffany hissed, tugging at Hedika's arm. She recognized the ghost's voice. "Don't."

Thankfully Hedika's blade hadn't roared to life. It would have been a beacon to the others still swimming through the shipping yard.

"It's OK. I know *this* ghost." Tiffany stepped between Hedika and the ghost. "I'm trying," she said to Matthias.

"Bones for bones," he replied softly and began backing away.

Matthias rose over the next container and his dark shadow disappeared. Hedika and Tiffany sank back flat against the container to watch the other ghosts slowly meander away.

"What was that?" Hedika whispered.

"He's on our side. He helped us find Bones."

"Some help."

"At least he didn't try to kill us."

"What if he tells the others we're here?"

"He won't. He wants us to kill Bones."

Hedika remained quietly tense as they watched the ghosts slink out of sight. Tiffany sighed when she could no longer see movement.

Hedika took Tiffany's hand and looked to the sky. "We should get out of here before something else—"

A bright light flashed in front of them. Two figures rose from the ground. Tiffany threw her hands up to cover her eyes. A second later, strong, rough hands grabbed her shoulders. She stiffened.

"Are you alright?" Franklin asked.

"I can't see again," Tiffany replied, blinking at the spots. Franklin chuckled softly. She lunged up to hug him around the neck. "I thought you were dead," she whispered into his ear.

"I'm fine. Are you fine?" he asked, prying her from him.

She nodded quickly, wiping at a tear under her eye.

"What are you doing down here?" Franklin asked. "Who's she?"

"This is my friend, Hedika. Hedika, this is Franklin, my mentor."

Hedika nodded toward him. Franklin nodded back.

Tiffany ducked. The presence of Bones erupted again, pushing through her, and over her, and in every direction at once. Franklin turned, drawing a staff from somewhere inside his overcoat. He didn't light it, but stood at the ready. A loud boom echoed throughout the interior of the mountain.

"How did you do that?" Franklin asked, glaring at Tiffany.

"I didn't do anything," Tiffany replied.

"I mean, how did you sense that before it happened?" Franklin put his hand on her shoulder and leaned forward to look her straight in the eye. "Why didn't you tell me earlier you could sense him?"

"I thought everyone could. When we were at the cemetery, you pushed me out of the way of Matthias. You knew *he* was coming."

"Because I saw him over your shoulder. I didn't *feel* him. Where's Bones now!?"

"I don't know. He's...everywhere. No! There." Tiffany pointed to the shipping yard terminal. "He's there again. He keeps going in there."

"A lot of ghosts just left there, too," Hedika offered. "One spotted us, but he left us alone."

"Matthias," Tiffany added.

"He left you alone?"

"Bones for bones," Tiffany said, nodding.

Franklin frowned.

"Where's everyone else?"

"Ghosts are roaming outside the mountain. All the hunters are protecting Sentinels, to keep up the barrier. I sent word to D.K., but I don't know when she'll get here. But if he's alone in there, we need to go get him now. Can you point him out for me?"

Tiffany took a deep breath. She swallowed a lump in her throat and nodded.

"Duke, can you bring us all in there?"

Duke nodded.

"Wait," Hedika started to protest, but the ground around them disappeared, leaving a dark void beneath their feet which pulled them all down like a vacuum sucking up lint. There was a bright flash of light and Tiffany felt herself listing on uneven ground. It bubbled beneath her bare feet, pushing her up again. As the bubbles popped and dissipated, she settled onto solid stone.

"I can't see," Tiffany whispered.

"Me neither," Hedika added softly.

"Duke, it's pitch black in here," Franklin grumbled.

A globe of blue-white light grew at the end of Duke's staff, pushing back the shroud of darkness surrounding them. Its glow penetrated the blackness, revealing the train of full slabs in front of them, the long walkway above, and scores of bones littering the floor. The slab closest to the pillar looked as though a bomb detonated on it. Crates were toppled, the water kegs shattered, and debris was scattered everywhere.

The most disturbing sight, however, were the bodies. A large wingless and tailless worker lay in a collapsed heap against a wall. Another lay on his stomach, face down, partially hidden by the shadows from the pillar. On the perch where the gate warden normally stood she saw Cardinal's body folded over the rail, his arms dangling straight down, his limp tail and legs acting as counter balance to keep him from falling over.

Tiffany looked down to block out the sight of so much death. Strewn across the floor at their feet were dozens more bones. Tiffany lifted her foot and kicked one away. Hedika shook her arc blade staff and it lit up, adding to Duke's light, casting a wider range that pushed back the remaining shadows.

"Where is he?" Franklin asked, no longer whispering. He must have figured the light gave them away.

Tiffany knew exactly where Bones was. She raised her training baton in the direction of the most chilling presence she'd ever felt. Bones had more strength than the last time she encountered him. He seemed to actually radiate with darkness.

"Ah, look who it is," an ominous voice echoed all around them. She recognized it to be Bones at once. His seething hate emanated from the ground and walls alike, rattling the very stone on which they stood. He'd grown more powerful by coming into the mountain, Tiffany realized. "Franklin Craft, in the flesh. Surprised to see me?"

"Stay with Duke," Franklin told Tiffany. He reached over his shoulder and tore away the Velcro strap to his overcoat. He shook his shoulders and the coat slumped to the ground. His white shirt stood out in the dark, making the leather holster she didn't know he wore all the more obvious. It looked like something an undercover cop might wear. It had six batons of various length strapped to his back, and what looked like two wooden pistols under his arms. He drew one of the pistols and it flared with blue-white light into the shape of a crossbow.

"And keep pointing his direction," Franklin said under his breath. He stepped forward, kicking one of the bones on the ground out of his way.

Tiffany held her breath. She expected Bones to rise up in front of Franklin, a black suffocating curtain that would wrap them all and crush the life out of them. The presence teleported to the far wall, to a dark recess filled with shadow. Tiffany turned her baton in its direction.

"I see you," Franklin taunted. He shot several bolts of lightning from his crossbow. Each arced across the room, slapping into the far wall in a burst of sparks, missing the black outline of Bones as the ghost dodged out of the way, retreating behind the pillar, away from Duke's light. The bolts fizzled out as Franklin gave chase, jumping into the air and sweeping his giant wings to surge him around the pillar.

Tiffany adjusted her baton to point where Bones was hiding,

but Franklin was out of sight. How would he know?

"He's next to the pillar," Tiffany called out. "In the—" Her words broke at the sight of a ghost rising in front of her. It appeared to come from one of the bones littering the ground. She gasped, stepping back, her wings pressing against Duke. It's shadowy, translucent form stretched like a tissue being tugged out of a box. Then it unfurled and turned toward them, an undulating substance crowned with a single glowing eye that fixed its gaze on Tiffany.

All around her she heard the shrieks and wails of frightened children. Tiffany covered her ears as best she could with the baton in her hand, but the sound didn't diminish.

Hedika yanked Tiffany by the arm to pull her aside, stepping in between her and the ghost. The ghost surged forward. Tiffany stiffened. The black shadow deflected, flattening over an unseen barrier in front of them. Hedika didn't hesitate. She swept her blade through the dark form. The blue-white light of Hedika's arc blade tore through the middle of the ghost's cloak-like form, shearing it like sharp scissors. A piercing scream echoed throughout the vast chamber. The white light at the head of the ghost pulsed. Hedika reversed her swing and turned her arc blade, carving upward at an angle. The white light of the ghost tried to move, but its severed black form seemed anchored to Hedika's light. She finished her stroke through the middle of the ghost's white-hot orb. A bright flash spattered sparks that rained over them as its scream ended instantly.

Tiffany sank behind Hedika's wings, breathing hard, her heart throbbing as adrenalin pumped through her system. Hedika didn't move. Smoke rose from the outline of the ghost's body as ash gently fell over them.

"It's gone," Hedika said with surprise. "I killed it." The light on Hedika's arc blade faltered and went out. Tiffany hoped it was by choice and not because her thoughts were as overwhelmed by everything as Tiffany's were. Tiffany still couldn't concentrate enough to light her own baton. If Hedika lost her light too, how would they ever survive until help arrived?

From the corner of her eye, Tiffany saw movement. She turned her head to see another dark form rising from one of the countless bones.

THIRTY-SIX

TIFFANY SANK FURTHER TO THE FLOOR as the new dark shade rose. Tiffany's arm burned under Hedika's vice-like grip. *Where was Franklin?* She still felt Bones lingering near the pillar, his chilling presence draping the darkness with despair. The lump in her throat choked her words.

"Hedika," Tiffany said hoarsely. Her friend didn't stir.

The ghost in front of them rose to its full, towering height and began to unfurl. *If she struck now,* Tiffany thought, *Hedika might be able to kill it, but where was its eye?* After seeing the light show Hedika put on, Tiffany finally knew how to kill a ghost. Hit its light.

"Hedika, you're hurting me," Tiffany complained, rolling back onto her knees to try to free her arm. She grabbed Hedika's fingers and pried at them. "Hedika!"

Hedika snapped out of her stupor. Her grip softened and she let Tiffany's arm free. Her eyes took on new resolve and she squared her shoulders toward their new foe. The ghost was an undulating blanket of shadowy darkness, a translucent obscurity that shifted like something hanging from a clothes line on a breezy day.

The ghost's eye finally ignited, glaring toward them like a distant lighthouse in a fog. It rolled over them slowly. Tiffany wasn't sure what it looked at, whether it was herself, Hedika, or Duke's ball of blue-white light at the end of his staff. It made sense to Tiffany now why Duke didn't fear ghosts. Whatever he was doing seemed to act like a barrier. Just like the dome surrounding the mountain out on the Endless See. That's what the Sentinels did. They made the wall that kept out the dead.

The ghost's eye continued to turn and it floated away from them, toward the darkness, toward where Franklin and Bones had gone.

"Franklin!" Tiffany called.

In answer, a bolt of blue-white light shot across the mouth of the pillar tunnel on the far side, carving through the shadowy darkness. A flash of light burst somewhere out of sight. Tiffany imagined the bolt slamming into the wall, erupting into brilliant shards that fizzled out as they fell to the ground.

Tiffany felt Bones wink out and reappear along the catwalk overlooking the train of slabs. She looked across the warehouse at his wavering shadow looming over the warden's pedestal, then saw the glow of Franklin's crossbow appear in the pillar tunnel as he stepped out cautiously.

"Where is he?" Franklin shouted, looking to Tiffany for direction.

Tiffany didn't point Bones out. She looked to where Bones hid and saw his single malicious eye undulating in his shadow, staring toward the tunnel. She looked back at Franklin. *Could Bones open a gate?*

"Don't move," Tiffany shouted.

"What?" Franklin grumbled, stepping closer toward Duke's light. He kicked aside a clutch of bones at his feet.

"Don't go into the pillar. It's a trap!"

Franklin stopped and spun around to face the dark shadows

cast by the pillar. He fired his crossbow twice into the darkness and took two quick steps in the same direction. Behind him, where he had been standing, the bones he'd disturbed swayed gently, one still spinning. Rising from two of the bones came more dark forms, billowing up as though some mystical black smoke had been uncorked from a bottle.

"Franklin, behind you!"

Franklin spun and took aim on the ghosts. Two bolts whisked through their forms, tearing out chunks of blackened fabric the size of hands. The bolts and dark fabric evaporated into puffs of dust and smoke as they sailed through the pillar, disintegrating into nothing.

The ghost Franklin shot wailed and shrieked as it rose to the ceiling. The other ghost charged Franklin like a tornado bending across the sky, its black body whirling wildly. Franklin dove aside at the last second, curling his wings as the shadow rushed past him. He fired his crossbow as he fell, shooting two more blue-white spikes into the air.

"We have to help him," Tiffany moaned. "He can't fight them all alone."

Hedika grabbed her arm to stop her from trying to leave the protection of Duke's barrier. She tried to shake Hedika's grip, but her fingers dug in like talons.

"Let me go!"

"To do what? You have no light, and if you so much as touch those bones, you'll just summon more ghosts. It's like a minefield out there!"

"I know, but—" Tiffany stopped struggling. Bones' whole plan suddenly became clear to her, or at least what she thought it to be. He'd hidden the remains of all these ghosts in the supplies. He'd hidden his own remains too, but which were his? *None of them, you idiot.* The broken water barrel carried his. The story of him grinding his bones along the river's edge made him sound insane when Hedika first read it to her, but turning his remains to powder meant he could go anywhere there was water—a lake, a river, the pipes of a home, or even just a barrel full of water.

He'd brought an army of ghosts into the hollow mountain with him, and if he got control of the pillar, he probably meant to bring more.

"Duke, do you have to be at the warden's stand to open a gate?"

"Yes," he replied.

"Can you take us there?"

"Yes. But not while I hold the wall."

Tiffany lunged for Franklin's coat, pulling Hedika with her. *Please, please, please.* She dug into his pockets, hoping to find the figurine. She felt something made of stone and yanked out the disfigured miniature statue of Matthias.

"Oh, thank goodness," Tiffany breathed. She stuffed it into Duke's free hand. "Can you open this gate?"

Duke didn't say anything.

"He's a Sentinel," Hedika replied as though Tiffany should know the difference.

"He had a tail," Tiffany snapped. Sentinels didn't open portals. That much Tiffany knew. But Duke was special—he'd been born with a tail—and she knew he must have learned how to operate the gates. She hoped he had, at least. "Can you?"

"It's been a long time," Duke admitted sadly.

"I know you still can," Tiffany said, touching his enormous hand to close his fingers over the figurine. "We just need you to send them all back. You already know where."

"Send what back?" Hedika asked.

"The bones."

"How's he supposed to do that? They're all over the—oh, no." Hedika shook her head.

"We can hide," Tiffany said, digging a hand into her bra to pull out the lock of hair. She held it reverently, and tightly. She didn't want to lose it now.

"Hair and a Hula-Hoop aren't enough against that many ghosts," Hedika argued.

Two more blue-white bolts of lightning arced through the air across the mouth of the pillar tunnel, followed by Franklin. He crouched low, the light of his crossbow now joined with a short sword in his other hand. He glared through the tunnel at the others.

"Where'd he go?" Franklin shouted. "Where's Bones?"

Tiffany pointed her baton at the gate warden's station. Franklin turned away and swung his sword warningly toward an approaching shadow. It dodged to the side to avoid being hit, giving Franklin room enough to turn the blade downward and plunge it into the ground. Glittering spark-fire burst from the stone, sending a shockwave through the floor that rumbled like distant thunder. The shadows trembled, stunned by the eruption.

Franklin abandoned his baton, leaving it lodged in the ground. He leapt toward the pillar tunnel, flapping in short, mad bursts, rocketing through the tunnel only inches from the ground. He bounded in long leaps through cackling electrical fingers that groped at his wings. He burst through the tunnel just before a white-hot ball of electrical mayhem erupted behind him. The bright light nearly blinded Tiffany, but she couldn't look away. Not with Franklin's fate hanging in the balance.

The presence she knew as Bones erupted with it, blasting through the warehouse in every direction, charging through her wings with a numbing chill. Tiffany ducked, but she couldn't avoid the sting. It burned to the very tips of her fingers, as though the ball of lightning in the tunnel had somehow struck her.

Hedika winced. She'd been affected by it too.

Duke's light wavered for a second.

Franklin's shadowy form banked. He swooped up to the gate warden's platform and landed, drawing another baton that flared into the shape of a sword, but Bones wasn't there. Tiffany felt Bones expanding in every direction like a sphere encompassing the entire mountain.

A distant boom echoed from above. Hedika ducked.

"Who opened that gate?" Duke demanded.

Tiffany didn't answer at first. She blinked several times while the blind spots faded from her eyes. She saw Franklin turning as he searched the shadows for any sign of Bones, but the ghost wasn't there. She felt him everywhere else, though. A sphere that surrounded the mountain.

"Bones," Tiffany whispered. "Somehow." *Probably the mind of the gate warden. Before Bones killed him, he must have gotten into his head and....*Tiffany shivered.

"This cannot stand," Duke said. The ball of energy at the end of his staff waned. "We must protect the wall."

The ground beneath them dissolved into a bubbling pool of sand that started to fall away into a void. Tiffany felt herself falling. *No!* Was Duke abandoning them to go to the wall!? She didn't want to leave Franklin. The last remnants of sand began to trickle under her toes. She jumped into the air, throwing her wings skyward to pull herself up. The room went dark for an instant and she felt weightless. She wondered if Duke had taken her someplace else, or if she managed to stay. A moment later she crashed to the ground in a heap.

Franklin's light still glowed atop the gate warden's platform, but now he was joined by Duke and Hedika. She didn't think of that. She thought Duke was going to take her outside of the mountain, to the other hunters. And now that all the light was up there, long shadows stretched across the warehouse floor and covered the whole wall beneath the catwalk. Worst of all, some of the shadows moved.

Tiffany pushed herself to her hands and knees. She shivered. The frigid air had somehow grown colder, boring into her skin now that she was outside of Duke's protective light. A dark shadow roamed the ground not far off, creeping her direction.

"Tiffany!" Hedika shouted.

Tiffany tugged some of the hair from the lock Hedika had given her and sprinkled it over herself. She hoped that was the right thing to do. Aside from hiding, she could only run, and she could just imagine how that would end.

Franklin put a hand on the rail and vaulted over it, his wings outstretched so he could glide down to her, but a shadow rose up from the wall and grabbed his boot like a feral dog, shaking him wildly. Franklin veered to the side, swinging his sword at his feet the whole way down. He crashed into one of the loaded slabs of supplies, tumbling over the crates with the shadow crawling over him.

Hedika's blade flared and she dove into the air, her wings lifting her high over the rail.

The ghost coming toward Tiffany shrank back as Hedika's light pierced the dark. The shadows of a dozen bones within arm's reach stretched away as Hedika landed beside Tiffany.

"Get up," Hedika said.

"Wait," Tiffany gasped, crawling forward. She let go of her baton and grabbed the nearest bone. She felt a twinge of pain, a chill run through her fingers that numbed her hand. She threw the bone ahead of her toward the tunnel. The bone bounced and slid to a stop inside the pillar.

"Don't touch them," Hedika hissed, pushing one of Tiffany's wings aside so she could put a hand on her shoulder. "Get up."

Tiffany heard Franklin cursing. A bolt of lightning shot across the warehouse, thwapping into the wall in a burst of sparks. One of his wings rose above the debris and swatted down, causing a stack of crates to tumble and crash over him. Another shadow rolled over the top of the crates towards Franklin's buried light. There were too many of them.

"We have to send them back," Tiffany said. "Before Bones returns."

Tiffany grabbed another bone and flung it into the pillar.

"Stop that," Hedika said.

"Help me!"

"I'm trying." Hedika let Tiffany go to yank off her bracelet. She smacked it on her hip and a metallic *shing* sang out as though she were drawing a sword from a scabbard. The bracelet expanded in an instant into a large circle over five feet wide. "Get up," Hedika said through gritted teeth.

Tiffany tossed the bone she just picked up into the pillar, then grabbed her baton and stood. Hedika dropped the silver hoop in front of them and stepped into it, pulling Tiffany inside with her.

"Here," Tiffany said, holding Hedika's hair between them. Hedika pinched some from the lock and threw it into the air outside of the ring. She shook out the light of her arc blade, letting the shadows draw across the room unhindered.

"The bones," Hedika whispered, pointing at their feet. A dozen bones were in the ring with them. "Get rid of the bones!"

Both girls squatted down and plucked one bone after another

off the ground and tossed them into the pillar. When Tiffany tried to reach for one outside the silver ring, Hedika grabbed her arm and pulled her back. A black shadow swam across the floor toward where Franklin fought with another ghost, ignoring them completely.

Hedika reached for the bone, but this time Tiffany grabbed her arm.

Hedika froze. "What?"

The presence rose like bile in her stomach. A fetid smell of death and rot fell upon the entire warehouse. Even Hedika gagged at its stench. The black pool of water darkened except where what appeared to be a subterranean glow fish meandered beneath the surface. A blue-white eye shimmered and grew brighter as it rose up past the surface, pulling a viscous black muck with it that dripped onto the pool. As it grew taller, it widened and formed itself into a draping cloak that billowed in the absence of wind.

"He's back."

THIRTY-SEVEN

FRANKLIN PUSHED OVER A CRATE in front of him while spouting out curses. He stood abruptly and leveled his crossbow at a shadow, firing bolts of lightning indiscriminately at its retreating form. It zigzagged across the floor. The bolts slapped into the ground like spikes of red-hot iron, shattering with fiery sparks. Another ghost tackled Franklin from the side, knocking them both into the debris of broken and upturned crates littering the ground alongside the train of slabs.

Tiffany cupped her mouth, afraid to yell out with Bones so close.

Ghosts began to rise from the other bones Tiffany and Hedika had thrown into the pillar tunnel. Each form billowed like heavy smoke pouring from a fog machine. The smoke fell to the ground, filling out into shadows that crept toward the vulture-like figure of Bones.

Bones didn't say anything, but waved an arm draped in what appeared to be a deep, hanging sleeve toward Duke, then another bell-wide sleeve toward Franklin. The majority of the ghosts swam toward Duke while a few darted for Franklin, with Bones following.

Now was the time to do something. *Anything!* Tiffany crawled halfway out of Hedika's circle and plucked another bone off the ground, then threw it into the pillar. "Duke, send them back," Tiffany shouted. "Quickly!"

The light in the warehouse dimmed as Duke's staff winked out. Tiffany retreated to lean against Hedika and both girls sat up on their knees. Hedika put an arm around Tiffany's shoulder. Only a meager glow of light rose from the crates that buried Franklin, enough to cast a dim pall over the entire warehouse.

The eye atop Bones spun, focusing first on the gate warden's station, then on the pillar itself. A chorus of shrieks and wails erupted as a ball of lightning appeared in the pillar, its static fingers groping at every bone scattered inside. The shadows outside stretched across the ground from where they were climbing the wall near Duke or nearly on top of Franklin, dragged back toward their bones. The orb inside the pillar expanded until it looked like an insect carcass wrapped in a spider's web, with the flailing ghosts its unfortunate victims. Then they were gone, and the room became still and quiet as death.

Tiffany stared with the same stunned amazement as Bones. They'd really sent the ghosts back! Not all of them, but enough to put a dent in their numbers. A hundred more bones littered the floor, but their ghosts weren't here. Only two ghosts other than Bones himself still lingered, both kept busy fighting Franklin, but even those stopped to gape in wide wonder, allowing Franklin a moment to climb out of the debris and draw another sword.

The ball of light at the end of Duke's staff relit the darkness.

"No!" a deep and horrible voice rumbled through the warehouse. Bones grew in size, ballooning to blot out every source of light reaching Tiffany and Hedika. "No!" he roared and fell like a hammer over Duke, igniting into a white-hot fireball before impact, pounding down on him with a thunderous boom that shook the ground. Duke shrank beneath the blow, absorbing it like Atlas holding the world, his blue-white ball of light sagging toward his shoulders as his long staff bent.

"No," Tiffany gasped.

Bones rose, his presence pressing Tiffany to the ground under an enormous weight as he swelled to blot out the light. He came down over Duke again. A boom echoed, shaking the walls and threatening to topple the entire building. All of Bones' dark form poured over Dukes' protective barrier. Duke fell to one knee under the weight, his staff bending nearly in half as Bones deflected like a bucket of water, screaming with rage as he dissipated. His oppressive weight lifted and Tiffany stood, wrenching herself from Hedika's hold to cup her ears.

"We have to do something," Tiffany shouted.

Hedika stood. "Quiet," she said into Tiffany's ear.

"But—"

"Shh!" Hedika stared at Tiffany and talked slightly above a whisper. "Some ghosts you hunt by letting them find you."

Tiffany glared at Hedika, but as her words sank in, she realized Hedika was right. Bones was entirely too powerful an adversary, and not just because of his mind games. His size alone made him an impossible opponent.

Bones shrank half his size and held his arms in front of him, casting long, shadowy fingers that reached out and rattled dozens of bones. He knocked them about, disturbing them as the shrouded light inside his overstretched body lit him up like fireworks going off inside a cloud, lighting even his fingertips.

A crack resounded behind Tiffany and Hedika. It came from where Franklin held one of his batons stabbed into the wall, its blue-white light fizzling out as he let it go. It remained fixedly stabbed into the stone, and a cloud of smoke rose from where he had slain a ghost.

"About time," Franklin growled loudly, his voice carrying easily through the warehouse. Tiffany felt a surge of joy at seeing her mentor still in one piece. "Now where were we?" he asked, looking up at Bones and firing several bolts of lightning toward the ghost without aiming. Bones was so big he seemed like an impossible target to miss.

Bones whirled like a tornado. His huge black form became a cone that bent and shrank to avoid the spikes of lightning arcing through the air. The bolts flew high over the ghost as he diminished in size, shrinking to the ground at impossible speed. He disappeared from sight completely, but Tiffany could feel him. He lingered inside the standing water.

"Where is he?" Franklin called out, jumping up and flapping his wings to glide to a higher perch atop a stack of crates. He looked to Tiffany for direction.

Tiffany pointed her baton at the wide pool.

Franklin aimed his crossbow, but didn't fire. His shoulders sank with what looked like defeat and he shook his head in disgust. More gaseous forms rose from the bones scattered near the pillar entryway. Their smoke billowed and spilled into dark forms that rushed for the nearby shadows beneath the ledge from which Duke's light spilled. Other shadows roamed along the floor behind the debris, slinking toward Franklin. He fired his crossbow at one of the shadows, making it retreat in fright.

"Anything else you want to throw at me?" Franklin shouted.

Tiffany swung her arm, tracking Bones as he rushed toward Franklin. The debris between them upheaved and burst as though being plowed over, knocking everything into the air and aside on a crash-course toward Franklin.

"Uh-oh," Franklin said, swatting his wings for air as he jumped off the stack of crates.

Tiffany sucked in a breath.

Franklin fired his crossbow at the approaching mass. Bones surged out of the debris. His black form thrust into the air like a whale breaching, spinning to avoid the bolts blasting past him.

"Franklin!" Tiffany shouted.

The black whale opened as it slammed into Franklin, engulfing him. Bones continued his diving arc toward the wall of the warehouse, Franklin trapped inside like Pinocchio. He fired his crossbow several times in the span of a second. Bolts of lightning pierced the black fabric of Bones' body, leaving a trail of smoke and ash. They slammed into the stone wall together. Franklin remained pinned as Bones washed through him. The agony in Franklin's expression was easy to see with her vision zoomed in close. His light stuttered out.

"Franklin," Tiffany gasped in horror.

Hedika's wings snapped open to shield the sight from Tiffany. Hedika curled her wings around them like a dome of protection as she stepped closer, close enough to hold Tiffany.

"No," Tiffany whimpered, craning her neck to try to see past Hedika. She tried to climb over Hedika, but her stronger friend held her firmly in place by the shoulders. "He's not dead."

Hedika didn't argue the point, but the room darkened without Franklin's light. And it didn't stop dimming either. Shadows rose along the walls and floor, obscuring the only other source of light. Tiffany pushed Hedika's wing aside to peer in Duke's direction.

Translucent, dark forms blanketed the sphere surrounding Duke, obscuring the light through his protective dome. The ghosts sparkled and shimmered as pulses of electrical current surged through their ethereal bodies. Tiffany knew it hurt them by the wails of pain they cried out each time the static flashed through their shadowy forms.

"No more gates from you," the chilling voice of Bones echoed through the warehouse. "Now where were we?" he added mockingly, rising once again to his enormous size. Tiffany shrank at the sight of him. He hovered where Franklin had been pinned to the wall. She couldn't see Franklin through Bones' black mass. She thought maybe he fell somewhere behind the debris.

Bones slammed down like a car crusher over Duke's sphere of protection, his white-hot light focused like a spike. He struck with a thunderous boom that rattled the bones throughout the warehouse and sent shivers up Tiffany's spine. Duke's sphere flattened measurably with the strike, but rebounded after Bones rose up again to his full towering height.

"We have to—"

"Shh," Hedika whispered in Tiffany's ear. "Hunters are coming."

Not fast enough.

Hedika held her arc blade out, but didn't light it. She still wrapped Tiffany in her wing and Tiffany sank low to hide beneath it, holding her own baton in front of her as tears fell down her cheeks. Franklin was gone. Bones was winning. The only reason she and Hedika were still alive was because they were like mice. Tiffany more so. She couldn't find her light. Not through the fury boiling inside of her. *Useless light!* She wanted to kick something. *I can't fight Bones! Not with this useless little body. I can't save Hedika or anything. I may as well be—*

"Hedika," Tiffany gasped as though life were suddenly breathed back into her lungs. Her eyes went wide at her own realization. Hedika even said it: *sometimes you hunt ghosts by letting them find you!* Bones liked to hunt.

"Shh," Hedika hissed. She glared over her own shoulder, watching Bones.

"Save Duke!"

"What?"

"Go save Duke. When Bones comes for me."

"Comes for you—?"

Tiffany pushed aside Hedika's wing and ran. She'd never run with such determination and power in her life, and yet she hardly moved. It felt like running through mud with her wings purposefully outstretched and dragging over the ground behind her. The strewn bones stung her wing fingers through the leathery membrane she brushed over them. She pushed harder against the floor to catch them instead, hauling a growing pile of human remains with her as she ran for the pillar, gaining more speed with each stride. She purposefully ran through Bones' water, whisking it with her wings as though they were a squeegee. Over her shoulder she saw the dark shadows around Duke swimming frantically, drawn to her, but held in check by Bones' will. Even Bones wavered, his burning hot eye shifting focus from Duke onto her. The wails and shrieking screams of all the ghosts echoed wildly, joined now by the maddening roar of Bones. She felt his white-hot eye bore down on her back like a laser.

Without looking back, she imagined Franklin getting up, shaking off the blow that only knocked him out for a minute. She imagined Hedika flying like a golden tiger through the air, her light blade carving a hole through Duke's barrier big enough to let her in. She imagined D.K. swooping in at the last minute, with a hundred hunters. She imagined Hedika's smile when Tiffany apologized for ever getting her into this mess. It felt real, and the warmth in her heart radiated to her limbs and to her hand. She opened her eyes and saw light. Her light!

She turned, sweeping her wings and brushing aside the pile of bones she'd dragged across the room. A wash of water slushed into the pillar too, and as she raised her wings, she felt them dripping a chilling acid that burned like ice.

Her own light warmed her. The burning of her wings was like the thawing of frozen fingers in a hot room. She held her glowing baton in front of her, a beacon for Bones.

"Haven't we already danced this dance, little girl?" Bones asked viciously, his voice pounding in her head. He was already there. Now that he could see her he was already digging through her thoughts.

"It's my turn to lead," Tiffany glowered. *Don't let him in. Don't let him know.*

"You're not that strong," Bones hissed, charging for her. She didn't expect his speed. He moved like a rocket, filling the space between them in the blink of an eye. Tiffany suddenly agreed with Bones and wanted to jump out of his way, but it was too late. She leveled her baton at him and held her breath. His shadowy form opened like a net being thrown over her. Wham! It felt like falling into an ice cold lake. Her whole body was enveloped by his cold, black, insubstantial form. He was nothing more than heavy air, but so heavy that when he tackled her, her legs gave out and she toppled backwards.

Her wings cushioned her fall, but she hit hard enough to knock the wind out of her. Her right arm flailed and her baton, drained of its light, smacked into the ground and wrenched itself out of her grip. It bounced away, thrown so far out of arm's reach it clattered against the line of empty slabs on the other end of the pillar tunnel.

Damn it!

Her left arm was pinned by Bones' pressing weight. He leaned on her and she gasped for air.

"Pathetic!" His words drummed in her ears. "I only ever killed

you to have your light, and look at you now. Frail. Weak. A *living* being. You could have been a powerful ghost under my tutelage, but in this form, any simpleton would be your undoing."

I'd take them over a coward like you, Tiffany thought.

"A coward!?"

I know you hid from the Dragon when he came for the son of Mehmed!

"Hid!? Ha!" Bones' eased his iron grip on her and she gasped for another breath. "I *led* him to my former master." Bones pressed down again, plying his full weight over her. "Which is why I don't trust anyone else to deal with the likes of you. You see, for some damnable reason you see me, and I can't have that. So it's time for you to die, Tiffany Noboru."

She felt his whole body constrict around her. Only her right arm, somehow free of his grip, could move. She must have stabbed through him with her light, she reasoned. She groped at her face, clawing and digging at the suffocating air, trying desperately to make a hole to breathe through. Her frantic swatting managed a quick, gasping breath, but the air was cold and burned like smoke.

Bones' white light flared in her eyes and his body twisted. She felt an icy grip on her right wrist. She fought against it, but it was so strong that it pulled her free hand against her own face to cover her mouth. She couldn't see through his blinding light. She closed her eyes against his seething rage.

I'm not dead yet.

"You will be shortly," Bones chuckled.

He may have held her arms, but she still had wings. She flailed her second set of arms, curling one side in and extending the other so she would roll. Maybe if she was on top she could pry herself free.

Her lungs burned. The only warmth she felt throughout her numb body came from her left hand, which was lashed to her body, just over her heart. In that hand, she still clutched some of Hedika's hair.

Hedika, please hurry!

She rolled onto her belly and felt the cold stone beneath her. It changed nothing. Bones squeezed even harder.

"Who's Hedika?" Bones taunted.

She swatted her wings, but it only lifted her a little off the ground. She fell back onto her face painfully. She thrust a wing over her head and lifted herself off the ground, trying to breathe, but no air came.

Duke! I'm not going to make it.

"Duke?" Bones asked, suddenly curious. "What's going on in that little mind of—?"

Tiffany felt the static all around her. Her hair stood on end. She smiled weakly.

"What?" Bones asked, astonished. She felt his weight slacken, but not quickly enough.

She heard a cackling *zot* and all her skin felt stretched.

And suddenly she could breathe.

THIRTY-EIGHT

BONES' SCREAM REVERBERATED in her thoughts so loudly that her ears rang. She no longer felt his weight pressing against her, or even his presence at all. She didn't feel any weight, actually, not even her own. But her wings felt wind, and her arms flailed in circles trying to find some semblance of balance, up from down, left or right.

I'm falling.

She cried out as her whole body careened into something. It hissed all around her and raked her exposed skin, biting with fangs and swatting her with sharp claws and whips as it slowed her fall. She felt her whole body sag and then lift, then sag and lift again. Her wings were outstretched above her, splayed out over something that poked and prodded.

And I'm blind.

She saw spots first. One enormous spot where the eye of Bones had born down on her moments ago. Other, smaller spots danced and faded quickly, revealing a night of utter darkness. She hung from her wings at the top of a familiar tree, her whole body trapped inside its thick canopy. Only her wings were outside of it.

She took a deep, revitalizing breath.

I'm alive!

"I'm alive!" she shouted. She took in a deep, refreshing

breath. Her lungs still ached, her heart beat uncertainly, but she was alive…and very much alone. Worse, she didn't know how to get back.

What, are you an idiot? You're up top. You can go home!

Then she sighed in disgust.

"You're stuck in a tree. How are you going to *ever* make it home on your own?"

Tiffany felt the branches with her feet until she found a sturdy one to stand on. It sagged under her weight, but her wings lifted off the leafy canopy. She took a deep breath, hoping this would work, then raised her wings and flapped hard. Her body lifted a little and she quickly stroked with the hands of her wings to try to get a little extra lift. Again and again she flapped as she pushed her body out with her normal arms and legs, scrambling to free herself. She rose as the wind from her wings sent wave after hissing wave of wind through the tree. She careened sideways out of the tree and fell again.

The spear-like tips of the cemetery fence rushed at her. She swung one wing abruptly to dodge them then opened both wings like a parachute to avoid crashing into the ground. She swooped over several rows of headstones. Ahead of her a crypt rose and she flared out her wings, stalling as her body swung forward. She slapped into the side of the crypt with her hands and feet taking the brunt of the blow.

She fell backwards to the cold, moist ground, her heart pounding at the fright of nearly impaling herself and almost running headlong into a crypt wall. The palms of her hands burned. She thought for a second she was feeling a little dizzy too because the ground next to her seemed to be moving.

Crap!

Tiffany rolled away from the meandering shadow. It moved

with her, swimming along the ground as it reached out where her hands and feet had just been. She trotted on hands and feet and flapped her wings, lifting off the ground as the shadow charged suddenly, racing by beneath her. Another building stood in her way. She flapped once as hard as she could, stretching her wings as wide as they would go. It lifted her over the top and her feet touched down on the stone roof of another crypt, her arms flailing to keep her balance.

The shadow rolled by below along the cemetery path, passing the building.

It wasn't Bones, or if it was, she couldn't feel him anymore. She shivered at the thought. Not being able to sense him would be far more nerve wracking than knowing where he was.

The shadow below the crypt wasn't alone. Dozens of shadows swam beneath her like hungry crocodiles surrounding a boat. She crouched low so that the things might not be able to see her from their vantage point. She knew the best thing to do was to fly someplace else, but she hadn't gotten her bearings yet. She looked for the front gate and found it. *Just fly out*, she told herself as she opened her wings.

A frigid air struck her, knocking her off balance. The black cloak of a ghost wrapped itself around from behind and yanked her off the roof. Her wings flared out and she plunged feet first onto the ground, landing on top of yet another ghost, which shrieked and reared up to grapple her legs.

Tiffany's heart raced. She didn't have any weapons. Just Hedika's hair still clutched in her hand—and a candle! Ghosts feared light. Any light would do, she hoped.

The weight of the first ghost shifted as it swam around her midsection, tugging her toward the ground. With her legs held by the other, she toppled forward, flattening Hedika's hair on a stone paver as she threw out her hands to avoid hitting her face on a headstone. She groped for her candle and yanked it free of her shorts, but she had no light. Not without concentrating, and her heart beat too hard, and the fear she felt constricted her throat even as the fangs of some unseen hound bore down on her calf.

She cried out in pain.

"Leave her be!"

She didn't recognize the voice, but the press of teeth against her skin slackened and the weight of the first ghost around her middle fell away. Another ghost poured over her, its icy body sending new shivers up her spine. It knocked the other two aside and swam onto the headstone in front of her.

Tiffany closed her eyes and thought of Hedika's touch, how she had cupped her hand at the lunch table, and how warm the girl's skin could be compared to the chill of ghosts. Now her candle shined like a beacon in the cemetery, casting long shadows in every direction, pushing aside all the natural darkness and leaving only pools of specters surrounding her, with one brave ghost by her side.

"She's freed you all," the ghost went on, unaffected by the light. "Take your remains and leave this place. This is *my* home, and she is under *my* protection here."

"Matthias?" Tiffany asked hopefully.

There was no answer, but she knew it was him. She stood again and raised her light in the direction of the nearest ghost. It loomed in a threatening manner, refusing to move, obviously unafraid of Tiffany's meager light. Matthias surged from the headstone, crashing into the other ghost and dragging it beneath the ground. The other ghosts scattered like frightened mice. Wails and screams echoed in every direction as though a pair of cats were fighting. Then the cemetery fell silent. A single shadow

bubbled up from the cracks in the walkway, and Tiffany pointed her light at it, unable to tell if it was Matthias or not. Other shadows loomed close by, edging up from the darker shadows to peer at Tiffany.

A hissing sound came from above and Tiffany turned her light in its direction. A dark shape descended on her, with great black wings that blew dust and wind over her. It was a gargoyle. A big one. Tiffany shielded her eyes against the air surge and turned her head.

"Any of you touch her, you're dead," Franklin growled as he landed. He drew a sword that flared to life.

"Franklin!" Tiffany bounded to him, throwing her arms around his neck.

"Criminy! Watch the arm," he said through gritted teeth. Tiffany eased her grip and let him move his left arm out of the way. He held his sword out to the side to avoid hitting her wings.

"I thought you were dead."

"Same here. Are you alright?"

"Yeah, a little beat up, but, yeah."

"Let me go," Franklin whispered, turning his body in her arms. She did and he stepped around her, levelling his sword of light toward the ghosts.

"Wait," Tiffany said, putting her hands on his arm. "Leave them alone."

"Alone!?"

"They're the ones we set free," Tiffany explained. "Go home!" She shooed the ghosts with a wave of her hand, but none of them moved. "You're free now."

"Is Bones here?" Franklin asked, his vigil unwavering. He looked past the ghosts that surrounded them, though, up into the trees and at the shadows behind a concentration of crypts.

"He's not in the shipping yard?"

"I don't know. Is he here?"

"I don't feel him."

"Then we need to get back. D.K. and some others finally showed, but we need to find Bones."

Tiffany nodded, but stepped past Franklin and approached the pool of shadow hovering a safe distance from Franklin's reach. "Thank you, Matthias."

"My bones are returned," the ghost's voice replied, resonating from the headstones and the ground and the very air above them. "Our debts are paid."

"We never had debts," Tiffany told him.

"Touch the headstone," Franklin said, stepping next to her. Matthias sank back, as did the other shadows. Tiffany put her hand on the headstone Franklin waved his sword at. He tapped the stone with his sword and its light burst all around her. She knew this feeling all too well now. Like when D.K. sent her back to the pillar in the obsidian dome, she felt a jolt and fell backwards on cold stone, landing on her butt.

"Is he here?" Franklin asked, his voice piercing the darkness.

"I can't see. Where's Hedika."

"*Is he here?*" Franklin reiterated angrily.

"No! I can't feel him anymore. He's gone," Tiffany said angrily. "I can't feel him."

"That doesn't mean he's gone."

"He was wrapped around me when Duke sent me through. He's…gone. I think."

Her blindness faded quickly and Franklin helped her to her feet. Franklin stood beside her, his light sword pulsing its blue-white light as he guarded her against the darkness just outside the shipping yard pillar's tunnel.

"Well, if he's dead, why don't you feel him?" Franklin asked.

"Huh?"

A light grew behind Tiffany and she spun to face it. Hedika, her arc blade lit and leading the way, swooped to the ground, landing only a few feet away.

"Hedika! You're alive!" Tiffany rushed at her blue-skinned friend, throwing her arms around Hedika's neck and pulling herself tight against her. Hedika stiffened, moving her arc blade aside and letting its light fade. "Hedika, I'm so sorry I got you into all this."

Hedika remained stiff as Tiffany embraced her. Tiffany thought of all the terrible things that might have happened to her friend, all the things that could have gone wrong. The ghosts could have attacked her, even killed her. And even if she managed to get into Duke's barrier, she might not have been able to scare away the ghosts long enough for Duke to open a gate. But she had.

"Thank you," Tiffany whispered, gripping her friend tighter. "You don't have to hug me back, but I can't let go just yet."

Hedika's wings curled around them both. "There are still ghosts," Hedika whispered back.

Tiffany eased her grip around Hedika's neck and stepped back, wiping at the tears running down her cheek. Hedika's wings rolled further, curling behind Tiffany to form a wide circle that gently pulled Tiffany closer, nudging her wings.

Hedika reached out her hand and touched Tiffany's cheek, wiping a tear away with her finger as she smiled warmly. "I thought you were dead for sure," Hedika said softly. "Don't ever scare me like that again."

Tiffany nodded, a broad smile stretching her cheeks. She felt flush, a warmth radiating inside her that helped push back the chill in the air. Hedika's wings retracted and she folded them to her back.

"If you're done, let's get out of the tunnel," Franklin said, ushering them with the light of his sword.

Outside, D.K. stood with Duke at the gate warden's station. Two other hunters stood guard beside her. Their combined light filled most of the warehouse, pushing back shadows beyond the debris and the tunnel. Scattered bones still filled the ground, except along the path Tiffany forged.

D.K. leapt from her perch and glided gently toward them, landing without so much as a gentle breeze blown upon them. Her wings didn't fold completely. She kept them poised for action, held high and partly extended.

"We need more Sentinels to secure this location," D.K. told them.

"Well, send Duke to the wall to get some."

"I'll need to go with him, or they won't—"

"No," Tiffany interrupted. "We need someone to open the gate."

"Young lady," D.K. said sourly, glaring at her. The matron obviously didn't appreciate being interrupted.

"We just need to get these bones out of here," Tiffany explained. She kicked one near her foot, sending it sliding into the tunnel. "And all that water," Tiffany added, pointing at the pools spilled over the floor. She shivered at the recollection of its icy touch on her wings. "Bones ground his remains to dust and mixed them in the water. We have to send it back."

"How do you know that?" Franklin growled.

"Because that's his anchor"—Tiffany pointed at the larger pool—"right there. That's where he came back after using the gate. I took some through with me. I dipped my wings in it and dragged it into the tunnel before Duke sent me up top. I think it stretched Bones to death."

"You did that?" Franklin asked, impressed.

Tiffany smiled, shrugging.

"We need a stone cutter and Sentinels," D.K. called to one of the other hunters. The tall woman D.K. addressed nodded and leapt into the air, flapping away out the main door. D.K. turned to face Tiffany, standing tall over her. "Now let's get up to that Sentinel's protection and you three tell me everything that happened."

THIRTY-NINE

FRANKLIN SAT PERCHED WITH HIS LEGS DANGLING on the edge of a stone square, ten feet to the side of Tiffany—a safe distance, as he called it. Tiffany stood in her sports bra and shorts with her dual-bladed practice baton in hand. In front of her were two practice dummies on the end of ropes that were tied to pulleys and gears which Franklin controlled. He held one rope in his good hand, the other arm still stuck in a sling.

"One more time," Franklin said, tugging on the rope. The practice dummy rose up out of her reach.

Tiffany shook her baton and it flared with long blades of blue-white light.

"I'm the ghost of Christmas Past," Franklin moaned and let the rope go.

Tiffany smiled, but didn't break her concentration. She side-stepped as the practice dummy swung toward her, and she turned her blade with both hands, thrusting it into the oncoming fake adversary. Her light sank in even as Franklin wrenched on the rope to change its course.

"You're definitely getting good at this," Franklin said with a smile. "Your light's grown really strong these past few days. I wish I could say the same for my arm."

Tiffany stood straight, letting the light of her baton fade. She took a deep breath, not looking at him. "Bones said he chose me for my light. It's why he killed me. I think he wanted to make me a ghost."

Franklin cleared his throat. "I'm sorry for all that."

"I didn't want to leave the world up top. That's why he picked me. Isn't it?"

"You're the kind of stubborn that could have been a ghost, yes," Franklin admitted.

She didn't like hearing it. If she hadn't become a gargoyle, she probably would have ended up haunting her own bedroom, and Bones would have used her to help conquer the gargoyle world.

She still wondered about Bones. Was he dead? What happened to him? Franklin told her one of the scholars was brought in to help investigate. He determined that the stretching of Bones through the portal somehow eviscerated his light, but there was only theory to support his conclusion. No one had ever stretched a ghost in a gate before. Regardless, they sent back all the water, and it didn't matter to Tiffany if he was still alive up top or not.

Franklin told her not to be afraid if she started feeling Bones again down here. Slain ghosts lived beyond the barrier surrounding the hollow mountain, he explained. That's why Bones attacked it. He wanted to break down the barrier to let the hundreds of thousands of lost souls in the Endless See loose on the hollow mountain, then he would have the gates and he could rule both worlds.

It made Tiffany wonder what Bones was really after. Did he want to destroy the living, or just gargoyles? She supposed she would never know, and that was fine by her as well. There were better things to do with her time than worry about whether Bones was alive or not, or where he was hiding. And even if he showed up in the hollow mountain again, she'd sense him for sure. D.K. explained that little trick. Her ability to sense Bones was a rare and little known phenomenon. The death of a person who became a gargoyle because a ghost killed them had an innate sense of that particular ghost. In the middle ages, it was considered a curse because they believe it meant that the ghost and gargoyle shared each other's light, that they could affect the other.

Tiffany was glad that little secret remained with D.K. and her and Franklin. Hedika knew too, but she trusted Hedika. The other girls in the bay, well, she didn't think they needed to know much of anything.

Life in the bay hadn't changed much. Hedika and Tiffany were told to keep their mouths shut. The gargoyle way. At least with it a secret, Corinne and the others wouldn't treat her differently. Hedika's mentor reassignment came a few days later, at the same time as two other girls who lost their mentors to Bones, so it didn't raise too much suspicion with the girls in the bay. Now, at least, they shared breakfast and dinner together every day, and Hedika even kept her company on her laundry day.

It made the hollow mountain feel a little more like home, and since this was where she planned on staying for a while, it felt good. She still wanted to go home, but she knew now there might be other ways of reaching her parents.

"You know," Franklin added, drawing her from her thoughts. "You're also the kind of stubborn that'll never be a ghost. You took Bones on with a clear head and a heart full of courage, and won. I've already said it a few times, but you know I'm proud of you. You're a special kind of gargoyle."

Tiffany nodded, pursing her lips to avoid smiling.

"What do you say we call it a day? Go get dressed."

Tiffany didn't need encouragement. She changed into her

flight gown in the locker room and found Franklin outside. They took off together and flew to the black dome in the center, landing outside its main doors at the courtyard. Tiffany jogged to a halt, nearly falling forward, but keeping her balance enough to furl her wings without toppling over. She grinned and turned with a feeling of achievement. Franklin grimaced and sat down at a bench, rubbing his shoulder.

Tiffany's smile waned. "You need to stop flying and let it heal," Tiffany said.

"Like you know," Franklin groused.

"The doctor said—"

"I know what the doctor said," Franklin interrupted.

Tiffany sighed and sat beside him. She knew not to press things with Franklin. He was the kind of stubborn that could *only* be a gargoyle, just like herself. Stubborn and persistent.

"Did you think about my proposition?"

"It's against the rules," Franklin said.

"Come on, seriously? Rules? After what we've been through?"

"You've only been good a few days," he grumbled.

"Argh! It's been two weeks."

"I never agreed I'd do it."

"Please," she pleaded, her hands clasped together in front of her. "I'll even get a different training baton. I'll do your laundry. I'm getting really good at laundry. I'll clean your bathroom, and you know that's a horrible...horrible—"

"Alright."

"Really?" Tiffany asked, brightening.

"Alright. One page. One side. And nothing revealing or I'll tear it up."

"Really?" she asked, shocked beyond belief that he finally

relented.

He fished out a pencil and a small sheet of thick paper from his pocket. *He came prepared!* Tiffany was too giddy to care, though, bouncing in her seat. She reached for the paper but Franklin snatched it back. "You still have to practice your flying...and landing."

"I will," Tiffany said. He closed an eye and glared at her skeptically. "I will!"

He handed her the paper. She took it from him reverently and slid to her knees so she could write on the bench seat. She knew what she wanted to say. She'd been thinking about it for weeks. The only trouble was keeping her fingers from trembling. She took a deep breath to slow her racing heart and started by writing the date of her death at the top:

Today I met someone who reminded me how much I love my Mom and Dad. She's a small girl, a lot like me, and a little afraid of being in a new place and having to make new friends. I know what that's like having moved twice. It's almost like everyone is out to make you cry, but not me. When that girl smiled at me because I sat with her, I just thought of Mom and how proud she'd be of me for doing what's right. I wanted to tell Mom how much I love her, but then she'd think something is wrong or something, and then tell Dad, and we'd have a big "talk" when all I really want to say is that I love them and that I appreciate them. They might embarrass me sometimes because they want to be a part of everything, but I'm not "embarrassed" embarrassed. I don't even mind Dad calling me Teeter, just as long as it's never in front of my friends. Thank goodness he's the best Dad on the planet and knows better. Yup, I love my parents.

She held the paper to her chest and dreamed of its arrival, her mother looking at a notebook on the counter where they refused to clean since her death, and seeing the paper peeking out. Tiffany hid her diary pages all the time. Mom knew that. Tiffany imagined her mother asking her father if he put it there, or where it came from, then reading it and gasping, calling her father over and their reading it together. They might wonder how they missed it before, and she hoped it would give them the same strength she felt in writing it.

Tiffany took a deep breath and held it out to Franklin.

"Sorry, but I have to read it, to make sure you're not saying too much."

"It's OK."

Franklin's eyes perused the page. "Teeter?"

"It's something only my Mom and Dad know. It was my nickname as a baby, because I fell over a lot."

"That explains your flying."

Tiffany grinned at him, which helped fight back the tears glistening in her eyes.

"I'll take care of this," Franklin said, waving the paper in front of him. "I think your Mom and Dad will appreciate it. Why don't you head on home?"

She looked up into the interior of the mountain at the waning light, zooming her vision in on the yellow perch of the barracks. Her vision zoomed back out and she looked through the door of the dome, into the hall toward the large doors at the end of the hallway, wishing she could see through them to get a glimpse of the pillar that could take her up top. Both homes; one old, the other new. She nodded and stepped away from Franklin, snapping out her wings as she crouched down to jump into the air.

"See you in the morning," Tiffany said with a broad smile.

"Good night, Tiffany," Franklin said.

The End

Girlgoyle Fan-Art & Fan-Fiction Handbook
The world of the Hollow Mountain Butterfly for artists and storytellers
ISBN-13 978-0692403969

If you love *Girlgoyle* and you love to draw or write, this book is a great companion to the *Girlgoyle* series. In its pages you'll discover character facts, detailed descriptions of the Hollow Mountain and beyond, and an endless source of inspiration for your own creations.

Girlgoyles
Book 2 of the Hollow Mountain Butterfly series
Coming in 2016

When her mentor, Franklin Craft, goes inexplicably missing, gargoyle cadet Tiffany Noboru and her best friend Hedika put their ghost hunting skills to the test in a harrowing journey across the world of gargoyles. To find him, they must brave what lies beyond the protection of their walls, but avoiding ghosts out on the Endless See is only the beginning. Strange and dangerous creatures roam the blighted landscape between the Hollow Mountain and their uncharted destination, the gargoyle sanctuary Freefall, whose dying populace guards a terrible secret about her own world that some are willing to do anything to protect.

Plagued: The Midamerica Zombie Half-Breed Experiment
Book 1 of the Plagued States of America series
ISBN-13: 978-1491216286

When Tom, the son of a powerful Senator, becomes stranded in the Plagued States of America while searching for his lost sister, his only hope of survival rests in the hands of a few grizzled veteran zombie hunters and a mysterious half-breed zombie woman he thinks may know where to find his sister.

CPSIA information can be obtained at www.ICGtesting.com
Printed in the USA
LVOW06s1953060815

449113LV00022B/1312/P